Marielle Brandt is an American woman

Marielle was the perfect Upper East Side wife who took care of all the domestic details of marriage and never worried about the finances—never realizing how dangerous that could be. Now a new chapter of Marielle's life is beginning: the age of resolution.

Her husband's death has left her without resources and with two small children to raise. Against all advice, Marielle has decided to start over, to make a new life for herself and to make it on her own. She doesn't know how she will make it—she only knows she must. For her own sake, for those who depend on her, Marielle won't give in and she won't give up.

Dear Reader,

This is indeed a special year for American Romance: it marks our fifth anniversary of bringing you the love stories you want to read. Stories of real women of contemporary America—women just like you. This month we're celebrating that anniversary with a special four-book series by four of your favorite American Romance authors. Rebecca Flanders, Beverly Sommers, Judith Arnold and Anne Stuart introduce you to Jaime, Suzanne, Abbie and Marielle—the women of Yorktown Towers.

They've been neighbors, they've been friends, but now they're saying goodbye, leaving Manhattan one by one, in search of their lives, in search of happiness, carving out their own version of the American Dream.

Jaime, Suzanne, Abbie and Marielle: four believable American Romance heroines...four contemporary American women just like you.

We hope you enjoy these special stories as much as we enjoyed preparing them for you for this occasion. It's our way of saying thanks for being there these past five years. We here at American Romance look forward to many more anniversaries of success....

Debra Matteucci
Senior Editor

Cry for the Moon
Anne Stuart

Harlequin Books

TORONTO • NEW YORK • LONDON
AMSTERDAM • PARIS • SYDNEY • HAMBURG
STOCKHOLM • ATHENS • TOKYO • MILAN

Published August 1988

First printing June 1988

ISBN 0-373-16260-X

Chapter One

Marielle Brandt stared up, way up at the building in front of her. Her five-year-old daughter Emily was gripping her challis skirt, her eighteen-month-old son Christopher was slipping off her hip. There was a cool Chicago breeze blowing around them, whipping off Lake Michigan and whistling through the autumn leaves that still clung to the trees. It would look even worse, Marielle decided gloomily, when the trees were bare.

The mansion in front of her was a crenellated, fenestrated old horror, tucked behind rusting iron fencing, set on grounds that seemed better suited to a jungle than a residential neighborhood in the heart of one of America's great cities. The gabled, multileveled roof was patched and stained, several of the diamond-paned windows on the five and a half floors were cracked or missing with rags stuffed in the holes, the stone walls were crumbling, the wooden trim peeling, the front porch sagging dangerously. Some of the steps were broken, limbs were down from the huge oak trees surrounding the place, and the whole building reeked of neglect and decay.

"I tried to warn you," Liam O'Donnell said primly, setting down the diaper bag he'd grudgingly carried on the cracked sidewalk. "You would have been better off staying in New York. Farnum's Castle is fit for nothing but a wrecking ball. I may not be your family attorney, but I've told you more than once my advice is to take that very generous offer and stay where you belong."

"I don't belong in New York," Marielle said calmly, allowing herself a brief glance away from the monstrosity in front of her to the fussy, elderly attorney who'd met her at O'Hare Airport. "Neither do my children. Farnum's Castle will do just fine. It can't be in as bad shape as it looks," she added on a more hopeful note, shifting Christopher's clinging body.

"Oh, can't it?" O'Donnell said. "Allow me to give you a tour of your new apartment building, Mrs. Brandt."

"Ms.," she corrected absently, still staring, still fighting the sinking feeling that was rumbling in her empty stomach. She'd been too nervous to eat, and she was paying for it now.

If she'd wanted to offend O'Donnell further she couldn't have chosen a better way. "You've only been widowed for six months!" he said, aghast.

But she didn't want to turn her one, albeit grudging ally in the unknown city of Chicago into more of an enemy than he already was. "Call me Marielle," she said somewhat desperately.

Liam O'Donnell stooped down and picked up the brightly colored box of Pampers and the diaper bag. "This way, Mrs. Brandt."

Marielle allowed herself a brief sigh. The lawyer had been disapproving from the start, pressuring her from a thousand miles away to sell the building to some anonymous conglomerate that probably wanted the place for a parking garage. If she'd had any sense she would have done so, but for once she'd grown stubborn. She didn't want to take anyone's advice, particularly any man's advice. For the first time in eight years her life was her own, whether she liked it or not, and it was up to her to make the decisions, up to her to make do with the hand fate had dealt her.

She took one more look at Farnum's Castle as she reached down to detach Emily's hand from her skirt and hold it tightly in her own. "What do you think, kiddo?"

Emily was a child of few words, particularly in the last six months since Greg had died. "It's okay," she said quietly, clinging close.

Marielle nodded. "It's an apartment building," she said brightly, following O'Donnell's prissy figure through the iron gate and up the uneven sidewalk. "Not much like Yorktown Towers, is it? And we won't just be living here, we'll be taking care of the place, just like Mr. Sanchez did in New York. But maybe there'll be some kids your age here."

"Maybe," Emily said, her voice not promising, and for the hundredth time Marielle felt the rush of anger and grief that she kept hoping she'd put behind her. Damn Greg. Damn him for dying like that, a thirty-three-year-old man dead of a heart attack. It was absurd, totally unexpected that a vigorous man such as Greg could suddenly be gone. Almost as absurd as the fact that the brilliant, workaholic husband she'd lived with since she was twenty years old had left her with a mountain of bills and just about no assets. He'd even cashed in his life insurance in the debt-plagued months before his death, and she'd never had the faintest idea they were in financial trouble. By the time the dust had settled and the debts were cleared, all she had left between herself and destitution was a crumbling old apartment building in Chicago and a very small bank balance.

"We're going to have a great time," Marielle said, climbing gingerly over the broken steps. "Mr. O'Donnell said we get half of the fourth floor. You and Christopher will share a room at first, but later, when we fix the place up a bit, you can have a room of your own. Won't that be wonderful?"

"Sure."

"Mr. O'Donnell had some of the furniture taken out of storage for us." She hated the falsely jolly note in her voice almost as much as she hated her daughter's quiet misery. "We'll have to make do with it for now, but after we start collecting a few of the back rents owed we might be able to buy you some new furniture. Maybe a bunk bed. You've always wanted one."

"Sure," said Emily.

"Sure," echoed Marielle, bouncing Christopher on her hip as she stepped inside the gloomy hallway.

The place was dark and deserted in the middle of the afternoon. The soot-encrusted windows let in only minimal light, and the dark-stained woodwork added to the atmosphere of dreariness and decay. Marielle managed to swallow the large lump in the back of her throat as she followed O'Donnell's natty little figure down the hall, past the wide, curving, decidedly dangerous looking staircase. Emily's hand was gripping tightly, Christopher was starting to slide off her hip, and all Marielle wanted to do was cry.

O'Donnell was standing inside a small closet that on closer inspection turned out to be an elevator. He was tapping one well-polished shoe, and she could just make out his disgruntled glare in the cramped space. "Get in, Mrs. Brandt. I assure you that at least the elevator works. A bill from the repair company arrived at our office. It's with the papers I have for you."

"It's a little small," she said, cramming herself and her two children into the coffinlike space along with O'Donnell, the diaper bag and the giant box of Pampers. The door shut, and an ominous vibration began to shake the *faux* wooden walls. There was a great creaking noise that seemed to come from the very bowels of the building, and then, with a jerk that flung Marielle back against the lawyer, the elevator started upward.

Marielle didn't like small, confined places. She took deep, calming breaths, but it didn't feel as if there was enough air in the tiny elevator. Christopher uttered an amiable protest as her arm tightened around him; she could feel her heart racing.

Marielle didn't like the dark much, either. As the elevator slowly creaked and jerked its way to the upper floors, the dim light bulb overhead flickered and went out. Marielle opened her mouth to scream, but the light came on just as she took a deep breath, and she let it out in a relieved *whoosh*. They shuddered to a halt, the light went off again, but at least the door slid open, revealing a hallway some six inches above the level of the elevator floor.

"After you, Mrs. Brandt," O'Donnell said testily. Of course he didn't have much choice in the matter, she thought, scrambling up into the hallway with more relieved haste than dignity. She'd been blocking the only escape route.

The fourth-floor hallway was a bit brighter than the main floor, and a great deal colder. The bottom half of the hall window was out completely, letting in sunshine and a vast amount of cold air. The oppressive wooden paneling had given way to wainscoting and wallpaper, but the fuchsia cabbage roses were only a slight improvement on the gloom downstairs. If she looked too closely the watermarks marring the pattern looked like nasty little worms crawling over the bright pink petals.

"What pretty flowers," she announced brightly, primarily for the benefit of her silent daughter.

O'Donnell's snort was his only comment as he pushed past her and pulled out a set of keys worthy of a Gothic chatelaine. The door opened with a sepulchral creak and

Marielle stepped inside, hoping for the best, expecting the worst.

She got the latter. The windows were intact but filthy, the walls painted olive green, the floor was covered with torn gold carpeting, and the furniture, culled from stuff stored in one of the empty apartments, resembled something out of *The Bride of Frankenstein*. There were a couple of very uncomfortable-looking baronial chairs, an old sofa, a chest that resembled a medieval sarcophagus and a Formica-topped table. One bedroom contained a portable crib with bars missing and a foldout cot, the other a dynasty-founding bed carved with salacious gargoyles and leering satyrs.

If O'Donnell was waiting for her to cry he'd have a long wait, she decided, letting Christopher down to inspect his new home as she finished her tour. "This will be fine," she said brightly. "It's lucky there was enough furniture to tide us over until we can afford to buy some."

"And when will that be?" O'Donnell stood by the door, clearly in a hurry to leave. "I understood that Farnum's Castle was all your husband left you."

She wanted to point out to him that it wasn't any of his business, but she was, as always, unerringly polite in the face of hostility. "There's got to be some income from this place. Rents...."

"The upkeep, such as it is, far exceeds any rent you might manage to collect from the bunch of weirdos and deadbeats who inhabit this building. I told you that in the first place and you didn't choose to believe me. Now that you've seen it for yourself, I'm sure you realize that anyone in his right mind who could afford rent would live somewhere else. The best thing that could be done would be to evict everyone and tear down the monstrosity."

Her politeness was beginning to slip. "Well," she said with just the trace of an edge to her voice, "I like it here. It has...character."

O'Donnell snorted. "Among other things. As far as I know the offer is still open for the place, but I can't guarantee that situation will last forever. Try it out for a while, if you must. But don't expect my office to be on twenty-four-hour call for every little emergency."

"I wouldn't think of it." She looked about her. "I think we'll be just fine."

O'Donnell just shook his silver-maned head. "I give you two weeks, tops, before you and your children are on a plane back to New York."

She considered explaining to him that she didn't have the airfare to spare—or the credit and she had no place to live even if she could get back to New York. A year ago she could have stayed with one of her friends in the bland new apartment building on New York's Upper East Side, but during the past few months they'd all gone their separate ways. Her parents lived in a very small condo near Orlando, and there simply wasn't room for herself and the two little ones for any length of time. And she wasn't going to ask for money, not unless her children's welfare truly was at stake.

She had yet to be convinced of that. She had her health, lots of energy and enthusiasm, and while her financial skills were a little shaky, all it would take was a little determination to get this place back to making a profit. She didn't need to be rich—she'd led the life of an upscale yuppie mother in New York and hadn't been happy. She just needed enough money to keep the three of them together while she decided what she wanted to do with her life. Managing a run-down apartment building would enable her to keep the kids with her while she sorted out her future. Then she'd sell Farnum's Castle to developers, move somewhere warm with a school system that didn't go on strike every other year, and never look back.

If Liam O'Donnell had shown her an ounce of sympathy, she would have explained all this. But from the start he had lectured her, wrinkling his patrician nose in utter fastidiousness, so she merely took his limp, unoffered hand in hers and shook it. "Thank you for your help. We'll try not to bother you again."

"I'll let you know if the offer is withdrawn," he said, removing his hand from her grasp. He moved into the hallway, pausing for maximum effect. "Perhaps I should mention one thing. I didn't think it pertinent, because I don't believe in such things, but you might be interested."

Christopher was climbing onto a kitchen chair, and Emily was wandering through the apartment like a lost soul, looking, Marielle suspected, for a television set. "Yes?" she said politely, thinking she probably didn't want to hear O'Donnell's parting salvo.

Her instincts were right. She didn't. "According to your rather bizarre tenants, not to mention the previous owners," O'Donnell said in his prissy little voice, "Farnum's Castle is haunted."

Marielle just stared at him. "By whom?" The question was just as absurd as O'Donnell's statement, but he took it seriously.

"Old Vittorio Farnum, of course. One of the most ruthless gangsters in Chicago's history before he found religion. They say he wanders the hallways."

"He'd better not wander my hallways," Marielle said. "I'll call the cops. I imagine he didn't like them when he was alive any more than his ghost will like them now."

"For that you'll have to get to a telephone. And the only phone in the place is upstairs in Simon Zebriskie's apartment."

"No telephone?" she asked faintly.

"No telephone. Good afternoon, Mrs. Brandt. I'll look forward to your acceptance of that offer."

He shut the door quietly behind him. Marielle stared at the peeling paint, the flimsy lock, the thin, cracked wood that wouldn't stand up to a strong breeze or a ghost, much less anyone more dangerous who happened to come in from the mean streets of Chicago to make a little mischief.

She felt a shiver race across her body, even though the apartment wasn't really cold. Another shiver followed, and the burning behind her eyes and in the back of her throat presaged another bout of impotent tears—one that would leave her exhausted, frighten the children and do no one any good.

She could wait to cry, wait until the children were asleep and she was alone in that Gothic horror of a bed. For now she had to somehow get the three of them settled, track down something for dinner and worry about ghosts later.

The knock on her door was so soft, so tentative that at first Marielle didn't hear it. When she finally answered it she didn't know what to expect—Vittorio Farnum's unearthly shade or the prosaic figure of the delivery van driver with the piles of luggage O'Donnell had refused to transport.

It was something in between. Standing in her doorway was a tiny old woman, with wild, flyaway white hair, dark, mischievous eyes, a wrinkled face and a nose and chin so pointed they almost met. Voluminous black clothing covered her sturdy little body, but by her side, instead of the expected black cat, stood a tall, dark-haired girl in her late teens and at an advanced stage of pregnancy.

"Welcome to Farnum's Castle," the apparition announced cheerfully, dragging her reluctant companion into the apartment before Marielle could recover from her amazement. "We're your neighbors. We live in the first-floor apartment on the right. I'm Esmerelda deCarlo and this is Julie. She's going to have a baby." This was announced in a breathless wheeze as her ancient face creased in an engaging smile. "And you have children!" she said, advancing on the fascinated Emily. "How delightful! Julie is wonderful with children, and it will do her good to practice. Not that she's planning to keep the baby. Some nice couple will get the fruit of her labor, but still, someday she'll have one of her own and I know she'll be a wonderful mother. Won't you, dear?"

"Esmy," Julie said in a soft, hesitant voice, her beautiful brown eyes watching Marielle suspiciously. "I don't know that we should barge in like this...."

"Of course we should," Esmerelda said, scooping up Christopher's chubby little form and seating herself on one of the uncomfortable chairs. She held out an arm and to Marielle's amazement Emily went, tucking her slender body against the old woman's voluminous garments. "How can she go down and get her luggage if we don't watch them for her? She can't very well cart them back and forth along with all those suitcases and boxes, can she?"

"My luggage is here?" Marielle cut to the heart of the matter.

"The man dumped it in the front hall. Guess he didn't want a tip," Julie announced. "We'll watch the kids for you while you bring it up. That is, if you trust us." Her eyes were bright with a belligerent suspicion, daring Marielle to voice her concern.

But Marielle could see beyond the anger to the vulnerability beneath. Besides, Esmerelda was right—she did need help. She'd simply have to take chances and learn to trust. And her instincts, infallible as usual, told her that her children would be safe.

"I'd really appreciate it," she said. "It shouldn't take long...."

"Are you kidding?" Julie said, her tight, defensive stance relaxing slightly. "If you can get the elevator working it'll take you four trips at least. If you try to carry it all up the stairs it'll take you longer. Maybe you should get what you need and wait for Simon to come home."

"That's a good idea. Simon will take care of it," Esmerelda said, rocking Christopher. "Simon takes care of all of us."

That was the last thing Marielle needed or wanted—a man to take care of her. O'Donnell had said every tenant in Farnum's Castle was an eccentric—she could just picture the mysterious Simon with the only telephone in the place. Some interfering old patriarch perhaps, or maybe a computer nerd. "I'll get it," she said, casting a doubtful eye on Emily. But Emily seemed perfectly at home nestled next to Esmerelda, so Marielle decided to take her chance while she could.

She ran down the stairs rather than deal with the claustrophobic elevator more than she had to. By the time she'd wrestled two suitcases and a box into the closetlike lift she was too out of breath to be nervous. She had just pushed the fourth-floor button when a hand shot out and caught the closing door, and a tall figure stepped into the cramped area.

She barely had time to see him before the door shut and the light began to flicker. The elevator began jerking upward, the groans and creaks of the machinery precluding conversation. Marielle held her breath, trying to still her heartbeat, telling herself she wouldn't suffocate, the elevator would stop, her unwanted passenger would get out, and she'd end up on the fourth floor with her possessions and her children and her safety intact.

The elevator stopped all right. Halfway between the third and fourth floors it shuddered to a halt. Then the lights went off, plunging them into darkness.

I won't scream, she told herself. *It's all right, it's just another tenant in here with me, not Farnum's ghost. He'll probably even know how to get the elevator going again.*

A deep, sepulchral voice slid through the darkness. "I was stuck in here three hours last time this happened," he said, his rich, eerie voice as chilling as his words. "How are you at screaming for help?"

Chapter Two

Marielle was frozen in a mindless, gibbering panic. Forcing herself to take a deep breath, she inquired of her faceless companion with deceptive calm, "Why should I scream for help?"

His cynical laugh was as funereal as his voice had been. "Because we could use some help getting out of this tomb," he said.

Marielle could feel the panic clawing at her as the darkness pressed around her in thick, smothering folds. The creature trapped with her was just one more threat, someone else to steal the oxygen that was rapidly disappearing. She struggled for breath, but there was none to be had. She pressed her back against the walls of the elevator, hoping to make herself smaller, but it did no good. Her heart was pounding so loudly it throbbed through the tiny space, and all she could think of was her children left abandoned to the mercies of two strange women while she suffocated in this airless box, stuck between floors until she rotted. . . .

"That's all I need," her companion announced to the walls. "A claustrophobic female on the edge of hysteria. For God's sake, calm down! Just breathe slowly and I'll get a light on."

She tried to listen to his words, to take slow breaths, but the fear was still beating at her. She needed light, yet she was afraid. The tall shadow in front of her had a voice like death—what if he had a face to match? What if she'd somehow stumbled into the twilight zone?

The shadow in front of her raised his fist and she flinched, pressing against the wall, waiting for him to strike her. Instead he gave the wall two sharp blows. The overhead light flickered dimly and then stayed on, illuminating the tiny space, illuminating her companion.

He was only a man, after all, not some harbinger of death. He was quite tall, but she'd known that even in the shadows, and he had the kind of rangy body that never put on weight. His hair was straight and dark, streaked with gray, and it brushed the collar of his freshly ironed blue chambray work shirt. His face was long, narrow and clever looking, with high cheekbones, slightly tilted eyes of a disturbing pale gray, and a wide, thin-lipped mouth that Marielle assumed some women would find sexy. He was looking down at her with a combination of irritation and compassion that she found deeply unsettling, and she tried to make herself even smaller. He reached out a hand to her, and she flinched again.

"Don't touch me," she managed to say in a tight, panic-stricken voice.

His hand had dropped the moment he'd seen her reaction. "Lady, I wouldn't think of it," he replied in that deep voice of his. "This elevator is crowded enough as it is without you screaming the house down. I suppose these are your things?"

She managed a nervous nod, half mesmerized by the voice.

He sighed wearily. "You're moving in, aren't you? Fourth floor, right? Esmerelda waved at me from the window, so I assumed someone was fool enough to rent one of the empty apartments. I'm just above you on the top floor. My name is Simon Zebriskie, and I can tell you right now you don't belong here.'' He didn't hold out his hand, just stood there, as far from her as he could manage in that tiny space, and Marielle felt a bit more of her panic melt away, to be replaced by a very real irritation with his unwelcoming attitude. If the rest of the tenants were like him, it was no wonder she had empty apartments.

"Marielle Brandt," she said, her voice still shaky. "And apart from this horrible elevator I happen to like it here. What makes you think I don't belong?"

"Maybe someone will fix it for good," he replied, his strange, tilted eyes staring at her with no emotion whatsoever. "But I wouldn't count on it. Farnum's Castle is a perfect place for people down on their luck, but the modern conveniences have a habit of breaking down at the most inconvenient of times. You don't look like you're used to inconveniences."

"You mean I don't look down on my luck?" She straightened her back, forgetting for a moment that she was going to suffocate.

"Not particularly. At least, not until one looks into those blue eyes of yours and sees beyond the princess."

By then she'd completely forgotten her panic. "I look like a princess who's down on her luck?" she demanded, half astounded, half outraged.

Simon Zebriskie smiled reluctantly, his wide mouth curving. He had big, strong white teeth and for a moment Marielle was reminded of the big bad wolf. "Exactly," he said. "Now that your panic attack is over, you want to help me get out of this damned elevator? Your suitcase is digging into my shins."

Marielle just looked at him for a moment. "I don't know if I like you."

"You probably don't," he said easily. "Once you get to know me you'll be absolutely certain of it."

"Who says I'm going to get to know you?"

"If you're going to stay here you will. For one thing, I've got the only telephone in the place, and even if you had the money, the phone company always makes excuses not to come here. So does everyone else, for that matter. For another thing, I'm the only one who can keep old man O'Donnell off your back when you can't meet the rent." Simon was deftly twisting the control panel plate off its moorings as he talked, exposing a complex mass of multicolored wires.

"Who says I can't meet the rent? Even a princess who's down on her luck has some assets. And the rent's not very high."

"Maybe not for you," he said, pulling out the wires and detaching a purple one. "But any rent at all is too much for most of the people here. They can just manage to pay the utilities and that's that. It's a good thing the newest owner is some New York socialite who couldn't care less about the money. These people would be in big trouble if they had to cough up the rent."

The narrow door began to open, with the slow, jerky movements that characterized everything about the elevator. They were smack-dab between floors, and Marielle could see curious faces staring at her feet, while she got a wonderful view of a pair of skinny ankles wrapped in woolen support stockings.

"Is that you, Simon?" a British voice demanded from the upper floor. The ankles and legs attached to them dropped to the floor, and another old lady peered at them. This one was the complete opposite of Esmerelda de-Carlo. Even folded sideways Marielle could see that she was very tall, very skinny and very aristocratic. Her clothes were wispy gray draperies, and her milky blue eyes were suspicious.

"It's me and your new neighbor. Marielle Brandt, this is Granita Dunkirk. She has the other first-floor apartment next to Esmerelda and Julie."

"That charlatan," Granita sniffed. "If you ever need any advice, my dear Mrs. Brandt, any connection with the spirit world, come to me. Esmerelda likes to think she has certain gifts, but we know the poor thing only deludes herself. On the other hand, I . . ."

"Mrs. Brandt?" Simon echoed, and Marielle couldn't miss the added edge to it.

"She has two of the most adorable children, Simon," Granita added with real enthusiasm. "Of course Esmerelda was her usual pushy self, forcing her way in, but I got a chance to visit with them, and they are the most precious things. It's so nice to have some children in the old place at last."

"I'm a widow," Marielle said, wondering why she felt the need to explain to this thoroughly cantankerous man.

"And we're sorry for your loss," Granita continued cheerfully, peering at her from the ceiling level of the elevator. "So young for such a tragedy. But he's not really gone, you know, dear, he's just on the other side. Any time you want to talk to him, to seek some comfort, we could try a little séance. I have much greater success talking to those who've passed over than Esmerelda has, no matter what she tells you. Maybe we could try it tonight after you get settled."

"Granita," Simon said, his deep voice firm and calm. "I think you should wait until Marielle asks you. Right now what she needs is to get out of this elevator and back to her children. Why don't you move out of the way while I give her a boost up?"

"Of course, of course. You know I only wanted to help, Simon. Sometimes I can be almost as tactless as Esmerelda," she said in a worried little voice, scrambling out of the way.

"Sometimes," Simon agreed with far more gentleness than he'd shown her, Marielle thought indignantly. "Granita and Esmerelda, in case you haven't figured it out yet, are our resident psychics. They do séances, palmistry, tarot reading and all sorts of useful things."

"Really?" Marielle said faintly, looking up at the cheerful old woman and wondering what the other one was doing to her babies.

Once again Simon seemed to know what she was thinking. "Your children are fine," he said in an undertone that was surprisingly reassuring. "Esmerelda's perfectly harmless, and Julie's great with kids."

She looked up at him suspiciously. "Are you sure those two are the only psychics around here?" she demanded.

"Lady, your face is absolutely transparent. Don't ever play poker." He peered up to the fourth-floor landing. "If I were a psychic I'd know what the hell you were doing in a place like this, with children, no less. While you don't look old enough to have much common sense, it doesn't take much to realize this isn't the place for someone like you. So why are you here?"

Marielle just looked at him for a moment, stubbornly reluctant to tell him anything. "Ask Granita," she said instead. "Maybe her crystal ball will tell you." She began climbing over her luggage and boxes to the elevator door.

Simon held out his hand and she took it, noting absently that it was strong and warm, the kind of hand you could trust. She scrambled up onto the upper floor, and that same hand reached behind her rump and gave her an enthusiastic shove. She was out before she had a chance to protest, but she didn't know whether to glare at him or thank him.

He was busy handing up her suitcases through the narrow opening, so she decided the impolite assist had been innocently meant. He followed her boxes with an agility that made her wish she was a little more limber, and walked behind her down the hall, carrying the things she and Granita couldn't manage.

If she'd expected tears or at least excitement upon her return, she got nothing more than a pleased smile from both her children. "You don't have to worry about dinner, Marielle. Fritzie's bringing a casserole up in another hour," Julie announced from her position on the floor beside Christopher. "Hey, Simon."

"Hey, Julie," Simon replied, his deep voice several degrees warmer. "So Fritzie's part of the welcome wagon? At least you'll be well fed. He's a great cook."

"Fritzie?" Marielle echoed. "What does he do for a living, exorcism?"

"You've already heard about the ghost of old Vittorio roaming the halls, have you?" Simon said. "Don't tell me you're scared of ghosts—you'll be in deep trouble living here. Not that Vittorio's been too active in recent years. He's just rumor—none of us have been lucky enough to see him since old Jesse passed away, and he used to see spacemen in the laundry and angels in the trees. No, Fritzie's a witch."

"A witch?" Marielle echoed faintly, knowing she was in over her head.

"A warlock," Granita corrected primly.

"Oh, God," Marielle moaned, carrying the suitcases into her bedroom.

Simon was right behind her again, dumping the boxes and giving her ornate bed no more than a raised eyebrow. "Then there are the Meltirks living two flights below you, and I'd as soon not know the details of their religion. It does seem to involve animals and odd-smelling fires, but they're basically harmless. They're from Baluchistan and don't speak a word of English, but Esmerelda manages to communicate with them quite well. If you manage to stand it here more than a couple of weeks and the animals get too noisy I'll do something about it."

"Sounds like you're the landlord around here," she said, looking up at him. Her earlier nervousness had faded, and once more her instincts had taken over. Despite his lack of welcome, Simon Zebriskie was no threat to her or her children. At least, not in any way she could think of.

"There is no landlord. We look after ourselves."

"So that explains everybody's otherworldly connections but yours. How do you earn your living, digging graves?"

He laughed, a short, reluctant sound. "I'm just a working stiff, if you'll pardon the expression. I work at a radio station here in town."

"Doing what?"

"Midnight to 6 a.m.," he said, watching her. "Better known as the graveyard shift."

"I give up. Maybe I should move back to New York."

"That's the smartest thing you've said so far. Why did you come here?"

A direct question, and this time she couldn't very well refuse to answer. "Let's just say that New York socialites sometimes need money, too."

If she expected his distrust and withdrawal to increase, she was disappointed. He merely nodded. "That explains it. The new owner."

"Exactly."

"And I suppose you're going to want people to pay their rents?"

"It's customary."

Simon shook his head. "You're living in a dream-world, Marielle Brandt. You'll soon find out that nothing about Farnum's Castle is customary. Half these people would be on the streets if they had to come up with the kind of money it costs to live in Chicago. That, or they'd be institutionalized, and that's no life for gentle, harmless creatures like Esmerelda and Granita."

"Do you pay rent?"

"As a matter of fact, I do. I send old man O'Donnell a hefty amount every month, just like clockwork. And the government pays for the Meltirks."

"The government?"

"Someone the government didn't like invaded Baluchistan. Mrs. Meltirk happens to be part of the ruling family, so someone like the CIA got them out and stashed them here until they can return."

Marielle just stared at him. "In Farnum's Castle?"

Simon shrugged. "Baluchistan isn't one of your more strategic countries. Besides, this looks like Shangri-la to the Meltirks. Anything with flush toilets has to be an improvement."

"How many Meltirks are there?"

"We lost count. Eight or nine. Three grandparents, two parents, assorted children, and her royal highness is pregnant again," Simon drawled. "Anyway, at least you're assured of the rent on two of the apartments. And Fritzie usually comes up with something. He's an antique dealer on the side, so he has another income."

"Will I get enough to live on?"

If she was expecting some sympathy she didn't get it. "I doubt it," he said. "Don't you have any money?"

"Do you think I'd be here if I did?" Marielle countered.

He shook his head. "I don't think the rents you're going to collect will even keep this place functioning, much less leave anything to cover your own expenses. Go back home."

"I have no home to go back to," she said, hating to expose herself to his unsympathetic eyes. "I'll have to sell," she added with a trace of desperation. She'd only been in the place a couple of hours, she'd been trapped in an elevator and bombarded with crazies, not the least of which was the cynical loony with the tomblike voice, yet she didn't want to leave Farnum's Castle. Not yet. Just a few months to pull herself together was all she asked for!

"Hey, not so fast!" Simon protested, finally jarred out of his remote disapproval. "Maybe some of us can come up with more money. Anything's possible. If we have to put up with having you here I suppose we can survive."

She looked at him for a long, thoughtful moment. "You're wrong," she said finally. "I do like you."

He shrugged. "I already told you, I don't think much of your common sense."

The bedroom was very small. There was room for the huge bed and not much else, and suddenly it seemed as if they were standing very close together. She was a bit above average height, but felt dwarfed by Simon's tall, wiry figure. For some obscure reason the effect was disturbing in a way she couldn't understand, and she felt a sudden warmth starting between her shoulders and moving downward.

She could see his eyes widen in surprised recognition. And then it vanished as quickly as it had appeared, and he was cool, distant, backing from the tiny room.

"Come on, Julie," he said, moving rapidly away from Marielle. "There are a few more boxes downstairs. Help me with the elevator while I get them and then we'll let Marielle have some time to get herself settled."

"Marielle likes company," Esmerelda announced.

"No one likes company all the time," Simon replied, pausing long enough to look at Emily, who was returning his gaze quite fearlessly. He opened his mouth to say something, then clearly thought better of it. "We'll be back." And he practically ran from the room, Julie sauntering along behind him.

"What's gotten into Simon?" Esmerelda demanded.

"If you were more in touch with your spirit guides you'd know," Granita sniffed.

Emily turned to her mother, and for the first time in months the shadows were gone from her clear blue eyes. "I like it here," she announced.

And Marielle decided then and there that nothing, not poverty, not lucrative offers, not Simon Zebriskie, not even the shade of old Vittorio himself would get her out of Farnum's Castle until she was ready to go. "So do I, darling," she said firmly. "So do I."

HALF AN HOUR LATER Simon Zebriskie shut the flimsy door of his fifth-floor apartment and leaned against it, muttering a heartfelt curse. Just his luck—another lost soul, this time equipped with children.

It never failed—every time life got to a point where things were tolerable, peaceful, even pleasant, something came along to disrupt the status quo. He'd just been thinking how easy things had become, and then Marielle Brandt had to show up. And he had to start feeling things he should know better than to feel.

How long had it been since he'd had that kind of schoolboy reaction? He would have thought that at the age of forty-two he'd be past such adolescent urges. But he'd stood there in that ridiculous little bedroom and looked down into those soulful blue eyes of hers and he'd almost lost it completely.

It didn't matter if she was a widow with two children; she was still nothing more than a baby herself. He'd be surprised if she was even in her mid-twenties, which made him maybe twenty years older than she was and a dirty old man into the bargain. On top of that, she looked about twelve, fifteen tops.

It wasn't just the age difference. He'd already failed at marriage and wasn't the sort of man to take that kind of failure lightly. He'd accepted the fact that he didn't have a talent for marriage, and rather than let some other woman down he planned to spend the next forty-two years steering clear of it. And Marielle Brandt, with her innocent eyes and her two babies, needed marriage.

But still, he thought, pushing away from the door and heading toward the kitchen, she had to be the prettiest woman he'd seen in as long as he could remember. The women he ran into were attractive, beautiful, striking, plain, but none of them were just simply pretty the way Marielle Brandt was. With her heart-shaped face, shoulder-length blond hair, shy smile and innocent eyes she was every adolescent's dream. Her body was small in the right places, deliciously rounded in others.

Did senility strike at age forty-two? he wondered, opening his nearly empty refrigerator and reaching for a Heineken. Maybe it was another midlife crisis. Except he didn't feel as if he was in the midst of a crisis—he still wanted his easy, solitary life. And he certainly didn't want Marielle Brandt and her children disrupting it.

He was overreacting and knew it. At his age he could recognize physical attraction when he felt it, but it didn't mean he had to act on it. He'd have to be in his eighties, not his forties, not to realize Marielle Brandt was a very attractive young lady. Certainly he was old enough to look without touching, particularly when someone was so patently off-limits.

Heading back into the living room, he switched on the FM before sinking onto the comfortable old sofa that his ex-wife had never been able to make him give up. Miles Van Cortland's too-mellow voice filled the room, and Simon snorted as a John Denver love song came on the air. "Annie's Song." Trust Miles to find the sweetest music the station owned. He must have another hangover.

Miles would leave all that soft, sweet, romantic music all over the place, and he'd have to put it away so he could get out stuff with a harder edge. The way he was feeling right now, he'd have to use every ounce of his determination to keep from playing some syrupy love songs himself.

She was too young, he was too old, she was too innocent, he was too jaded, he told himself, moving from the couch and flicking off the radio. And if she expected the tenants of Farnum's Castle to support her she wasn't going to be here very long, thank God. All he had to do was make himself scarce and wait it out. And continue to be as unfriendly as he could manage.

He could hear the soft murmur of voices beneath him, the quiet thump of people moving around, and once more he pictured her, her controlled panic in the broken elevator, the widening of her big blue eyes when she finally saw him in the bedroom. And he knew, deep in his heart, that she was as scared of him as he was of her.

She'd leave, he'd be safe from temptation. All he had to do was wait.

Chapter Three

Blessed peace and quiet settled around Marielle like a warm blanket. It was ten-thirty at night, her visitors had left ages ago, and the children were asleep, Emily on the foldaway cot and Christopher in the portable crib in the bedroom next to Marielle's. Fritzie, the infamous warlock, had turned out to be a very sweet middle-aged man who resembled Winnie the Pooh more than something out of *The Exorcist*. And his Peruvian chicken casserole had been so delicious that even Emily hadn't balked.

Granita and Esmerelda had spent the evening squabbling, over their professions, over Marielle's future love life, over the children, but it hadn't taken Marielle long to realize that beneath the bickering was a real devotion between the two old women, and she felt more than a pang of guilt at the thought that her presence threatened their security. She didn't want to threaten anyone, she thought, sinking onto a hard little chair in the now-empty living room. She just needed enough money to survive. If Granita and Esmerelda couldn't afford to pay their rent, maybe they could qualify for some sort of government assistance. She could even help them fill out the myriad of forms most bureaucracies required.

It would work out. For all its inconveniences and shady history she'd already grown attached to Farnum's Castle.

All she needed was enough energy and just a little bit of money and she could make a go of it. Tomorrow she'd call O'Donnell's office and see what sort of income the building brought in. She had a couple of thousand in savings, enough to make it through perhaps a month or two if she was very careful, and maybe even allow a little bit for repairs on the place. At the very least she needed a telephone of her own.

She sighed, looking around her at the bare walls, the bricked-up fireplace, the peeling paint and cracked windows, and suddenly felt very alone. Her friends were miles away, scattered over the country, and there was no one she could talk to, no one she could turn to for comfort and encouragement. Jaime was off in New Orleans, living, as far as Marielle understood it, with a witch doctor. Abbie was in California and Suzanne was where she'd always wanted to be, somewhere on the road. There was no one left in the old building in New York any more—her life there had vanished. But right then she would have given anything for a familiar voice.

If she had a phone she could always call her parents. It would have been worth putting up with her mother's non-stop helpful suggestions, none of which Marielle planned on following, just to hear from someone who'd known her for more than five hours. But she couldn't feel comfortable leaving the sleeping children to wander around looking for Simon Zebriskie's telephone.

She slumped in her chair. There was no coffee in the house, no food besides the leftover casserole, and she was no longer in the mood for black olives and onions. She'd have to borrow something from the ladies downstairs for breakfast before she attempted dragging both kids out to the grocery store. She could only hope they'd have something reasonably normal like toast. She wouldn't put it past the witchlike Esmerelda to breakfast on bat wings in milk.

She smiled to herself at the thought. The wind was whipping around the building, sliding through cracks and crevices in the old windows. There was heat from some source, though it wasn't particularly effective, and with a sudden sinking feeling Marielle realized that as owner and manager of this place she was responsible for heat. She could only pray it continued to work properly until she was able to orient herself better, or else that Chicago had a particularly balmy autumn.

Branches were tapping against the window, ghostly fingers rapping at her peace of mind, she thought. Then she realized someone was tapping at her door.

Her first thought was Simon, and the instinctive rush of pleasure surprised her enough to effectively wipe that emotion away before she could think about it. She wasn't ready to be vulnerable again—she'd spent too much of her life in reflecting someone else's, rather than being her own person. And if she were going to get involved with someone again she'd certainly have enough sense to choose someone with at least a trace of charm, a speck of warmth for someone other than old women and pregnant teenagers. Still, there was something about his eyes....

She ran nervous hands through her tangled blond hair before answering the door. Julie's stolid gaze met hers. "You expecting someone in particular?" she inquired.

"Not a soul," Marielle said.

"Esmerelda thought you might want to use the phone, let your family know you were settled in all right. I can stay with the kids while you go upstairs."

"I couldn't ask you to do that," Marielle protested.

"You aren't asking," Julie said flatly. "I'm here, sounds like your kids are asleep, and I brought a book." She held up a slightly tattered-looking romance. "Go ahead and call if you want."

"I haven't asked Simon...."

"He's probably gone by now. Besides, the phone's in the hall where anyone can use it. You won't be bothering anyone." She tapped her foot with all the impatience of youth. "You wanna call someone or not?"

Marielle didn't hesitate any longer. "Thank you, Julie. I appreciate it."

"No problem." Julie pushed past her, her shape making her slightly unwieldy as she headed for the chair. "Take your time."

The light bulb in the hall was dangerously dim as Marielle started up the final winding flight of stairs. Replacing a light bulb was one thing she could certainly manage to do, she thought, holding on to the railing as she went. Someone could fall and break his leg, and then she'd really be up a creek without a paddle. No one ever hurt themselves in a public building nowadays without suing, and she'd be lucky if the price offered for Farnum's Castle equalled damages awarded.

God, she was being gloomy tonight, she thought as she reached the top-floor landing. She needed Abbie's brisk common sense to help clear away her obnoxious self-pity. She only hoped she'd be able to track her down somewhere in the heart of Wheeler, California.

There was a comfortable chair sitting in the hallway, better than anything in her threadbare apartment, and the telephone even had an adjustment for the hard of hearing. Marielle stared at it a moment before dialing. More of Simon's charity work. The man was an enigma.

No answer at Abbie's father's home. No answer at her apartment in Yorktown Towers, either, but that had been a long shot anyway. It was too late to call her parents, and her younger sister was on a retreat in some Buddhist commune in northern Vermont. There was no one she could turn to.

She set the receiver down quietly, sat back in the chair and closed her eyes, trying to blink away the sting of tears. And then her eyes shot open again as the door to Simon Zebriskie's apartment opened.

He looked as surprised to see her as she was to see him, and fully as uncomfortable. She couldn't figure out why—at least he hadn't been crying.

"I was using the telephone," she said. "I hope you don't mind. Julie said you'd probably be gone by now...."

"Anytime," he said. In the dimly lit hallway he seemed almost sinister, with his clear gray eyes in shadow and his eerie, deep voice. He was still wearing the chambray work shirt and faded jeans, and his boots had seen better days.

Maybe he hadn't seen she was crying. Maybe if she sat there in the shadows and waited until he was gone he'd think she was waiting for another phone call and ...

"You've been crying," he said.

So much for that thought. "Just feeling sorry for myself," she said brightly, rubbing away the dampness from her face. "I don't usually give in to it."

He moved closer, standing over her. "Everybody has the right to feel sorry for themselves sometime," he said slowly. "Even I indulge in a little self-pity every now and then."

She wished she could see him in the darkness, but the shadows were too deep, he was too tall, and she didn't trust herself to stand up. They would have been close, dangerously close, and there were things going on that she didn't understand, didn't want to understand.

And then he backed away, suddenly, as if burned. "This won't work," he said, his deep voice very definite.

She didn't move, staring up at him, confused and uncertain and still tingling from an unlikely awareness. "What won't?"

"I'm not going to take on one more lost soul. There are too many in this apartment building as it is, and there isn't room for a vacationing socialite trying to find herself. Go back to New York. Go back to your upscale life and let us deal with our own problems."

She stared at him, a slow-growing anger burning away the last of her miserable self-pity. "I don't have an up-scale life to go back to," she said between her teeth. "I'm a widow, remember? No husband, no apartment, no money. All I have is this damned monstrosity, and some-how or other, I'm going to make the best of it."

"By sitting in my hallway crying?"

"If I had a telephone in my apartment I'd be sitting there. Crying," she added defiantly.

He moved into the light, and she expected his eyes to be cold and gray and angry. They were still gray all right, and the irritation was plain to see. So were the unwilling con-cern and compassion. Marielle's anger vanished.

"You don't belong here," he said more gently. "Surely you can see that as well as I can?"

"Whether you believe it or not, I have no choice in the matter. I'm here and I'm going to make it." She wished she could summon up a glare, but his sudden compassion stripped away her righteous indignation.

"And nothing I say will change your mind?"

"Nothing." This time she could glare, but it was a poor excuse for anger.

"Great," he said wearily. "You want to do me one more favor?"

"Sure thing."

He put his hand under her chin, turning her bemused face up to his. "Don't cry any more," he said gruffly. "You shouldn't have to cry."

She didn't say a word, just looked up into those pale gray eyes. And then, before she realized what was happening, his head moved down, his mouth lingering just above hers for a long, breathless minute. She shut her eyes, waiting, but he moved no closer. And then he was gone.

"Damn," he muttered, practically falling down the wide, curving stairs in his haste to get away from her. "I'm not going to do that."

She leaned over the bannister, watching him go, prey to reactions and emotions she couldn't begin to understand. She rubbed her eyes, taking a deep, calming breath. It was no wonder she was confused. The uncertainty of the last few days and months had taken its toll. Add to that the last few sleepless nights, and it was a wonder she could function at all.

One thing was certain—she didn't understand Simon Zebriskie. With his bristling anger, his sudden kindness, he was an enigma. An unsettling one.

Maybe after a decent night's sleep this would begin to make some sense. Maybe that odd, irrational awareness would resolve itself into something she understood and could cope with. For now all she could do was head back to her apartment and try to put everything out of her mind. Particularly the mystery that was Simon Zebriskie.

IT WAS A COLD, WINDY NIGHT as Simon drove his '72 Mustang down Michigan Avenue toward the elegant old building that housed WAKS, and a chilly rain had begun to fall. The old oil furnace at Farnum's Castle usually chose nights like this to conk out, and he could only hope it wouldn't run true to form. Marielle wouldn't know how to deal with it, and old people like Esmy and Granita couldn't afford to be without their heat.

Marielle probably thought he was a coldhearted bastard and a half. It couldn't be helped. He didn't need any dilettantes distracting him from the people who really needed his help. He didn't need an impossibly attractive young woman making him forget all the things he had to remember, making him think he could have... God, what was that awful word nowadays? A relationship? There were no relationships in his future, not with the likes of Marielle Brandt.

He'd handled her well, he thought, with more hope than self-assurance. Until he'd almost kissed her he'd done very well, trying to get rid of her. Now she probably thought he was crazy.

That was the least of his worries. In his forty-two years on earth plenty of people had thought he was off the wall, and plenty would continue to think so. No one would ever understand why he'd given up a job at the biggest station in Chicago, with a salary in the six figures, for the nighttime shift on a small independent station that had trouble making ends meet. Of course, WAKS wouldn't have as much trouble if Miles Van Cortland, the program director and station manager, didn't insist on paying himself such a hefty salary.

And people didn't understand why Simon stayed on at Farnum's Castle when he could definitely afford some nice bland condo on Lake Shore Drive. He didn't bother to explain. It was something in his past, and it was nobody's business but his. He'd learned long ago to accept the fact that he was out of step with yuppie society.

Which was where Marielle Brandt belonged, he thought gloomily. In some nice, elegant place with nice, elegant people. She wasn't the sort to be scrambling for a living, game though she was. She hadn't wanted him to see her crying, and with his unfriendly attitude he'd done his best to make her cry some more.

But she hadn't cried. She'd straightened her shoulders and glared at him, and he had to admire her pluck. Maybe she wouldn't be another drain on his increasingly limited reserve. Maybe she wouldn't even prove a distraction, a temptation. Maybe he could think of her with the same impartial concern that he thought of all the others in the building. And maybe not, he thought gloomily. Maybe not.

MARIELLE SLOWLY MADE HER WAY back down the flight of stairs to her fourth-floor apartment, her brow wrinkled in thought. Simon Zebriskie had to be the oddest of all the extremely odd people living in Farnum's Castle. An extremely attractive sort of odd, she had to admit, despite his gruff manner. If she didn't know better she would have thought he was attracted to her. For a moment it had almost seemed as if he was going to kiss her. It had to be her overwrought imagination, of course. Why would a man who was clearly intent on getting rid of her want to kiss her?

It was a good thing he wasn't interested. The last thing she wanted was another relationship so soon after Greg. Not that her marriage had been so tumultuously wonderful—in fact, quite the opposite. Greg had been a workaholic, a man with an overwhelming personality who was seldom home, and when he was, spent most of his time issuing orders. They'd met in college, when she'd been young and stupid enough to be attracted to his masterful ways. In the last years of their marriage they'd been little more than bedmates, and after Christopher had been born, not even that. He'd been on the verge of moving out, the separation in the hands of the lawyers when he'd died. She was still coping with the nagging guilt and regret, with grief for Greg's lost youth, for the failure of a marriage that had seemed to hold so much promise, for the loss of her children's father. For the loss of her illusions.

No, there'd been nothing so marvelous about married life that she was tempted to repeat the experiment, at least not for now. She wouldn't marry a man for security—it would be doomed to failure. She wouldn't marry a man to provide a stepfather for the children—he could turn around and be just as uninterested as their real father had been. And she certainly wouldn't marry a man for the sake of sex. She knew only too well what a farce and a sham that was. Making love was a messy, disappointing business. She liked the kissing ahead of time, the holding afterward, but as far as she could see the central act was vastly overrated.

No, celibacy suited her just fine for now. In a few years, if she wanted some companionship, she might be willing to pay the price. But right now she needed to prove to herself that she didn't need anyone else telling her what to do, laying claim to her time and her body.

"Did I hear Simon in the hall?" Julie questioned, looking up from her book as Marielle reentered the unlocked apartment.

"He hadn't left yet." She knew her cheeks were still slightly red from her peculiar encounter, and Julie's flat brown eyes were far too observant. "He's a funny guy."

"Simon's the best there is," Julie said, bristling. "He's just a little grumpy sometimes. He likes his privacy."

"I didn't say he wasn't a wonderful human being," Marielle said mildly. "I just said he was peculiar. I can't get over the feeling that I know him from somewhere."

Julie said nothing, shutting her book with dignified deliberation and heaving her bulk from the chair. "The kids are still sound asleep. If you need anything, just run down and get me." She paused by the door. "When are you going to tell the others who you are?

"I beg your pardon?"

"I saw you arrive with old man O'Donnell. You own this rattrap, don't you?" Her eyes were accusing.

There was no point in lying. "Yes."

"You planning to evict Esmy and Granita?"

"No."

Julie relaxed a little. "What about me? I don't pay any rent either."

"I'm not going to evict anyone, whether they pay rent or not," Marielle said wearily. "I just want to make a home for me and my children."

"We help each other around here. We take care of each other. We can take care of you, too."

"I don't want anyone to take care of me...."

"All right, next time you can forget your damn phone call."

"I didn't mean to sound ungrateful."

"Forget it," Julie said grudgingly. "You've got nice kids. You're not too bad yourself. As long as you're not planning to hurt anyone it's okay with me."

Once again Marielle had to swallow the smile that threatened to spill over. Julie was very jealous of her dignity, and she wouldn't appreciate Marielle's reluctant amusement.

"Thank you," she said gravely.

"Tell you what," Julie said. "Anytime you need babysitting, you come to me. It's the least I can do."

Marielle stared at her for a long moment. How could she turn this tough, vulnerable teenager out on the street? How could she evict two harmless old ladies? At least the Meltirks and Simon paid rent. Maybe they could all get by.

"I'd appreciate that," Marielle said, knowing that any polite demurrals would be taken as a dire insult. "Maybe you could stay with them while I buy some food tomorrow?"

"Sure," Julie said. "Just come and get me."

Marielle shut the door behind her. The locks didn't work, but that didn't surprise her. At least if no one paid rent no one could expect her to do much maintenance.

Of course, she thought half an hour later, she'd have to put up with minimal hot water, sporadic heat, drafty windows and flickering electricity herself. Maybe tomorrow she'd better include a bookstore in her shopping trip. She was going to need a self-help manual on home repair or freeze to death in her apartment.

She hadn't unpacked any sheets, so she had no choice but to wrap herself up in an afghan and curl up on the old mattress. The gargoyles overhead would be bound to give her nightmares, and the wind whistling through the eaves of the old building sounded unpleasantly ghostlike. At least the children were sleeping soundly.

She had brought a small portable radio. She turned it on and was randomly flicking the dial when she stopped, mesmerized by a familiar voice. It was Simon's voice, deep and sepulchral, coming through the tiny box on the floor beside the bed.

"It's twelve thirty-three in the morning," he said, his voice melting over her like warm honey, "and here's something I should have enough sense not to play." And coming over the airwaves, in all its sensual sweetness, was John Denver singing "Annie's Song."

Chapter Four

Marielle's eyes shot open. She'd fallen asleep with the meagerly watted light bulb still shining, and in the early morning glow it cast strange shadows over the gargoyles adorning her bed. She was still fully dressed in jeans and a cotton T-shirt, and she was soaked with sweat, her heart pounding, adrenaline shooting through her body.

Her first thought was the children. Within seconds she was off the bed and into the other room, but her panic had been groundless. They were both sound asleep, Christopher with his diapered rump in the air, Emily sprawled sideways across the folding cot.

Marielle stepped back into the hallway, leaning against the wall to catch her breath. And then she heard it again, the sound that must have awakened her in the first place.

It was a hollow, scraping noise, quiet enough, eerily so, and it seemed to emanate from the walls. Marielle took another deep breath, placing her palms against the plaster, and was rewarded with the barest hint of a vibration. Moving along the corridor she followed the noise into her own room, over to the bricked-up fireplace.

There was no question as to where the sound was coming from. Marielle pressed her ear against the brick, holding her breath to listen. Somewhere below her in the chimney that presumably ran the full height of the house, someone was scratching and tapping.

She moved away, climbing back onto the bare mattress and pulling the threadbare quilt around her. The gargoyles and satyrs above her leered down, and she found herself keeping her back to them, leaning against the headboard and staring fixedly at the old fireplace.

"Squirrels," she said out loud, the sound of her voice in the silent apartment drowning the scratching noises. "Or mice," she added, less pleased with that possibility. "Or rats," she had to be honest enough to admit. "Maybe I'd prefer ghosts."

The scratching stopped abruptly. Whoever, whatever it was had abandoned its efforts, maybe scared off by the sound of her voice. Marielle scrunched down on the bed, wrapping the quilt more tightly around her, and waited for the sound to resume.

Silence closed around her like a thick, velvet cloak. In her sleepy mind she tried to reconstruct the layout of Farnum's Castle. There were two apartments on each floor. The first floor held Granita's and Esmerelda's apartments, the Meltirks and Fritzie lived on the second, and the entire floor below her was empty, as was the second apartment on her floor. Simon Zebriskie commandeered the entire floor and a half above her, but that wasn't bothering her at the moment. It was the empty apartment beneath her where the trouble was located.

A sensible, committed landlord would go downstairs immediately and investigate. But just then the most sensible thing in the world was to stay right where she was, away from mysterious noises and things that went bump in the night. If she did go roaming around like some Gothic heroine she'd deserve to be committed.

She huddled down further on the lumpy mattress. She could hear a steady thumping, but this time she knew it was only her heart. Whoever, whatever had been in the chimney was gone, leaving her to reclaim what sleep she could.

She peered out the curtainless windows, but the Chicago night was artificially bright, so she couldn't tell if it was anywhere near dawn. Her watch was in what passed for a kitchen, and the clock radio she'd listened to earlier still flashed 12:00 with monotonous regularity. She reached out to turn it on, then pulled her hand back. The last thing she needed, alone and nervous in the middle of the night, was Simon Zebriskie's deep voice comforting her. She didn't need to know what time it was—the kids would wake up at seven o'clock on the dot. Or, God help her, six o'clock Central Time. She'd better grab what sleep she could, and forget about harmless creatures resting in her chimney.

She shut her eyes, allowing a weary sigh to escape her. Sleep, blessed sleep. And as she began to drift off, the scratching and tapping began once more.

WHEN MARIELLE FINALLY WOKE UP again, three pairs of eyes were staring at her. Christopher was on the floor, dressed in a disposable diaper, a T-shirt and a big grin, Emily was sitting beside him, her Pound Puppies nightshirt smeared with what looked like strawberry jam, and in the doorway stood Esmerelda, her raisin-dark eyes both wary and reproachful.

"Julie told me who you were," she said, her voice quavering slightly. "Are you going to kick us out?"

Marielle shook her head slightly, more to clear the fogs of sleep away than as an expression of negation. Christopher raced over to her, his gap-toothed grin endearing, and Emily plopped onto the bed beside her, swinging her long legs. "I'm not going to kick anyone out," Marielle said, pulling Christopher onto the bed as well. She wished there was some way she could skirt the issue rather than make an outright promise. But the fear in Esmerelda's dark eyes and the bravado in Julie's made polite nothings useless.

"You haven't seen your electric bill yet," Simon's deep voice called from the living room. "You shouldn't make promises you can't keep."

"Good heavens, is the entire apartment building visiting me this morning?" Marielle demanded, pushing back her covers and climbing from the bed, hoisting Christopher onto her hip.

"Fritzie's gone on a buying trip," Granita announced, appearing in the doorway, her tall, skinny body draped once again in gray. "And the Meltirks probably aren't even aware you're here. Come on out and have some coffee. Fortunately Simon brought enough for all of us."

"Oh, he did, did he?" Marielle muttered, wishing she could at least look in a mirror, knowing the results would only depress her.

"And he brought me Froot Loops," Emily said, her voice rich with satisfaction.

Simon was sitting by the window reading the paper, a Styrofoam cup of coffee beside him. The look he cast her was far from welcoming, a fact that managed to spark some irritation in Marielle's tired brain. After all, it was her apartment.

"Finish your cereal, Emily Brandt," Julie admonished, taking Christopher from Marielle's arms and handing her a cup of black coffee. "And then we'll go out and find the park. Your ma's got a lot to accomplish today, and she doesn't need us underfoot."

Marielle waited for Emily's tears and an attack of clinging. Instead Emily climbed back onto the chair, tucked her plastic spoon into her cup of cereal and announced with a beatific smile, "I like Froot Loops."

"You've got a slave for life," Marielle told Simon, sinking to the ratty carpet and taking a sip of coffee. It was absolutely awful—watery and bitter—but at least it contained a good dose of caffeine, so she swallowed half the cup, shuddering.

Simon looked down at her, his light gray eyes distant and unreadable. It was as though the odd conversation in his hallway last night had never happened. "I can always do with more groupies," he said, folding the paper and setting it down. "How'd you sleep?"

"Fine except for the ghosts," she said, draining the coffee.

"Ghosts?" Granita murmured, suddenly alert. "You were blessed with a visitation?"

"I wouldn't call it blessed and I wouldn't call it a visitation," Marielle replied, stretching her legs in front of her. "I'm sure it was just squirrels."

"In the chimney?" Esmerelda questioned.

Marielle had thought her nerves from the night before were gone, but Esmerelda's bright question brought them back. "As a matter of fact, yes. Has there been a problem with them before?"

Esmerelda opened her mouth to speak, but Simon was ahead of her. "Julie, why don't you get the children dressed for outdoors? I'm sure Emily would like the carousel in the park, and you could stop for an ice-cream cone on the way there."

"She's already had too much sugar," Marielle protested, but with her customary efficiency Julie had already whisked the children from the room. Marielle stared after them, wishing that just once she might accomplish something as simple as getting the two of them dressed without arguments and discussions and a wrestling match from her younger child. Julie made it look so damned easy.

"I wasn't going to say anything, Simon," Esmerelda said plaintively. "I wouldn't want to scare the children."

"Of course you wouldn't, Esmy," he said with more patience than he had showed Marielle. "But sometimes accidents happen, and people say things they shouldn't."

"Say what?" Marielle demanded, incensed. "Don't tell me old Vittorio's ghost haunts the chimneys?"

"Not exactly," Granita said. "Though something definitely does."

"Rumor has it," Esmerelda said delicately, "that old Vittorio might have disposed of one of his enemies."

Marielle just stared at her. "I would have thought he'd disposed of a great many of his enemies. He was a Prohibition era gangster, wasn't he?"

"No, my dear. I mean one particular victim. In the...chimney."

Marielle could feel her face turn pale and the nasty coffee churn in her stomach. "You're kidding."

"It's just a rumor," Simon said, unmoved by her horror. "Probably started by my boss. I sincerely doubt it's true."

"Yes, but you can't ignore what he says. Miles Van Cortland is an expert on Chicago in that time period," Esmy insisted. "You know how he's always poking around here when he comes to see you."

"Miles isn't an expert on anything," Simon grumbled. "Except on being charming."

"He is that," Esmerelda said soulfully. "You'll have to meet him, Marielle. The most delightful man. And he's a bachelor," she added significantly. "All he needs is the right woman and he'll be more than ready to settle down."

"I'm not looking for a new husband," Marielle replied absently, turning her attention to weightier matters. "You don't mean there's really a dead body stuffed in the chimney?"

"Of course not," Esmy soothed. "We would have felt the vibrations. It's probably just squirrels looking for a nice warm place to spend the winter."

"They won't find it here unless she does something about the boiler," Simon muttered.

"The furnace?" Marielle echoed in a strained voice.

"It's on its last legs," he announced with an air of satisfaction.

"And the electric bill?"

"I believe it's up to four figures."

Marielle slumped to the floor with a strangled moan, but Simon reached down, caught her hand, pulled her up again—and instantly released her. It was a good hand, she thought. Warm and strong and capable.

"You're in over your head," he said. "You should get out while the getting is good."

"I can deal with it. All I need is another cup of that horrible coffee and I can deal with anything."

"Hey!" Simon protested, insulted. "At least it's better than instant."

"Maybe," said Marielle.

"What do you mean, you don't want a new husband?" Esmerelda demanded, still working on that statement. "Of course you do. You don't want to have to struggle for a living yourself, and your children need a father."

"My children will do just fine without a father."

"If you don't like Miles I can think of several other possibilities," Granita said, not to be outdone. "There's Mr. McFarlane who runs the dry cleaning establishment down the street, if you like them mature. Or there's Mr. Davies from the State Department who comes to check on the Meltirks. I don't think he's married, and he's young and quite presentable, besides having a decent job. Or there's that nice young man from the tax assessors' office who was here last month, or..."

"Tax assessor?" Marielle asked faintly.

"Or there's Simon!" Esmerelda broke in on a note of triumph, casting a fond glance at both of them.

"Esmy!" Simon said in a dangerous voice. "Don't you think it's up to Marielle to find a new husband? When she's ready?"

"But Simon," Esmy said, fluttering her crepey eyelids at him soulfully, "some people are so diffident! Here Marielle thinks she doesn't even want a new husband, when I'm certain nothing would make her happier. If you don't want her I have no doubt I could find any number of suitable men...."

"Don't!" Marielle protested in a strangled tone.

"What makes you think you're the only one capable of matchmaking?" Granita broke in huffily. "I'll have you know there are some remarkably successful marriages that have been a direct result of my machinations. And I don't know that we should rule out Simon entirely...."

"Ladies!" Simon thundered, his deep, rich voice rattling the windows. "Stop meddling! You seem to forget that Marielle has been widowed for only a short while. Don't you think you ought to respect her grief?"

"She doesn't seem to be grieving," Esmy pointed out with damning practicality. "But you're right, Simon. We've been too precipitate. Come along, Granita. We have plans to make."

The two old ladies, one tall and elegant, the other short and round, stalked from the apartment, leaving Marielle alone with Simon Zebriskie.

She swiveled around on the tattered carpet, looking up at him quite fearlessly. "I don't think they're going to drop it," she said gloomily.

He watched her out of hooded gray eyes, and his mouth wasn't smiling. "They seldom do. The two of them are like a dog with a bone—they won't let go of something that takes their fancy. Be prepared to have a whole crew of suitable prospects paraded in front of you."

"Just what I need," she sighed.

"Maybe it is."

"I beg your pardon?"

Simon shrugged. "Maybe Esmy and Granita are right. Maybe the best thing you can do is find a new husband to take care of you."

"I don't want anyone taking care of me." Her tone was fierce. "I have no intention of getting involved with anyone for a long, long time."

"Did you love him that much?" he asked, as if he couldn't keep his curiosity at bay any longer.

"Whom?" Marielle was honestly mystified.

"Your late husband?"

The last thing she should do was confide in Simon Zebriskie, but for some reason she couldn't help herself. "No," she said. "We weren't going to stay married."

He still didn't move. "You hated him so much that you don't want to try again?"

"No. Frankly, it just doesn't seem worth the trouble. True love and marriage are vastly overrated commodities. I can do without."

Simon rose, towering over her, and she once more felt that strange flutter, a pleasant sort of apprehension in the pit of her stomach. "What about making love?" he said with what sounded like no more than casual curiosity. "Are you going to do without that, too?"

Marielle couldn't believe she was having this conversation with a total stranger. But since she'd started, she might as well make her position clear. "The most overrated commodity of all," she said firmly.

He stared at her for a long moment. "If you say so. Let's go see if there are any goblins downstairs."

"Sounds promising." She moved to the hallway. "Julie, could you watch the kids while I go see the third-floor apartment? It should only take a few minutes."

"Go right ahead. I thought I might take them to the park. That is, if it's all right." Julie was looking defensive again, but Marielle had already learned to read her.

Marielle's smile didn't waver. "Wonderful," she said, squashing her doubts. "I'll be here when you get back."

Simon didn't say a word until they were standing in the third-floor apartment and Marielle was trying to sort through ten pounds of keys. "She's a good kid, you know. You don't need to worry."

"All mothers worry. If I didn't trust her I wouldn't let them go. I'm just going to worry anyway. Do you mind?" The third key worked, and she reached for the tarnished brass doorknob.

"It's a waste of time," he said, leaning against the wall. Some of his open combativeness had vanished, Marielle recognized with gratitude, not bothering to try to figure out why.

"But it's my time I'm wasting," she said, tossing her hair over one shoulder. "Let's see if there are any ghosts in here." She pushed the door open, and a wave of cold air washed over them.

Whether it was another broken window or the notorious chill that accompanied supernatural occurrences Marielle had no way of knowing. But foolhardy or not, she was glad Simon Zebriskie was one pace behind her as she stepped into the deserted apartment and faced the demon from last night.

Chapter Five

He was getting in deeper and deeper, Simon thought, looking around the deserted apartment and out the cracked, grimy windows, in fact anywhere but at the slender female figure beside him. Why couldn't he trust his first instincts—to keep as far away from her as possible? The more he was around her, the more he was drawn in.

It was probably just part of his paternalistic feeling toward the people in Farnum's Castle. Marielle was simply another lost soul who needed his help while she served her time in the decrepit old place. But looking at her, the slender, defiant back, the tangle of blond hair, the long legs, he knew his feelings weren't the slightest bit paternal. And he ought to be up in his apartment, letting her fend for herself.

"God, it's cold in here," Marielle said, moving over to the window and wrapping her arms about her slender body. "Why isn't anyone in this apartment? It looks in better shape than the one I'm in."

"The pipes broke last winter," he said, following her and peering into the overgrown yard that surrounded the old place. "The plumber capped them off, but that was it. No one thought it was worth the trouble to fix them."

"Who was taking care of the building? Didn't you have a superintendent, a landlord or something?"

"We had one. He spent all his time in the basement doing drugs and watching soap operas. Life in the big city isn't pretty."

"I lived in New York," Marielle said absently. "I'm not used to hearts and flowers."

"Where in New York? I can't see you anywhere but the Upper East Side."

She grinned ruefully. "Guilty. Did you live in New York?"

"At one point in my checkered past."

"Were you always a disc jockey?"

He grimaced. "I did other things."

"Like what?"

"Nosy, aren't you? I thought we were down here looking for ghosts."

She looked around, wrinkling her nose. "The place looks empty to me. What did you do?"

"Why do you want to know?" He was stalling, knowing that sooner or later he'd have to tell her.

"Because you look familiar. I can't get over the feeling I know you from somewhere, but I can't place it." She seemed to have forgotten all about skeletons and ghosts in the chimneys. "Who are you?"

"Did your parents let you watch television when you were a kid?"

"Of course. What's that got to do with anything?"

"What about horror movies? Maybe when you were about ten years old?"

She stared up at him in dawning realization. "Simon Zee," she said, her voice awed. "You used to dress up like a cross between a vampire and Frankenstein and introduce old horror movies. Was that really you?"

"Throwing spaghetti and calling it veins? Yes, that was me."

"But that was so long ago," she said artlessly, then blushed.

He hadn't seen a woman blush in more than a decade. "I told you, I'm an old man and you're a child."

"You're full of . . . spaghetti," she amended, staring up at him in disbelief. "I can hardly recognize you."

"I wore lots of makeup. Not to mention the fact that almost twenty years have passed since I used to do that."

"What did you do after you were Simon Zee?"

"If you'd like I'll drop my résumé off at your apartment," he snapped.

"I'm just curious."

"You're too curious."

She waited, saying nothing, and finally he sighed. "After the horror movies I hosted a dance show on cable. If you think the old movies were scary, you should have seen disco at its height. From there it was a logical step to FM radio." He moved away from the window. "Enough? Or would you like references?"

"How come you're so touchy about your past?"

"You want to tell me more about your sex life with your husband?" The moment the words were out of his mouth he regretted them. He wasn't used to hurting people; all he wanted was to stay in his nice, safe shell. The expression on Marielle's face was like a knife thrust to his heart.

But he wouldn't apologize. To say he was sorry would be to let down boundaries he needed to keep firmly in place. "Which chimney do you think the sounds were coming from?"

"There's more than one?" she inquired, after only a moment's hesitation.

"There are four or five. Not to mention seventeen fireplaces. If Vittorio stashed a victim in one of them, it's going to take a while to pinpoint which one."

"You don't really think he did?" she asked.

There it was again—that absurdly vulnerable streak in her that brought forth all sorts of unwelcome feelings. "It's highly unlikely. Despite all you've heard about Santa Claus, people can't fit into chimneys."

"If they're in one piece," Marielle added gloomily.

Simon grimaced. "With that kind of imagination it's no wonder you hear noises at night."

"You've got to admit it's a possibility."

"I don't have to admit anything. Let's check out the fireplaces and get out of here. It's too damned cold."

"Ghosts are supposed to make places unnaturally cold," she said, rubbing her bare arms beneath the threadbare T-shirt.

Her arms were too skinny, he thought, watching her, but even the bagginess of the oversize shirt didn't disguise her curves.

"Broken windows do an even better job." He squatted beside the boarded-up fireplace, poking at it. "Seems intact."

"It wouldn't have been from that chimney. I heard it in my bedroom—if there's a fireplace directly below it . . ."

"Are you sure it wasn't the effect of that horrific bed you were sleeping in? I think that was part of Vittorio's stuff that no one would take."

"I'm not that gullible. I just . . ." She stopped dead still in the bedroom doorway so that it took all Simon's balance not to careen into her.

"No, I guess you're not." With his superior height he could easily see over her shoulder into the room, where a pile of bricks littered the stained and pitted wooden flooring. The window wasn't broken, but it was wide open to the chilly autumn air, and the metal fire escape swung gently in the breeze, clanging against the outside wall.

She looked over her shoulder at him, and once again he could see her eyes widen in surprised reaction to his closeness. He knew he should back away but held his ground. She didn't seem capable of moving farther into the room. "Do we want to look?" she whispered.

"At what?" He kept his deep voice at a normal level, trying to break the eerie atmosphere.

"To see if there's anyone in the chimney. Or part of anyone," she added, with a shiver not attributable to the cold air.

"Sure thing." He pushed past her into the room and squatted by the fireplace. Someone had done a fairly effective job of pulling out the old bricks and mortar that had been blocking it. He peered up into the chimney, saw that bits of twigs and shredded newspapers still clung to the inside, then backed out.

"No skeletons, no corpses, no miscellaneous body parts," he said, standing up and brushing his hands against his jeans. "Want to take a look?"

"I'll take your word for it." She still hadn't moved from the doorway. "Who do you think did this?"

"Not the ghost of old Vittorio." He went over and shut the window. "He doesn't need to use fire escapes."

"Then who?"

He shrugged. "I expect those old rumors are circulating again. Every few years we have incidents of vandalism, and then people forget all about it."

"Forget all about what?"

"Vittorio Farnum was one of the meanest, nastiest, dirtiest SOBs to ever set up shop in Chicago. In his heyday he could make Al Capone look like a choirboy. But then he found religion, gave up his wicked ways, and died in bed at the ripe old age of seventy."

"Not my bed, I hope," Marielle said devoutly.

"I wouldn't count on it." He was clearly unwilling to give her any comfort.

Marielle shivered. "Go on."

"So the old guy left most of his money to the church. But there was a huge portion missing. And Vittorio had always said his treasure was in his castle, where even the fires of hell couldn't reach it. Maybe someone took the story literally and thought he'd stashed the loot in the fireplace."

Marielle moaned, slumping against the wall. "That's all I need. Treasure hunters vandalizing the place."

"I think," said Simon, "that's the least of your problems."

She raised her head. "Why do you say that?"

"I shut the window and it's still getting colder. The boiler must have conked out again."

For a moment he thought she might cry. He didn't know what he'd do if she did. If he put his arms around her to comfort her he might not be able to maintain his gruff, avuncular attitude. But he couldn't just let her stand there and weep.

He'd underestimated her. She stiffened her back and sighed. "Okay," she said. "You want to show me the boiler?"

THE DAY, MARIELLE THOUGHT later, had gone from bad to worse. If being ripped from a sound sleep after a restless night wasn't bad enough, the strange things going on in Farnum's Castle added to the strain. To top it all off the boiler proved to be just as mysterious and on its last legs as she'd suspected it would be, the price of replacement mentioned by the repairman would just about empty her savings account, and that still left the four-figure electric bill looming over her.

Still, there had been compensations, she thought as she leaned against the wall, stretching out her legs on the threadbare carpet and taking a deep sip of coffee. For one thing, the expensive repairman *had* come promptly, and he had managed to coax a modicum of heat out of the antique machinery. And Christopher and Emily had had a wonderful day, going to the park with Julie, eating their fill in Esmerelda's tiny kitchen, and were now sleeping soundly in their cozy little bedroom.

She'd met the Meltirks, or at least been introduced to her serene highness and her consort. Her highness was in the middle stages of pregnancy, a few months behind Julie, and her communication consisted of smiles and nods and an incomprehensible babble that only Esmerelda seemed to understand. Marielle thought she could hear livestock in the distance, behind the closed door of their apartment, and the smoky smell was a cross between incense and burned cabbage, but who was she to quibble with people who paid rent? She'd smiled and nodded too, hoping to God the Meltirks were careful with their fires.

And in the stack of bills forwarded from her old apartment in Yorktown Towers, there'd been a postcard from Suzanne. Marielle had looked at it and laughed, her first genuine laugh of the day. On the front of the postcard was a cowboy, complete with chaps, lariat, oversize Stetson and pointy-toed boots. The postmark was Laramie, Wyoming, and on the back was a message in Suzanne's typically brief style.

"Would you believe I've fallen in love with a cowboy? Not with the guy on the postcard—Billy's cuter. We're living together in a house in Laramie, of all the remote places. I'm going to college and I'm very, very happy. Mouse married the cop I told you about and sends her love. With my luck I'm going to be a grandmother before I'm forty. Take care, Suzanne."

Marielle allowed herself a full five minutes to miss her, to miss her other friends who had been closer than her spacey sister had ever been. Suzanne with her funny, wisecracking nature, finally in love. And Jaime engaged to a doctor, settling down in her hometown of New Orleans. Happy endings for both of them. She still didn't know what was going on with Abbie, and could only hope the same luck held for her. If her three best friends could find happiness, maybe there was still hope for herself.

Surprisingly enough, one of the day's compensations had been Simon. For all his odd manner and his gruff, cynical nature, she'd begun to understand him. Or at least to make her peace with him. She still didn't quite understand what a man with his background would be doing living in a decaying hovel like Farnum's Castle, babysitting a lot of people who were, to put it politely, not enjoying the fruits of the burgeoning economy. Right now she was surrounded by the weirdest people she'd ever known in her fairly sheltered life, and surprisingly enough, she was enjoying it. Most of all she was enjoying Simon, Simon of the dour outlook and gentle charm with the old ladies. She could have done with some gentle charm herself, but apparently he didn't have enough to go around.

At least they seemed to have settled into some sort of truce. It was reassuring to know he was up there within shrieking distance if whoever vandalized the fireplace in the apartment beneath her decided to go one floor higher.

"Damn," she said out loud, sitting up and pulling her legs under her. "Why did I have to think of that?" She cast an anxious glance at the window, but all was darkness and gloom beyond the newly washed glass.

She ought to go to bed. The kids had been asleep since eight, it was now half past ten and Marielle was exhausted. Once she'd dealt with the furnace and the highway robber who called himself a repairman, she'd tackled the apartment, stripping off decades of grime and filth from the walls, the windows, the floors. Aesthetically it wasn't much improvement, but at least she knew that if she leaned against the wall now she wouldn't stick to it, and that was some consolation. She hadn't even minded the distinctly chilly shower she'd indulged in once the kids had gone to bed. She'd managed to unpack sheets for everyone and a few kitchen utensils, but heaven only knew where the hair dryer was. She shivered slightly as her damp hair drifted in the breeze wafting from the tightly closed window. How much would storm windows cost? Maybe she could at least dig up enough money for insulated curtains. And it was only October.

She didn't bother to get up when she heard the knock at the door. It could be no one but Julie, who'd promised to check back and see if she needed any last-minute help. Back in New York Marielle wouldn't have been caught dead answering the door in wet hair, no makeup, sweatpants and a stretched-out T-shirt with Virginia Woolf's faded visage plastered across her chest. But things had changed, Marielle had changed, and she had no standards to live up to but her own.

"Come in, Julie," she called lazily, stretching out on her stomach on the carpet. It was still slightly damp, but at least no longer had things crawling in it, and anything was more comfortable than the sturdy wooden chairs that had to date back to old Vittorio himself, probably in his penitential days.

The door with the broken lock opened, but instead of Julie she got a perfect view of a man's beautiful leather shoes. She didn't for one moment suspect they could belong to Simon—he was clearly a devotee of running shoes and Frye boots, and besides, the man wearing these shoes had small, neat feet. She looked up past perfectly tailored legs and a thick knit sweater that had to have come from Ireland to the handsomest face she'd ever seen. Mesmerized, she sat up, her mouth hanging open as her disbelieving eyes took in the vision in front of her.

He had thick blond hair, tumbling rakishly across his high forehead. He had beautifully sculptured lips, curling back in a smile that exposed straight white teeth. He had a short, perfect nose, a golden tan and blue eyes shining with intelligence and humor. Marielle simply stared, not even noticing Simon's taller figure directly behind the glorious apparition.

"What on earth have you been doing?" Simon demanded, striding into the apartment with his companion.

"I cleaned the place," she said.

Simon looked around him. "I guess it's an improvement. Are you just going to roll around the floor like Little Egypt or would you like to meet Miles?"

"Simon, your social graces leave a great deal to be desired," Prince Charming murmured in a voice as thick and rich as imported honey. He crossed the room and reached out a bronzed hand to the benumbed Marielle, pulling her gently to her feet. "You'd never guess that he really knows how to behave, would you?"

Marielle shook her head. Simon snorted, moving past her to the kitchen area and peering inside her aging refrigerator. Finding nothing more exciting than Diet Pepsi and milk, he shut it again. "This is Miles Van Cortland," he said, his tone offhand, his gray eyes alert. "You remember, the one Esmerelda said you should marry?"

"He is a beast, isn't he?" Marielle had by this time recovered her equilibrium, and she gave the gorgeous Mr. Van Cortland a friendly smile.

"He's just trying to protect his turf," Miles said. "Never mind that he's insulting his boss."

"You're his boss?" Marielle echoed, walking past him into the kitchen. She pulled Simon out of the open refrigerator which, after an afternoon's defrosting, was already building up a new coating of ice, and firmly shut the door.

"He is," Simon rumbled, looking down at her. "He's also an expert on old Chicago architecture, not to mention certain legends surrounding the gangsters in the twenties and thirties. I thought maybe he could tell you a bit about Farnum's Castle. I never paid much attention to details, but Miles can be downright compulsive. Can't you, Miles?"

"I wouldn't put it that way, Simon," he protested politely. "Just because I happen to like trivia..."

"Whatever," Simon said airily. "Tell Marielle what you know about the castle, make a date with her for later, and then let's get to the studio."

Miles smiled faintly. "Simon asked me to stop by on my way to the studio to meet an absolutely beautiful young widow, but I think he's forgotten he wanted to set us up. Are you sure you haven't got designs on her yourself, old man?"

"I haven't," Simon said flatly, adding, "young man." He pushed away from the counter, moving past Marielle without another glance. "I'll meet you downstairs in fifteen minutes." And without another word he was gone.

"My, my," Miles said, sinking gracefully into one of the uncomfortable chairs. "I seem to have tweaked the lion's tail. I've never known Simon to be so touchy."

"Really? I thought he was always that grumpy," Marielle said, staring after the tightly shut door, no longer interested in the refugee from *Gentleman's Quarterly* ensconced in her living room. Just when she was thinking she was beginning to understand how Simon's mind worked, he did something completely unexpected.

"Not usually," Miles said.

Marielle was still staring at the door when she realized an uncomfortable silence had fallen over the room. She turned back to her guest, once more the perfect hostess.

"I'm sorry. My mind's been wandering. Did you say something?"

"I said, you don't really want me here, do you?"

Marielle stared at him for a long moment. "I'd have to be mad not to," she said bluntly, secretly appalled at her own outspokenness. For years she'd been the model of discretion; now suddenly she seemed to have no sense of polite behavior.

Miles Van Cortland grinned in appreciation. "Clearly you weren't expecting visitors. But despite Simon's heavy-handed matchmaking, which was clearly intended to do more harm than good, I would love to take you out to dinner sometime. I think we'd do better without his disapproving ghost hanging over us."

"I think it's Vittorio's ghost that worries Simon."

"No, it isn't. Simon doesn't believe in him."

"Do you?" she questioned.

The humor was suddenly, chillingly gone from Miles Van Cortland's beautiful blue eyes. "I don't want to," he said seriously.

Tiny tendrils of fear were beginning to creep up Marielle's scantily covered backbone, and she wished she could fling open the door and call for Simon to come and take Miles away before he could scare her further. But Simon was probably out of earshot and might not pay any attention even if she yelled. "You're scaring me," she said in her most even voice.

"I wouldn't want to do that. Warn you, perhaps. Things have happened here, things without rational explanation. It wouldn't do to be too smug."

Marielle just stared at him, thinking of the nightmare bed she'd be sleeping in, thinking of the midnight visitor in the deserted apartment beneath her, thinking of what might be hidden in the closed-off chimneys. "I think I'd rather discuss this in the light of day."

"What about lunch, then?"

"I think I'd better say no," Marielle said slowly, knowing she was out of her mind. The best-looking man she'd ever seen was asking her out, and she was telling him no.

"Dinner?"

"Sorry."

"What about a guided tour of your new domicile, complete with architectural history? With Simon along for moral support? Though I assure you I'm not the slightest bit dangerous. I haven't thrown myself on an unwilling female in at least ten days."

She laughed. All those beautiful features and humor, too. She was out of her mind. "I'd like that. If you have the time."

"I have the time." He rose, and Marielle realized he was exactly Greg's height, a few inches taller than her own five foot seven. "What about Saturday for the grand tour? Neither Simon nor I work and we'd have plenty of time."

"That would be terrific."

He looked at her, his eyes slightly troubled. "In the meantime, would you do me a favor?"

"If I can."

He smiled, a rueful, self-deprecating smile. "I know this sounds crazy," he said, "and if you're feeling nervous I know you won't want me to go into details. Whether you believe in the supernatural or not, please, for your own sake, keep away from the fireplaces."

Marielle, her throat choked with creeping nervousness, could do nothing more than nod.

Chapter Six

Another miserable, disrupted night, Marielle thought with a groan, pulling herself out of bed and shivering in the cool morning air. It was six-thirty, the children were still asleep, but she didn't want to risk awakening to an audience of half the tenants two days in a row. She wasn't going to get any more sleep, no matter how desperately she needed it, and the best thing she could do was brew herself a pot of strong, dark coffee, throw on some clothes and prepare to face the day—and the myriad of problems Farnum's Castle would no doubt present.

It wasn't that she'd stayed awake listening for the eerie *tap-tap, scrape-scrape* that had never come. It wasn't that she'd been tormented by the suspicion that evil old Vittorio had breathed his last in the very bed she was lying in. Nor was she worried someone would break into her apartment if she allowed herself some desperately needed sleep.

She'd tossed and turned, dozed and then been jarred awake, for the simple reason that she couldn't get Simon Zebriskie off her mind. She was oddly attracted to him, though she knew she shouldn't be, and it was only the knowledge that it was impossible and the last thing Simon wanted that made her even entertain some fleeting, wistful thoughts. As far as she could tell, Simon was just as strange as the rest of the odd people holed up in Farnum's Castle; his eccentricities were just a little better hidden.

What she should do, she thought, pulling on clean clothes and a thick sweatshirt, was to keep her distance from him. But that left her essentially alone and friendless in the huge city of Chicago, and she didn't fancy prissy old Liam O'Donnell would offer much help. Whether Simon paid lip service to polite conventions or not, she knew she could count on him. And faced with the overwhelming problems and complexities of her new life, she needed some sort of help. Or at least a reluctant shoulder to cry on.

The children were still soundly, blissfully asleep. It was icy cold in the hallway outside their bedroom, with a sharp wind whistling through the predawn apartment. Marielle paused with her hand on the light switch. The artificial Chicago light barely penetrated the tree-filled grounds and thick, crumbling walls of Farnum's Castle, but even in the murky darkness she could tell something wasn't right.

"You've got two choices," she informed herself out loud. "Both rotten. One, the furnace conked out again. Two, your window's open, which means someone got in here last night while you were sleeping. Take your poison." And she flicked on the light switch.

Parenthood was a strange and wondrous thing, she thought absently, not moving. When panic and horror made you want to scream at the top of your lungs, some inner guard clamped down, keeping you silent, keeping you from terrifying your children when caught up in your own fright. She stared at the rubbled pile of bricks and mortar on her once-clean carpet, stared at the open window letting in a chill morning breeze, and let the stray shiver of unadulterated panic wash over her silent body.

She was still standing there, frozen in time and space, when she heard the footsteps on the creaking wooden stairs. Someone was moving stealthily, trying not to be heard. For a moment Marielle was torn between the desperate desire to rush into the children's room and make a last stand against the creature of the night stalking her, and the equally strong desire to face whatever person or persons were tormenting her.

She didn't allow herself time to hesitate. On silent bare feet she raced across the room and flung open the door to the hallway, prepared to confront chain-wielding hoodlums or the shade of old Vittorio himself. What she saw was a weary-looking Simon, trudging up the stairs, his gray-streaked hair rumpled, his eyes shadowed, a Styrofoam cup of what was no doubt the same hideous coffee in his hand.

He paused, looking at her in surprise. "What's wrong?"

It might have been the relief that it was someone safe and not the creature she'd been fearing. It might have been silliness from lack of sleep, or just something as simple as Simon knowing there was something wrong from the expression on her face in the dimly lit hallway. Whatever the reason, she hurtled across the empty hallway and threw herself into his arms.

The hot coffee went flying, splattering the hallway, splattering both of them, but Marielle was scarcely aware of it, and if Simon noticed he was too busy wrapping his long arms around her, holding her trembling body close against his own.

His jacket still held the cold from outside. He smelled of coffee and night air and clean male flesh, and he was strong and solid against her. For a long moment she closed her eyes and breathed in the smell and strength and comfort of him, allowing herself a few short moments of weakness.

And then she pushed away, just as his arms began to tighten, as his hands began to move. He let her go with unflattering haste, and she had no trouble reading his expression. It contained both relief and regret, and the relief was by far the stronger emotion.

"I repeat," he said, his deep voice unemotional as he brushed at his coffee-stained clothes. "What's wrong?"

She should have had more sense, but for some reason she couldn't resist touching him again. And he didn't seem to be able to pull back. She took his hand in both of hers and pulled him into the apartment without a word.

He stood surveying the mess, his expression inscrutable. Pulling off his venerable denim jacket and covering his hands with the material, he crossed to the window and closed it. The cessation of the cold draft was an immediate relief, and the knocking and clanging of the old radiator assured her that for now the furnace was still working.

"Did you hear anything?" Simon demanded.

"Not a sound," Marielle said. "And I was awake half the night listening for it."

Simon stared at the fireplace for a long, thoughtful moment. "This time we call the police. Stay put while I go get Julie to watch the kids."

Marielle had no intention of moving. Much as she wanted to clear away the debris, to clear away any sign of her privacy being violated, she knew better than to do so. Even Simon had had the immediate good sense not to mess with possible fingerprints.

She listened to his footsteps descending the stairs. He was no longer making any attempt to be quiet, and in retrospect she realized he'd been trying not to wake her when he'd been creeping up the stairs. The tantalizing aroma of coffee was strong in the morning air, and it took her a moment to trace it to the wet stains across her chest.

She stumbled to the kitchen area, flicked on the light and began making coffee with numb ease. Probably she shouldn't even do that—the intruder might have left fingerprints in her kitchen, but right then caffeine was even more important than catching the vandal. By the time Simon returned with a sleepy-eyed Julie she was already inhaling the perfectly brewed coffee.

"You shouldn't have touched anything," Simon said, accepting a mug.

"If I didn't have coffee I would have died, and then it wouldn't have made any difference if they caught the person who did this," she said flatly. She could see the coffee stains across his chambray work shirt, and she suspected they were a mirror image of the ones across her chest. After all, the coffee had been plastered between them during that too-brief embrace in the hallway, and it only made sense they'd be matching inkblots. If she looked at the splotchy stain with her eyes half closed she could imagine all sorts of things, none of them particularly healthy for her peace of mind.

"There's milk in the refrigerator," Simon informed Julie, ignoring Marielle as he drained half the mug of steaming coffee without flinching. "Drink some, and then you can have coffee."

Marielle waited for Julie to take offense, but all the young girl did was stick out her tongue at him. "I prefer Diet Pepsi."

"Bellywash," Simon sneered. "After you drink some milk. Marielle and I won't be gone too long."

"Take your time," Julie said with an airy wave, moving into the kitchen and peering into the refrigerator. "If the kids wake up I'll take 'em down to Esmy's to watch cartoons."

Marielle considered protesting, then swallowed her objections. So what if her kids had eaten more sugar and watched more TV in the last forty-eight hours than they had in their entire lives? The two of them were thriving, showing more life than they had in the six months since

Greg had died, and she could just make them brush their teeth six times a day. As for television, it would take more than a little black box to put a dent in Emily's fevered imagination.

She refilled her mug of coffee before she followed Simon's rangy figure out the door. On a day that had begun as inauspiciously as this one, she was going to need all the caffeine she could get. She wondered briefly what her friend Jaime would say if she could see her now. Jaime had always had the ridiculous notion that Marielle could deal with anything, and do it with calm good humor. Right now Marielle felt like flinging herself onto the winding stairs and weeping in frustration and worry. But she wasn't going to let Simon see her anxiety, just as she had never let Jaime see it. Coping was second nature to her, and there were times that came in awfully handy, times like these. But she wished to hell there was some point when she could just give way and howl and let someone else cope, for a change.

Simon ignored the telephone in the hallway, opening his apartment door and gesturing for her to enter. Marielle stopped, staring suspiciously. "You don't lock your apartment?"

"Who would I keep out? Esmy?"

"Maybe whoever trashed my apartment and the one beneath me," she suggested, still not moving.

"I hate to point this out, but locked doors didn't do any good in either case. Besides, I always lose my keys."

"Aren't we going to use the telephone?" she stalled.

"We're going to use the one in my apartment. That way if someone comes up to use the telephone they won't overhear something that will put them in a panic."

"I thought you put the telephone in the hall because you couldn't stand having one in the apartment?"

He stood in the doorway for a long moment. "So I lied. The people in the apartment building need a telephone, and no one else can afford one. I tried to get the phone company to put it on the first floor so it would be easier to reach, but they were, as usual, obstructionist. If there's one thing I've kept from the sixties it's a strong distrust of the phone company." He tilted his head to one side, staring at her through hooded eyes. "Are you going to stand there in the hallway asking more questions or are we going to call the police?"

"We'll call the police."

His apartment wasn't at all what she would have expected, but when she thought about it she realized it was exactly right for him. While she might have thought he'd live in austere, Eastern simplicity or modular, streamlined yuppie heaven, the jumbled, cluttered, homey feel to the place attested to a man who knew what he wanted. At least one apartment in the decrepit old building had recently been painted, and the old horror movie posters on the white walls were an oddly cheerful splash of color. The furniture was old and comfortable, the bookcases were piled haphazardly with books and magazines, the Oriental rug had the pattern almost walked off it. And it was warm, blissfully, gloriously warm.

"How come you've got the only apartment with decent heat in it?" she demanded, sinking onto the old sofa and wrapping herself in its sprawling comfort. She let out a surreptitious sigh, setting her coffee on the cluttered table in front of her. There were times when she'd thought she'd die for a bed as comfortable as this tattered old couch.

He had an odd expression on his face as he stood by the window, watching her nestle into his sofa, one she couldn't begin to read and didn't have the energy to try. "That's one of the problems of old-fashioned steam heat. There's one thermostat, all the heat rises, and the people on the top floors roast while the people lower down freeze. Esmy and

Granita need the heat a hell of a lot more than I do, but they don't need a five-floor climb. So we all live with it.''

"Will the new boiler even things out? Assuming I can even dig up the money for it." She stretched out her long legs on the cushions, surveying her dusty bare feet for a moment. When she'd gotten dressed that morning she hadn't expected to be leaving the apartment so soon, and it was the first time she'd realized she was barefoot.

He was watching her feet, too. "I don't know. It couldn't hurt."

"I don't want to spend that much money on something that has only a vague chance of helping."

"Do you have any alternative?"

Marielle shut her eyes for a pained moment. "Let's not talk about it now. Do you want to call the police or shall I?"

"Oh, you can definitely do the honors. I'm not crazy about the police, either.''

"Along with the phone company," she said. "What sort of life of crime did you lead?"

Simon's smile was wintry. "Let's just say they wouldn't let me on the supreme court."

Marielle sat up abruptly. "I hope this was all part of your sordid past?"

"It's none of your damned business," he said, leaning against the wall, his shoulder resting against Colin Clive as Dr. Frankenstein. "But yes, it's all part of my distant past. Sins, however, have a habit of backfiring on the sinner."

"Yes, they do," she said. "Do you have any other sins waiting to catch up with you?"

He pushed away from the wall. "Maybe," he said, his deep voice giving nothing away. "The telephone's beside the couch. But don't expect a whole lot of help from the cops. They've been here too many times checking out treasure hunters to get too excited about the latest rash of breaking and entering.''

"Even though I and my children were asleep in the same apartment?" Marielle demanded, incensed.

"They didn't bother you, did they? Didn't even wake you up. I don't think Chicago's finest are going to break their hearts over it. There's too much real crime going on."

Marielle crossed her legs under her. "I think you must be the most cynical man I know."

"Maybe. But if I were you I wouldn't take Miles Van Cortland at face value, either. Beneath that golden yuppie charm lurks the heart of a shark. Are you going to go out with him?"

"Why don't you ask Miles?"

"He wouldn't tell me. Are you?"

"Why do you want to know?"

Simon shrugged. "I went to all that trouble to match-make for you; I'd like to know if I was successful."

Marielle reached for the phone. "You got just what you wanted, Simon," she said obscurely, dialing 911.

Simon glared at her. "I'm very happy for both of you. Let me know when the big date is and I'll make sure Julie can baby-sit."

"I can take care of my own baby-sitters, thank you," she said in a tranquil voice that was calculated to drive him crazy. "Julie and I have an understanding."

"Great," growled Simon. "Terrific." And he stomped into another room, presumably the kitchen, and began banging pots and pans around with great enthusiasm.

She found him a few minutes later, staring disconsolately into a mug of black coffee. The jar of instant sat out on the counter, and Marielle gave it a passing grimace. "You were right," she said, hoisting herself onto the spotless butcher-block counter and swinging her legs. "The police weren't very excited about the whole thing. They promised they'd send someone over later today, but I don't think we're going to get the full attention of the Chicago police department."

"I warned you," Simon said.

"Want to say 'I told you so' just to make things even pleasanter?" she suggested sweetly.

A small smile tugged at the corner of his mouth. If she'd been into mouths she knew she'd find his mouth particularly attractive. It was lucky she didn't care about such things, or Simon Zebriskie might be extremely distracting.

"I told you so," he said.

"Wretch. And don't even bother to offer me instant coffee. I'd rather drink Drano."

"I don't think I have any."

"What I don't understand," she said, looking around her at the spotless little room, "is why you keep your kitchen so neat? I've never in my life known a man to have such a clean kitchen."

"Sexist," he said mildly, pouring the rest of his coffee into the sink. "I don't think you want to know why my kitchen is so clean."

Marielle just stared at him. "Why?" she asked in a doomed voice.

"Cockroaches."

"Oh, God!" she moaned. "I thought that was one thing I left behind in New York."

"I didn't think cockroaches lived in the Upper East Side. I thought they were confined to the West Side and the Village."

"Sometimes," Marielle said, "they get forged papers and cross Central Park at night where they take over nice new apartment buildings like Yorktown Towers and drive fastidious housekeepers crazy."

"Are you a fastidious housekeeper?" Simon asked with real curiosity.

"I am when someone's holding a gun to my head. Be it a demanding husband or an army of cockroaches. I thought I could relax my standards a bit here."

"Be my guest. That way my cockroaches will always know where they can find a good meal."

"Damn," she said, shaking her head. "A dying boiler, a huge electric bill, poverty-stricken tenants, vandals, and now cockroaches. What else can possibly go wrong?"

"You haven't talked to the tax assessor yet."

She glared at him. "You know," she said in a conversational tone, "you're so nice to Julie and the old ladies. Don't you think you might consider being nice to me, too?"

He shook his head. "Can't do it. I have a very limited supply of kindness for my fellow man, and they use it all up. You'll have to make do with what's left. Besides, you're not in need like the rest of them."

"Not in need of kindness?" Her voice came out just the tiniest bit rough. For some totally bizarre reason she felt like crying, she who never cried, she who was calm and capable and good-humored and always in control. "Don't you think everyone needs a little kindness?"

If she didn't know better she would have thought that was guilt shadowing his gray eyes. "Sure," he said. "But maybe being kind to you would prove dangerous to my peace of mind. You'll have to count on Miles for kindness."

"I don't think that's a very good idea," she said. "I don't think I'd trust Miles not to be out for number one."

"Would you trust me?" The moment the words were out of his mouth it was clear he regretted them, but Marielle answered before he could call them back.

"Yes," she said. "I'd trust you." He wasn't very far away, less than a foot from where her legs hung over the counter. His eyes had a fine network of lines fanning out from them, and she wondered if those lines came from smiling, if there was someone he smiled with, laughed with, joked with. For some odd reason she wanted to reach out and smooth the frown away from his narrow, clever face, to push the thick, straight hair from his high forehead....

She jumped back, shocked at her wayward thoughts. There was a strange light in his eyes, and for a moment she wondered if he'd read her mind. But the moment passed.

"I don't know if you should," he said, and she stared at him blankly. "Trust me, that is."

"I don't think I'm going to get much help from the police," she said, deliberately changing the subject to one more prosaic. "Are you telling me you won't help, either?"

"I'll tell you what." He moved closer so that his hipbone was millimeters away from her knee. "I'll help you find out who's breaking into the apartments, I'll help you get things sorted out with the electric company, the tax assessor and the heating contractor. I'll help you get everything under control," he said, "and then you can leave."

"Why should I want to leave?"

"You do, don't you? You don't want to spend your life in this ramshackle old building with a bunch of crazies. You want to live someplace clean and warm and sunny. Like New Mexico."

Marielle stared at him for a long moment. For a moment she hated him, hated herself for being that transparent. But her anger would have been a waste of time, and she prided herself on being levelheaded and practical. "How am I going to do that?"

"I'm not sure. But I'm going to do everything I can to help you, starting with finding out who's been haunting Farnum's Castle. If worse comes to worst we'll find someone who'll buy you out, someone who won't tear down the place and turn it into a high rise or a parking lot. We'll find an answer," he said, "and you'll find your freedom."

"You'd be going to a lot of effort to get rid of me," she said evenly.

He didn't even blink. "I consider it a worthy investment of my time."

"I accept it. I'm not in the position to turn down anyone's help." She started to scoot down from the high counter, and almost instinctively his hands went around her.

Then he stopped, so that she was halfway off the counter, his long, strong fingers wrapped around her waist, his eyes level with hers, his mouth level with hers—and dangerously, enticingly close. For a moment neither of them moved, and the silence grew and stretched in the small, spotless kitchen. And then she deliberately broke the moment, pushing away from him, landing on the floor, moving from the room with undignified haste.

"Will you come down when the police show up?" she asked, tugging down her sweatshirt, keeping her eyes on her toes.

"Just send Julie up."

"What if you're asleep?"

"I'll wake up."

"Okay," she said, looking at the faded carpet in the living room, looking at the bottom of the apartment door. "See you."

"If you don't lift your head you're going to bump into the wall," he drawled.

She did lift her head at that, staring at him defiantly. "New Mexico," she said sharply, "will be a definite improvement."

"Keep remembering that," he said. "And I'll keep reminding you."

Chapter Seven

Simon was dead wrong, Marielle thought hours later as she hurried along the sidewalk, ducking her head into the wind as she headed for the closest thing to a supermarket this side of Evanston. The police had been blessedly, wonderfully helpful, so much so that she was practically dancing down the street. In a fit of good humor she'd even promised the kids Alpha-Bits, telling herself that if they weren't nutritional at least they were educational, and she had every intention of buying *TV Guide*. Simon had sent down an old thirteen-inch color television, insisting that he had no need for it, and the children were in seventh heaven, absorbed in *Sesame Street* while she dealt with the late-arriving police.

And now she was on her own in the early evening streets of Chicago. The area around Farnum's Castle was genteelly run-down—an old residential area becoming gracefully seedy, not unlike the tenants of her decrepit apartment building. Not that she'd call Simon gracefully seedy, she thought with a smile. She could think of a thousand adjectives, words like cynical, nonconformist, gruff, bad-tempered, charming, protective, attractive....

Not that she was attracted to him, mind you. She had too much common sense for that. Eight years of married life had been enough, enough to hold her for at least eight years of single life. She wasn't going to let herself in for more disappointment if she could help it, and she was too levelheaded to fall into any romantic traps. Not that Simon would set one for her. He had no intention of getting involved with her, thank heaven. All he wanted to do was get her out of there, and she'd accept his help quite happily.

Traffic was light that time of night—rush hour had ended early and midweek wasn't prime shopping time. The crisp autumn air had just enough bite to be invigorating, Marielle knew her kids were safe and sound with Julie watching them, and she'd had her first bit of good news concerning the old wreck she'd inherited. She couldn't wait to tell Simon, to have her own chance to say "I told you so."

She was spending much too much time thinking about Simon, she thought absently. She was almost more interested in his reaction to her good news than the import of that stroke of luck itself.

Simon had been true to his word, coming downstairs when Officers Toody and Muldoon had arrived. While he'd gone off with the tall, skinny Toody, Marielle had been left with the rubicund Muldoon—the cheery Muldoon who, along with his wife and three children had a brother-in-law crammed into his small suburban house, a brother-in-law who was a licensed plumber and electrician. Licensed, that is, in the faraway hills of New Hampshire, not in the union-dominated heart of Chicago. On top of that, the young man was no longer interested in practicing such noble arts—instead he wished to find himself by writing hard-boiled detective novels. There not being a vast market for unwritten novels, Dennis McMurtry was sponging off his long-suffering brother-in-law and fast wearing out his welcome.

And blessed Officer Muldoon, upon viewing the empty apartment with the broken water pipes, had suggested a trade. A free apartment in exchange for Dennis McMurtry's precious talents.

"What makes you think he'll go for it?" Marielle had asked, not daring to believe her luck.

"He'll go for it," Muldoon had said grimly. "Have you ever shared a bedroom with a five-year-old and a seven-year-old? Mind you, he's great with them. But the man's ready for a place of his own. I'll have him call you the moment I get home."

"I don't have a telephone."

"I'll have him appear on your doorstep the moment I can get him out of the house," Muldoon promised with a streak of ruthlessness. And Marielle had not the slightest doubt that he would.

She'd still have to pay for supplies, pipes and fittings and wiring and the like. But at least, if this worked out, she wouldn't be saddled with a hundred dollars an hour or whatever plumbers and electricians cost nowadays. Once Dennis turned into the next Elmore Leonard and moved to Lake Shore Drive she'd have a usable apartment to rent. And chances were a plumber-electrician even knew about boilers and heating systems. Things were definitely looking up.

She wasn't quite so sanguine half an hour later as she struggled back up the sidewalk, cursing her own stupidity. She'd lived in a city long enough to know you couldn't buy too much at a grocery store if you had to carry it all yourself, but remembering her empty refrigerator and enticed by the rows of food, she'd simply forgotten. The Diet Pepsi alone weighed at least five pounds, the Alpha-Bits kept slipping out of the bag, the gallon of milk that would last her not much more than a day weighed a ton, and the Ben and Jerry's Ice Cream was melting, pressed as it was to her breast. To top it all off, some lowlife in a beaten up old Mustang was slowing down as she did her best to hurry along, clutching the bags that seemed determined to take a suicide leap to the cracked sidewalk.

Marielle kept her head averted, knowing with a sinking heart that the unseen driver was rolling down his window, bracing herself for some obscene proposition or at least a sexist comment. The streets were relatively empty and she allowed herself a tiny tendril of fear. Would the unknown people of Chicago help a woman in trouble, or were they just as apathetic as New Yorkers?

The driver leaned his head out of the window. "Don't you know better than to buy too much at one time?" Simon's deep voice demanded. "You could at least have asked me to drive you."

Marielle stopped dead still, and the bag with the Pepsi slid to the ground with a clang. "I didn't realize you had a car," she said. Then her eyes surveyed the battered old wreck. "I'm still not sure you do," she added dubiously.

"Beggars can't be choosers. Do you want a ride back to the apartment or not?"

"I want a ride back to the apartment." She slipped into the cracked leather seat, dumping her groceries at her feet. "Why in heaven's name do you drive such a rattletrap? I thought you were some lowlife about to come on to me."

"I drive it because it runs," he said, pulling into the nonexistent traffic and heading toward Farnum's Castle. "And what makes you think I'm not a lowlife?"

Are you coming on to me? she couldn't help but wonder, then quickly wiped the thought from her docile mind as she settled back in the bucket seat. The dashboard was cracked and so was the windshield, the engine had clearly seen better days, and she knew if she looked behind her there'd be a trail of greasy black smoke. The radio was turned so low it was almost inaudible, and without think-ing she reached forward to turn it up.

His hand shot out and caught hers. "I'm not in the mood to listen to Miles Van Cortland," he grumbled.

"Why not?"

"All he plays is stuff calculated to put you to sleep. Soft, easy-listening garbage that's been proven to melt your brain."

Marielle laughed. "What do you play?"

"Anything I damned well please. That's one of the rea-sons I work at WAKS. There's no playlist, no restriction. I can play Erma Franklin singing 'Piece of my Heart', and I can play yuppie muzak like George Winston. I can play Miles Davis and Otis Redding and Queen Ida and even Reba MacEntire if I'm in the mood."

"I heard you playing John Denver a couple of nights ago," she said. "The one about 'You fill up my senses.'"

"A momentary aberration. I'm over it. Why didn't you ask me to drive you to the store?" he asked abruptly.

Marielle shrugged. "Several reasons. Number one, I didn't know you had a car—such as it is," she added mis-chievously. "Number two, I'm already asking a lot from you. I didn't want to wear out my welcome."

"I told you, I'm willing," he said, turning onto the rut-ted driveway and speeding past the old house to a tumble-down three-stall garage behind it.

"I hadn't even realized this was here," she marveled as she climbed out of the car.

"If you decided to evict the old ladies it could be a strong selling point, if you want to rent to yuppies." There was no mistaking the disapproval in his voice.

"I've got a better idea," she returned sweetly. "Why not make Esmerelda and Granita sleep out here? We'll get a little straw, maybe even throw in a sleeping bag or two...."

"Okay, okay. I realize you're not going to kick them out."

"You, on the other hand, are more than expendable. And you could always sleep in your car."

"I'm six feet three inches tall, Marielle. I don't fit in a Mustang. A Cadillac, maybe."

"Then it's a shame your tastes don't run to Cadillacs." She struggled toward the house with her two bags clasped to her chest, but Simon blocked her way.

"Are you going to give me one of those bags?"

"No."

"All right." Without any warning he reached out to take one, his hand slipping down between the bag and her chest, sliding against her breast before he pulled the groceries away. He grinned at her shocked expression. "It's best not to thwart me," he said. "I don't put too much stock in polite conventions when I want my own way."

A bra, a camisole, a turtleneck, a flannel shirt and a sweatshirt lay between him and his momentary, supposedly inadvertent caress. So why was her flesh tingling? "Do that again," she said in a strangled voice, "and I'll break your arm."

"You and who else?" he taunted, clearly enjoying her temper.

There was a full moon that night, and a strong breeze sent the leaves scudding from the trees, lifted the mane of hair from the back of her neck, tumbled his gray-streaked hair into his too discerning eyes. It was all cool and crisp and strangely beautiful, and Marielle let out her pent-up breath and her anger with a sigh. "You're going to drive me crazy, Simon," she said, shaking her head.

"Not me. Maybe your midnight intruder, but not me. Are we going in, or are we going to stand out here like something out of *Wuthering Heights*?"

"We are going in."

"Good," he said. "Then you can tell me who the hell Dennis McMurtry is."

Marielle merely smiled mysteriously. "Is he here?"

"He is. With three suitcases and a typewriter. He says he's a writer and he's come to live with you."

"Well," she said, scuffling through the leaves as she headed for the front of the house, "that's true. I don't suppose there's a back entrance to the castle, is there?"

"Don't change the subject. The back porch is boarded up—it's unsafe. We almost lost a meter reader there a couple of years ago. How long have you known Mc-Murtry? I didn't realize you were involved with someone. I wouldn't have bothered to set you up with Miles if I'd known."

Marielle stopped for a moment to smile back at him. "I'm not going to tell you a thing, Simon," she said. "So stop asking."

"Why aren't you going to tell me a thing?" They'd reached the front door by then, and Simon blocked the door, clutching her battered bag of groceries and glowering at her in the unnatural light.

"Because it drives you crazy." She ducked under his arm and went inside, not even considering the death trap of an elevator. Simon wasn't far behind her, and she could sense his disapproval spreading over her like a vast dark cloud. That disapproval was oddly like jealousy. For a man who said he was determined to both match her up with someone and get her out of the state, it seemed a pretty strange emotion. But then Simon Zebriskie, like most of the people in the building, was slightly, delightfully strange.

It took Marielle one look at Dennis McMurtry to realize what was bugging Simon. As she dealt with two small figures hurtling themselves at her in an excess of delight, she glanced up and saw her new tenant. And she saw the light shining in Julie's eyes when her young friend thought no one was looking.

Not that Dennis had anywhere near Miles Van Cortland's phenomenal good looks. He appeared to be in his late twenties, with curly auburn hair, a pugnacious tilt to his jaw, frankly freckled skin and a pair of merry brown eyes. But he was young and strong and handsome, and even if Marielle had not the faintest interest in such things, Simon didn't know that.

"You must be Mrs. Brandt," Dennis said artlessly, coming up and shaking her hand with boyish enthusiasm.

"Marielle," she corrected. "This is another one of the tenants, Simon Zebriskie."

"Simon Zee!" Dennis said, dropping her hand and grabbing Simon's with even more delight. "Man, I used to watch you when I was a kid. Used to scare the bejesus out of me when you'd throw cauliflowers around and call them brains."

"What happened to that fun-loving creature?" Marielle murmured plaintively.

"And I listen to you on the radio whenever I'm up late. What're you doing on such a chicken-feed radio station like WAKS, anyway?"

"Yes, I wondered that myself," Marielle said, enjoying Simon's discomfiture. Clearly he wasn't used to hero worship, but he was having a hard time disliking such an obvious fan.

"Penance," said Simon obscurely. "If you didn't know Marielle, how come you're moving in with her?"

"I'm not. I'm moving into an empty apartment so I can finish my novel."

"A writer," Simon said in a resigned voice. "I don't suppose you have any money?"

"Not a cent," Dennis said cheerfully.

"And you're not planning to pay rent?"

"Not a cent."

Simon nodded as if his worst fears were confirmed. "Not that we aren't thrilled to have you, Dennis," he said, his voice deep and slow, "but none of the empty apartments are habitable. If they were, I'd think Marielle would rather have someone with a little more wherewithal...."

"Shut up, Simon," Marielle said sweetly. "Dennis is Officer Muldoon's brother-in-law."

"I see. So we get special police protection by giving you shelter?"

"I imagine Francis will have a vested interest in keeping this place safe and keeping me out of his hair," Dennis agreed. "But I think Marielle was more taken with the fact that I hold licenses as both a plumber and electrician. The licenses are only good in New Hampshire, but I don't imagine my lovely landlord cares about that. And I've even had some experience with your type of heating system. I took the liberty of checking it out on my way up here. I'm a firm believer in staying warm."

"So am I," said Marielle, taking in Simon's reaction with absolute delight. It was even better than saying "I told you so."

"By the way, if I were you I'd keep that basement locked. The whole place is wide open to whoever might wander in off the street. If you're having trouble with breaking and entering you ought to at least use a few locks. It might discourage some of the less dedicated criminal element in our fair city."

"You're an expert on that, too?" Simon grumbled.

Dennis grinned. "Didn't like me calling her lovely, did you? Message received, over and out. But I've picked up a few pointers from Muldoon. And locking doors is only common sense."

"I don't have any claim on Marielle." Simon was instantly defensive. "You can call her anything you please."

"Sure thing, man," Dennis said. "Hands off."

"Listen. . . ." Simon's voice was definitely warning, and Marielle decided it was time to intervene. Julie was still practically hiding in the kitchen, watching Dennis McMurtry out of absurdly vulnerable old-young eyes. Hiding, Marielle realized, behind the chest-high partition.

Sorrow and sympathy knifed through her, and she wished with all her heart that there was some way to spare Julie, to shield her from the hurts that seemed to be hanging over her like a dark rain cloud. But there was no way she could, and no way Julie could spend the next two or three weeks hiding behind partitions whenever an attractive man turned up.

"Why don't you take Dennis down and show him the apartment, Julie?" she suggested.

"Hey, that would be great," Dennis said. "We were having a good time talking, waiting for you. Your folks live here, Julie?"

"I'm on my own," she said with her usual defiance, moving slowly from behind the barrier.

Dennis didn't even blink, and Marielle's initial positive response positively blossomed. "I know what you mean," he said. "I left home when I was seventeen. Joined the navy and saw the world when I was too young and dumb to know any better." He continued chattering in an amiable voice as he followed Julie's cumbersome figure out the door. "See you tomorrow, landlady," he shot back over his shoulder.

"Tomorrow, Dennis." The door shut behind them, leaving her alone with Simon. "He wasn't coming on to her, was he?" she added, a sudden worry assailing her.

"I doubt it. He's nothing more than a great friendly puppy dog. The only one he'd be coming on to is you."

Marielle shook her head. "Trust me, Simon. He's not interested."

"That's good," he growled.

"Is it?"

"Yup. I'd hate to have my matchmaking for Miles go down the tubes."

"That would be a tragedy," she said in her iciest tone.

Her obvious hostility seemed to cheer Simon. "In the meantime, maybe I'll check out the basement and lock everything I can. The boy's right—it doesn't hurt to take a few precautions, even if your midnight caller has been coming in through the windows."

"Dennis has to be thirty if he's a day."

"Dennis," Simon said, "is young enough to be my son."

"Go away, Simon."

"I'm going. You going to call Dennis if old Vittorio's ghost comes visiting?"

"You'll be gone, won't you?"

"Not tonight. Even the graveyard shift gets a few nights off every now and then."

"Then I'm going to call you," she said. "Unless you have some objections."

"No objections. I promised to help, didn't I?"

Marielle stared at him for a long, breathless moment. "Do you always keep your promises?"

He didn't even need to think about it. "No," he said, and there was an odd note of pain in his voice. "But I'll keep that one. Good night, Marielle. Have a peaceful night."

"If Vittorio will let me," Marielle said. "Good night, Simon." And she stood there a long time without moving as she listened to the sound his footsteps down the hallway outside her door.

Chapter Eight

Marielle slid between the chilly sheets, deliberately averting her gaze from the gargoyles overhead, prepared to enjoy her first decent night of sleep since she'd packed up the kids and moved to Chicago. There were no guarantees, of course, but her instincts told her that there'd be no midnight visitors, no ghostly tappings, no open windows and trashed fireplaces.

Maybe it was the knowledge that Simon would be home tonight, right above her, well within screaming distance. And Dennis would be underneath, Dennis who looked strong and brave and had a cop for a brother-in-law. Marielle felt safer than she had in a long, long time, and she was fully prepared to enjoy the effect by sleeping soundly through the night.

She could hear the rumble of voices in the apartment beneath her—Julie and Dennis must still be talking. She was a fool to worry about Julie's well-being. The girl was far more levelheaded than most women twice her age. She might have made a mistake once, but Marielle knew for certain she wasn't about to repeat that mistake. And Simon was right—Dennis certainly didn't seem the type to take advantage.

No, they'd be fine, she assured herself, sinking into the soft mattress. Julie needed all the friends she could get in her current predicament, and Dennis was nothing if not friendly. Things were finally beginning to improve.

Three hours later she wasn't so sure. The bright full moon shone directly in her window, into her eyes. She lay there, jarred out of sleep, cursing the moonlight and wondering which of her sheets she could turn into curtains, when the sound came again. Someone in her apartment was crying.

Adrenalin shot through her body, as it had in similar situations since the day her first child had been born. Within seconds she was out of bed and in the next room. Christopher slept as soundly as he always did—nothing short of a nuclear war could wake him. But Emily lay in her cot, eyes shut, face contorted in grief, tears pouring down her face.

"Oh, baby," Marielle murmured, bending over the precariously unsteady little bed and scooping Emily into her arms. Her little body was hot, damp and tense, the tears rolled down her pale face, and she huddled against her mother for nameless comfort. Marielle realized with sudden shock that her daughter was still soundly, deeply asleep.

Her own form of despair washed over Marielle. In the six months since Greg had died Emily had been as quietly in control as her mother, and Marielle had hoped her instincts were wrong, hoped that beneath Emily's quiet, calm demeanor there didn't lurk a ravaged heart. Clearly her hope had been vain. When sleep came and ripped away her five-year-old daughter's defenses, grief took over, and she wept against her mother's chest with all the hopelessness of a child who has lost her father.

They sat that way for a long time, Emily weeping in her mother's lap, Marielle murmuring meaningless, soothing phrases as she smoothed the tumbled hair away from her daughter's sleeping, tear-streaked face. Gradually the tears abated, the tense little body relaxed into a deeper sleep, and with a great, shuddering sigh Emily released Marielle's flannel nightgown from her tight fists.

Slowly, carefully Marielle settled her back into the folding cot. Emily's breathing was deep and peaceful once more; the pain that had surfaced through her sleep had for the moment left her. But Marielle's pain had just begun.

She left the children's door ajar as she tiptoed into the hall, hugging herself in the cool night air. And then she heard the crying again. This time from her living room.

LATE-NIGHT TELEVISION STANK, Simon thought, pressing the remote control that was one of his few concessions to the video age. The nineteen-inch screen went blank, and only the overhead light from the kitchen illuminated the sprawling apartment.

He was stretched out on the overstuffed sofa, dressed in baggy gray sweatpants and an old black T-shirt, hot as always. If Dennis really could even out the heating system in Farnum's Castle he'd be a friend for life, despite the overwhelming cheeriness of the man. Simon sincerely doubted he could deal with that engaging grin first thing in the morning, but with luck their hours would be very different and he'd only have to put up with Dennis's overwhelming bonhomie when he'd already spent part of his day dealing with the other petty annoyances of life in the nineteen-eighties.

Of course, Simon thought, flipping onto his stomach, maybe Marielle liked that good-natured boyish charm. If Dennis could just abandon his literary pretensions, get his Illinois license and join a union, the guy would make more than enough to support the Brandt family in decent style. Maybe he should forget about Miles and see what he could do about matchmaking for his newest neighbors.

No, that wasn't an option. He couldn't see Marielle in the midst of middle-class suburbia, married to a plumber. Actually he couldn't see her married to an elitist sleaze like Miles, either. Maybe he should give up matchmaking altogether and concentrate his energies on simply getting her out of Chicago. The longer she stayed the more tempting she was, and he was too old and too smart to give in to temptation. Wasn't he?

It was after three in the morning. Instead of lying on the couch thinking about the woman beneath him, he should go to bed and try to get some sleep. That was the problem with working nights—he never could sleep on his day off. If he were a reasonable person he'd take one of the jobs offered him at the bigger stations in town. Jobs that offered benefits, a much higher salary and whatever hours he chose. Jobs that offered fame and fortune. Jobs that he simply wouldn't allow himself to take.

Penance, he'd told Dennis earlier, knowing there was too much going on for anyone to take him up on it. And in the dark of night, with the bright full moon shining in and the wind whipping the leaves off the trees, he knew he hadn't completed his atonement. Old Vittorio would have approved, he thought with a mirthless grin. The old scoundrel had spent the last fifteen years of his wicked life atoning for his sins. Maybe there was something about Farnum's Castle that brought out the penitential in all of them.

He couldn't see Marielle donning sackcloth and ashes. He probably didn't have to worry about fixing her up with anyone. A few more months of widowhood and she'd get tired of a cloistered existence. She'd go out and find someone on her own. It was up to him to remind her she'd have an easier time of it in New Mexico.

Why did life have to get so complicated? Twenty years ago he couldn't have cared less about scruples and penance; twenty years ago he would have taken the best-paying job he could find, have gotten Marielle Brandt into bed as fast as he could, and dropped both when something better came along. Nowadays he thought about consequences and debts and honor and fairness, not money and lust. Well, he amended, not so much about lust.

If only he at least had the satisfaction of knowing he was a better person for it. But the truth was that he'd been much more self-satisfied at twenty-two than he was now. Nowadays he saw himself clearly, too clearly. And if that clarity of vision meant his life was a little less comfortable than it could have been, then that was his choice.

He pushed himself off the sofa, heading through the dim, moonlit apartment for his bedroom. Maybe if he pulled the curtains he'd be able to sleep. Maybe if he could just think about something pleasant, like *Night of the Living Dead*, he wouldn't have to think about Marielle Brandt. But maybe nothing in this world or the next was going to keep him from fantasizing, as hopeless as he knew it was.

MARIELLE HESITATED for only a moment. It didn't matter who was crying in her living room. Whether it was some petty criminal regretting his vandalism, the ghost of one of Vittorio's victims or one of her hapless tenants, her course was clear. Someone was in pain, in need of comfort, and Marielle was too much of a mother to ignore that need.

She didn't turn on the living-room light, but there was no need. The moonlight pouring in the windows illuminated Julie's bulky figure huddled on the sofa, and the muffled sobs and groans sent a sudden panic through Marielle.

She rushed to her side, sinking onto the cushions and drawing the girl's trembling body into her arms. "Julie," she whispered, hugging her tightly. "Is it the baby? Is the baby coming early?"

Julie lifted her tear-streaked face, trying to swallow her choking sobs. "No," she said in a hushed, raspy voice. "The baby's fine."

"Then what is it? Did someone hurt you? Did Dennis...?" She finally allowed her doubts to surface.

"Dennis didn't do anything," Julie said, fiercely defensive. "He's good and kind."

"Then what is it?"

"I just wish," Julie said on a choked sob, "that I'd met him some other time." And her strangled weeping began again in earnest.

Marielle held her tight, brushing the tangled hair away from her brow, murmuring soothing, meaningless words, the same words she'd just murmured to her daughter. She could come up with no answers, no easy solutions, either for Emily or for Julie. Greg was dead, and all a child's misery or a mother's wanting couldn't bring him back. Julie was eighteen, alone and eight and a half months pregnant, and nothing but time would change that. All Marielle could do was comfort the wounded and curse her own helplessness.

Finally Julie's tears slowed to a halt. "Tissue," she mumbled, and Marielle released her to go in search of a box. Then she sat down beside her again, waiting while Julie blew her nose, wiped her face and pulled her courage back around her.

"Feeling better?" Marielle murmured.

Julie's shy, embarrassed smile was a revelation. "Yes, thank you. I'm sorry I had to bother you like that, but Esmy sleeps very lightly, and I don't like her to know when things get too much for me sometimes. She takes things so to heart, you know."

"What about you? Don't you take things to heart?"

Julie tossed back her tangled length of dark hair. "I'm tough," she said, and Marielle had no doubt about that one. "I've had to be, growing up around here."

"Julie, where are your parents? Where is your family? Shouldn't they be with you at a time like this?"

Bleakness shuttered Julie's features. "Not if you ask them. My ma's dead, my old man's ashamed of me, and his girlfriend was glad of an excuse to kick me out. I wouldn't go back there if they crawled on their hands and knees; I wouldn't go back there if they paid me. If you kick me out I'll work the streets before I'll..."

"No one's going to kick you out, Julie," Marielle said firmly. "We're your family now."

Julie managed a watery grin. "It didn't take you long to figure that out. How long have you been here—two days?"

"Three." *And I'd kill for a decent night's sleep,* Marielle added to herself.

"Do you mind if I spend the rest of the night here? I told Esmy you thought you might need some help."

"Sure. But I don't have a bed...."

"I like the floor. My back's been killing me, and the only place I can get comfortable is on something hard. Trust me, I'll be fine."

"Okay," Marielle said. "As a matter of fact, I did want to use the telephone...."

"Don't worry; I'll keep an ear out for the kids. They trust me; I don't think they'd mind if they woke up and found me here."

"No, I don't think they would. Thank you, Julie."

"No problem."

Marielle looked down at the tough, determined woman-child in front of her. "No problem," she echoed.

She grabbed the first thing she could find, an old black shawl, and wrapped it around her flannel nightgown. She didn't bother with slippers—it grew progressively warmer as one headed up the last flight of stairs, and she knew she'd be quite comfortable curled up in the chair outside Simon's apartment. She was suddenly in a desperate hurry to get out of her apartment, away from witnesses, away from her own overwhelming need to be strong and nurturing.

"Emily's been awake once," she said, pausing at the door, surprised to feel the tightness in her own throat. "She shouldn't wake up again, but come and get me if she does. I'll be in the hallway...."

"She'll be fine," Julie said. "Take your time."

It was cold in the hallway, as it always was. For one brief moment Marielle considered ghosts, considered whether she ought to be roaming Farnum's Castle in the middle of the night with no more protection than a pair of powerful lungs. She could have at least taken a rolling pin from the kitchen. Except that in her unorganized kitchen there were no rolling pins. There was nothing more lethal than a paring knife and a pizza cutter.

Simon would be sound asleep, she thought as she ran swiftly, silently up the stairs. She could hide out in that comfortable chair and do what she'd needed to do for the past hour, for the past week, for the past year. She'd cry.

There was no one she could turn to, no one's shoulder she could cry on. Somewhere downstairs in one of the unpacked boxes was her address book with Jaime's new phone number. But Jaime would have been the last person Marielle would have chosen to call. Jaime thought Marielle was strong and wise and brave, in control of everything, the perfect earth mother, everything her own glamorous mother hadn't been. It would probably do her some good to find out Marielle had feet of clay.

But at that moment Marielle had no interest in anyone else's well-being. She was burned-out, incapable of taking care of one more lost soul. For an hour or two, alone in

Simon's hallway, she was going to think of nothing but herself.

She didn't even have Suzanne's phone number. Not that Suzanne would have been much help in her current predicament—she wasn't the nurturing type, either. She'd offer Marielle a few wisecracks to cheer her up, suggest she take up smoking, and probably offer to send her daughter Mouse back to baby-sit.

Of all her friends Abbie was the warmest, the most likely to give her a sympathetic ear and a shoulder to cry on. Abbie was the one person she could track down, and with the time difference it wouldn't even be that late a phone call.

But she wouldn't call Abbie. Much as she needed help, she couldn't ask for it. She was a fine one to mourn her daughter's defenses when her own were so firmly in place. Once she started to let her vulnerability show there'd be no stopping it. She'd be weeping all over Chicago, and Emily was feeling insecure enough without a waterworks for a mother.

She curled up in the comfortable chair, leaned back and willed the tears to come. Nothing happened. Her eyes still burned, her throat felt tight and miserable, her chest throbbed, but everything was still locked up tight inside. She thought about Emily's miserable expression. She thought about Greg's funeral, the look of blame on his mother's face. Sara Brandt had known they were about to separate. Without question she blamed that stress for her son's unexpected heart attack, ignoring the fact that he'd lived with an undiagnosed heart defect for his entire thirty-three years.

She remembered the phone call, the shock, the disbelief, the pain of knowing someone she'd once loved dearly was gone. But still she sat alone in Simon's hallway, dry-eyed.

She thought of Julie crying for the moon, for all the lost chances, for young men like Dennis, for the baby she was too wise not to relinquish.

And she thought of her four-figure electricity bill and her very tiny savings account.

Not a tear. The fist around her heart tightened, clamping down until she was gasping for breath. But still the relief of tears was beyond her.

It was sort of like sex, she thought distantly, huddling deeper into the chair and wrapping the shawl around her body. The only person she'd ever made love with was Greg, and during the last few years that hadn't been very often. But even in the rush of youth it hadn't been very exciting, though there had been times when it seemed as if there was something else, something just out of reach, something absolutely wonderful that she couldn't quite accomplish.

Her feelings at the moment were almost identical. She was wrapped in a tight little ball of misery, not even certain if the tears she sought would bring her any release at all.

There were advantages in having no one to turn to. She had no witnesses, could sit here all night if she had a mind to, and no one would have to know. She could tell Julie she fell asleep in the chair, waiting for someone to return her call. And if Julie didn't believe her she was too much of a good person to say so.

She took a few tentative, deep breaths, hoping to ease the iron band around her chest. It released its grip a few centimeters, and Marielle drew in a deeper breath, struggling for the calm that was her second choice, since an orgy of weeping seemed to be denied her.

Her usual calm self-control was within her grasp now. A few more moments and she'd be fine, able to return to her apartment and her surprisingly comfortable bed, able to tend to Julie and Emily if they should need her again during the long predawn hours. It wasn't even four o'clock yet—hours to go before the autumn sun rose over the city. If she were lucky she'd still manage another few hours of sleep.

She took another deep breath, willing the tension to leave her, willing calm to return, when without warning the door to Simon's apartment was flung open and a dark, menacing form loomed over her like a vengeful ghost.

And Marielle, looking up into Simon's dark, distant face, burst into tears.

Chapter Nine

"Damn," said Simon. "I thought I told you not to cry."
But his tone of voice belied the harsh words, and before
she even realized what he was doing he'd scooped her up
in his arms and carried her into his darkened apartment,
the shawl trailing on the floor behind them.

If Simon's appearance had broken through her blocked
tears, his touch destroyed the dam entirely. She let loose a
torrent of weeping, burying her face against his shoulder
and releasing all the pent-up misery and despair that had
been so well battened down. For a few short moments all
her responsibilities vanished, for a few short moments
there was someone else to shoulder them for her. She was
hardly aware of him sinking onto the huge old sofa; all she
knew was the warmth and comfort of his arms around her.

He didn't utter the soothing phrases she specialized in.
He didn't push her damp hair away from her tear-soaked
face, didn't rub her shoulders or pat her back or murmur,
"It's all right." He was just there, a solid, dependable
presence, there as no one had been for her since she'd
grown up and had to be everybody else's mother. He was
there, and the sensation was such a delightful relief that she
cried even harder, her hands clinging to him, to the soft,
stretchy cotton of his T-shirt, to the hard, muscled flesh
beneath.

At that point he did say something, but Marielle couldn't quite hear it beyond her tears. It might have been her name, it might have been a strangled protest, perhaps even encouragement. She wasn't paying much attention, being too busily awash in an absolute riot of misery. She knew he was lying back on the couch, knew he was taking her with him, stretching her out beside him, tucking her against his body and holding her, but all these things were part of the dream state she seemed to be in, a dream state brought about by overwhelming emotion and not enough sleep.

She couldn't see—the room was too dark and she was blinded by tears. She could smell, though, the faint, soapy smell of him, the lingering traces of whatever he'd had for dinner, the pleasantly musty scent of the old sofa. And she could feel him, the oddly comforting textures, the juxta-position of soft and hard, the softness of his T-shirt and sweatpants, the hardness of bone and muscle beneath the garments.

Abruptly her tears vanished, swallowed in sudden surprise. Her eyes flew open, and the room was brighter than she'd realized. Moonlight was shining in, flooding Simon's face as he leaned over her, mere inches away, his breath smelling of brandy and toothpaste, his eyes absolutely opaque as he stared into hers.

Her flannel nightgown had somehow ridden up her legs, her bare thighs were pressed against him, but the over-heated air of his apartment was only partially responsible for the flush that suffused her body, for the flaming color in her face and the burning ache in the pit of her stomach. The tightness was back in her chest, but it was a different kind of tightness, an odd sort of yearning she couldn't and wouldn't understand.

"Let go of me," she said, her voice a hushed command in the still room.

"Yes," said Simon, not moving.

"We can't do this."

"No," he agreed.

"Simon." Her voice held a very definite note of warning.

"Yes," he said. Then, "No." And then he dipped his head, blotting out the moonlight, and his mouth caught hers.

Unbelievably, it had been years since she'd been kissed. Possibly not since the night Christopher had been conceived, and she wasn't even sure of that. And she'd never been kissed the way Simon was kissing her, all urgency gone now, slowly, thoroughly, his mouth touching and teasing and tasting, nudging away her panic until she had no choice but to soften her mouth, to part her lips for him, to let him take possession with a sudden sly ferocity that left her trembling beneath him.

Somehow he'd managed to maneuver her into the corner of the couch, and his long, hard body was stretched over hers, pressing her against the frayed upholstery. One of his arms was still around her, holding her against him, the other hand was cupping her chin, keeping her face still for his leisurely, totally devastating kiss.

She could do no more than accept that kiss passively, willingly, too overwhelmed to do anything else. Her own hands were up, an ineffectual barrier pressing against his chest, pushing him away, but her fingers were kneading the soft material over his hard chest like the paws of a cat in heat. She even sounded like one, she thought dismally, listening to the tiny whimper of denial and desire that was swallowed up by Simon's hungry mouth.

But she didn't want the kiss to end. She wanted to drown in it, to lose herself in the mesmerizing power of his clever, hungry mouth on hers, just as she'd lost herself in his warmth and comfort moments before. She was still ready to relinquish all responsibility, just for a little while, even though that distant, conscious part of her knew better. But right now she didn't care; he was in control, not she, and nothing mattered but the nagging, worrisome, over-whelming pleasure he was coaxing from her with nothing more than his mouth laying claim to hers.

And then he pulled his mouth away abruptly, laying his head beside her own. She could hear his rasping breath in her ear, feel the tension trembling in the body covering hers, and she could feel her own intense response, her own labored breathing.

"Damn," he muttered hoarsely, his voice not much more than a whisper in her ear. "We weren't going to do that."

Marielle swallowed the protest that rose to her sensitized lips. "Let me up," she said, suddenly desperate.

"Please." Simon's voice was strangled. "I won't touch you again. But just stay put for a minute. Please."

She stayed where she was. The body pressed so closely against hers felt tense and almost feverish. She could practically feel the nerves jumping underneath his skin, and each deep, shaky breath he took pressed against her breasts beneath the flannel nightgown.

Then he moved, slipping away from her off the couch, and was halfway across the room before she even knew what had happened. Her hands were reaching out for him, and she quickly drew them back, wrapping her arms around her suddenly chilled body. The overheated top floor no longer felt so warm without Simon's body heat.

He was silhouetted in the moonlight. His face, his expression were hidden in the shadows, but she could see the faint gleam of his eyes watching her, could see the tell-tale rise and fall of his chest as he slowly brought himself back under total and rigid control.

She was a woman who could understand and respect self-control, but Simon's self-possession was curiously wounding. She lay on the couch without moving, her flannel nightgown still halfway up her thighs, and waited for him to say something.

It wasn't what she expected. Leaning forward, he turned on a light, flooding the room with an unwelcome brightness. "Do you want to go into the bedroom with me?" he asked bluntly, his face absolutely emotionless. "Or do you want to go back to your apartment?"

"I want," she said carefully, "to slap your face."

"Why? I didn't do anything you didn't want me to do. What I want to know is, do you want me to do more?"

She sat up slowly, pulling down her nightgown around her ankles, pulling up her knees to her chest, reaching for the shawl and wrapping it around her. "Go away, Simon."

"This is my apartment, remember? I actually pay rent on it."

"Then I'll go." Her feet had barely touched the floor before he'd crossed the room and shoved her back with ungentle hands. "You'll stay put," he snapped. And then he stopped himself. "Sorry," he said. "Let's start all over again. What were you doing in my hallway trying not to cry?"

"You've got it all wrong." She watched him warily as he sank back onto the large sofa, a nice safe distance away from her. "I was sitting there trying to cry and getting nowhere. At least until you showed up."

"Always glad to be of service. I scare babies and make people cry," Simon growled. "Why did you want to cry?"

"Everybody else was. Why not me?" She decided not to look at him. Looking at him reminded her of what they'd been doing just a short while ago, and thinking about that had the strange effect of making her want to do it again, irrational as such a wish might be.

"Who else was crying, Marielle?"

"Emily. Crying for her father. And Julie, crying for things she couldn't change."

Simon nodded, leaning back against the high-backed sofa with a weary sigh. "Which did you want to cry for? Your dead husband? Or were you crying for the moon?"

"Definitely the moon," she said. "Greg and I were in the midst of separating when he had his heart attack. That doesn't mean I didn't mourn him or greatly regret his death. But I'd already let go of him, said goodbye to him."

"So what were you crying for?" he persisted.

"It's none of your business."

"If it's none of my business, why did you come up here for comfort?"

"I didn't. I came up to the hallway because it was the only place I thought I could be alone."

"Why?" he pushed.

He'd pushed too hard. "Damn it!" Marielle said, turning to him. "I needed to stop being everybody's mother for a few minutes, okay? Responsible for my children, for Julie, for this whole decaying apartment building and all the indigent people living here. For a few minutes I only wanted to think about myself. Is that a crime?"

"No," he said. "Come here."

"I thought we decided this wasn't a good idea."

Simon reached out and caught her arm, tugging—no, hauling—her across the couch. "I'm not going to make another pass at you," he said, tucking her against him, wrapping his arms around her. "You just need a little comfort on a cold night. I'm giving it."

"You're just as bad as I am." She sniffed. "You took on all these old people before I ever did. Now you seem to be taking on me and my family as well."

"It's just temporary." His deep, rich voice rumbled in his chest. Marielle gave in to the sleepy temptation of rubbing her face against the soft, stretchy cotton of his T-shirt, nuzzling against the warm, hard flesh beneath. "We'll get this old place in decent shape so that you and the children can go off and live somewhere warm and sunny and just cash the rent checks while someone else takes care of the dirty work."

She was so tired, the room was so warm, and the body beside her was so comforting. "What if we don't want to live somewhere warm and sunny?" she murmured sleepily. "What if I like cold, windy cities and derelict buildings?"

He didn't bother to answer, and she didn't bother to notice. She was, astonishingly, trustingly, sound asleep.

ANOTHER LOST SOUL to add to his collection, Simon thought with a stifled yawn, careful not to jar her sleeping body. He was going to be hard-pressed to keep up his feelings of animosity at this rate. As long as he could view her as a dilettante, someone who didn't really need to be here, someone who was playing at being self-supporting before she gave up and cashed in her trust fund, then he could keep those treacherous feelings at bay.

But it was damned hard to distance himself from a warm, clinging body leaning so trustingly against his, to distance himself from the sleeping, endearingly pretty face that still bore traces of tears. Her lips were slightly swollen, and he wanted to crane his neck and kiss her again to see if he could make them respond.

He needed to remind himself that she was just like Esmy and Granita, like Julie and the Meltirks. Nothing more, nothing less. If he viewed her as one more responsibility, like the others, then maybe he wouldn't be so damned tempted.

But she wasn't like the others; that was the problem. It wasn't that she was young and pretty—Julie was young and pretty too, despite the advanced pregnancy. And it wasn't that she needed him—they all needed him. And it wasn't that she was trying to make a go of it. All the residents of Farnum's Castle were trying, in their own ways, to make a life for themselves and those around them.

It was the fact that she was taking responsibility, not just for herself and her family but for the others, just as he had. Right now she might be a little burned-out by it all, but he already knew that by tomorrow she'd be facing things once again. He hated to admit it, but Dennis McMurtry was a brilliant addition to their extended household. He'd never thought of bartering living space for plumbing and electrical expertise. Not that it would have been his place to do it, but Farnum's Castle had been ignored for so long that he pretty much did what he pleased. Fritzie was there because of him. So, for that matter, was Granita.

Sweet, elegant Granita with the noble carriage and the British accent and the impeccable manners had been just this side of becoming a bag lady. The residence she'd lived in had been closed down by the city, she had no family, no money, and her only possessions were stuffed into an old suitcase that was held together by rope. She hadn't eaten or slept in days, and she'd been sitting in the Pan Am terminal at O'Hare Airport, dodging the security guards. He'd brought her back with him, settled her in with Esmerelda, and time had taken care of the rest.

Esmy and Granita's relationship particularly amused him. They had a great deal of fun squabbling, arguing over everything from how to cook meat loaf to whether God was a woman. Esmy's interest in the occult had always been marginal until Granita had shown up, but it had been one-upmanship from then on.

The only real fight they'd ever had had been over Julie, and it had been severe enough to make Granita move across the hall into a recently vacated apartment. Granita thought Julie should try to patch things up with her father and stepmother, while Esmerelda was convinced she should turn her back on them, just as they had turned their backs on her. It had been a bitter fight, with the two old ladies not exchanging a word for over two weeks, but in the end it was Julie who'd had the final say. Her father had cleared out her room, thrown her belongings into the street, and told the parish priest she'd died in a car accident in California. She'd had no choice and no desire but to accept the situation.

Simon had been paying for Julie's prenatal care. Maybe that was part of his sensitivity about age. The one time he'd gone with Julie the nurse had given him a condemning, disgusted look, one that despite his complete innocence, made him feel like the worst sort of lecher. It didn't matter that Marielle was more than ten years older than Julie—he still felt like a dirty old man.

Not enough that he'd wake her up and send her back downstairs, however. Julie was there with the children, and Marielle needed a few hours of sleep. He had complete faith in Julie's ability to deal with Christopher and Emily. She'd be a wonderful mother—it was a damned shame she couldn't keep her own child.

Marielle stirred, sighing, and the warmth of her breath brushed his bare arm, stirring the hairs. Simon let himself settle back and she went with him, still sound asleep. Despite what she said, she must miss her husband, Simon thought. Otherwise she wouldn't sleep so peacefully and well with a strange body wrapped around her.

Of course, just because she had been in the middle of a separation that didn't mean she wasn't involved with someone else, he reminded himself, then dismissed the idea as soon as it came. For one thing, Marielle simply wasn't that kind of person.

For another, her response to his kiss fitted exactly with what she'd said yesterday afternoon. She'd said sex was the most overrated commodity of all. If that was how she usually responded to a kiss, it was no wonder she thought the whole thing was a big fuss over nothing.

Of course, he could be kidding himself. It could be *his* kiss she was so passive about. Except that he could feel the stirring tendrils of response deep within her, in the clinging of her fists to his T-shirt, in the restlessness of her hips beneath his, in the dazed expression in her clear blue eyes when he'd moved away.

It was more than obvious that someone hadn't done it right. And the temptation to show her just how delicious, how exhilarating, how overwhelming it could be was just one more barb in his lacerated soul. He had to keep his hands off, damn it. Someone else would show her, sooner or later. Someone would take the time and care that were needed to make her realize that sex, when it was done right, when it was done with love, simply couldn't be overrated.

But he didn't have the love, the time or the caring to spare. And when he thought about it clearly he knew that he didn't deserve Marielle Brandt or her two children, any more than he deserved a more upscale job. Penance, he reminded himself again, breathing in the faint, flowery scent that lingered in Marielle's hair and sent a sharp fist to his gut. He wondered if there'd be a time when he'd ever feel as if he'd paid enough. And if he'd ever trust anyone enough to tell them exactly what he did.

Actually, it was a particularly nasty kind of slow torture to be wrapped around Marielle Brandt and to know he couldn't touch her again, shouldn't have her no matter how much his body, mind, and yes, his very soul were beginning to ache for her. So maybe it was okay to let her sleep like that, to endure the torment for just a little bit longer. All in the name of penance, he reminded himself.

The full moon had disappeared, and the sky was beginning to lighten with the first streakings of dawn. He wished he hadn't turned on that damned light that kept shining in his eyes, but he wasn't about to get up and do anything about it. He was going to sit there and watch the sun come up and breathe in the enticing scent of Marielle's perfume. In a few hours he'd be his usual irascible self. For now he was going to have a brief indulgence, a moment or two to pretend the past never happened. And resting his stubbled cheek lightly on Marielle's blond head, he drifted into sleep.

It seemed like moments later when his eyes flew open. The room was flooded with daylight, Marielle was standing a few feet away, her eyes panicked, her body in its ridiculous granny nightgown tense with fear. A terrified scream still echoed in his sleep-drugged consciousness, and he wondered if that scream had come from her when she awoke and realized where she was.

And then it came again, a loud, terrified shriek, floating up the flights of stairs and in through the open door of his apartment. "Granita," he identified the voice, leaping to his feet. But Marielle was already out the door, racing in the direction of that frightened voice.

Chapter Ten

Julie was standing in the doorway of Marielle's apartment, panic and indecision on her face. "What's wrong? I thought I heard Granita...."

"Stay put," Marielle ordered, not stopping her head-long pace down the angular flights of stairs. "Watch the children. We'll find out what's happened."

"But..."

"Stay put." Simon's voice behind her repeated the order. He'd caught up with her between the fourth and third floors, passed her at the Meltirks' apartment and raced on ahead to the first, to Granita and Esmerelda's apartments. Half a dozen Meltirks were roaming the hall in various stages of undress, the most alarming of which was her serene highness, with a purple velvet nightgown flowing around her impressive bulk and a head full of pink plastic curlers. Since her highness always wore a turban the curlers might have seemed a bit redundant, but Marielle didn't have time to ponder the matter as she caught her foot on an uneven stair tread, began to tumble, and barely caught herself on the wide bannister.

Granita was stretched out on the sofa in her overstuffed apartment, with Esmerelda bustling around, fanning her erstwhile competitor's ashen face, clucking and muttering in counterpoint to Granita's intermittent moans. Dennis was already there, already being marvelously efficient, pouring a glass of ice water down Granita's throat, chafing her long, bony hands.

Marielle paused inside the apartment long enough to take in the scene. She would have thought Simon might not be too pleased at having Dennis take over as dispenser of aid to the needy, but he seemed surprisingly unaffected, even going to give Dennis a nod of approval that was free of the underlying hostility of the night before.

"Simon," Granita moaned piteously—a bit too piteously, Marielle thought—and held out a shaking hand. Simon sat down on the couch beside her, still dressed in his old gray sweatpants and black T-shirt. His feet were bare, as were hers, and she suddenly realized that she was even more scantily dressed than the others, enveloped as she was in the flannel nightie.

She could feel her face turn a bright crimson, and could only be thankful all eyes were on Granita and not on her own miserably guilty countenance. But if she'd been where she should have been, fast asleep, alone in her own bed, she would have been dressed just the same, and she doubted she would have had the sense to grab her bathrobe before she responded to Granita's shrill scream. As a matter of fact, she hadn't even unpacked her bathrobe yet.

The shawl, however, was still lying on Simon's floor. And Julie would know she'd been coming down at dawn from the fifth-floor apartment, and not her own bed.

Where Marielle Brandt spent the night turned out to be the least of her worries, however, when Granita could finally be persuaded to gasp out what had happened. With Simon beside her, holding one hand, and Dennis still patting the other, she managed to pull herself together enough to enjoy the attention, and Esmerelda emitted a disparaging sniff.

"I don't sleep well," Granita said by way of preamble. "I'm usually up by half past four, and this morning was no different. I feed the cat, make myself a pot of tea, and write a few letters. Then I meditate for a bit...."

"Get on with it, Granita." Esmerelda spoke the words everyone else wanted to but was far too polite to utter. "What happened?"

"The cat was outside. I could see her from my bedroom window, and I knew without a doubt that she'd been in when I went to bed last night. When I went to let her in I heard a noise from the dining room. You know I hardly use it, only for an occasional reading or a séance. Not that it isn't a nice enough room, even though it is a bit drafty despite the bricked-up fireplace, and I'm lucky to have the space...."

"Granita!" Esmy shrieked. "Get to the point. What was in the dining room?"

While Granita's distress was clearly very real, she couldn't resist the melodrama of the moment. Her long, horsey face quivered, her faded blue eyes widened, and her voice grew low and hushed. "Vittorio Farnum."

"No!" Simon said instantly.

"Who?" Dennis asked at the same time.

"Oh, God," murmured Marielle.

"Damn," declared Esmy. "You have all the luck."

Granita allowed herself a small, satisfied smirk before she resumed her tragic queen pose. "You wouldn't call having your apartment vandalized a stroke of luck," she informed her friend with great dignity.

"Oh, wouldn't I? By old Vittorio himself? Guess again, Granita." Esmy was beside herself with envy.

"Granita," Simon said, and his deep, sepulchral voice was firm but gentle. "Tell us exactly what happened. What made you think it was Vittorio?"

"How do you even know what Vittorio looks like?" Marielle couldn't keep from asking.

She should have kept her mouth shut. Everyone turned to stare at her from the tips of her bare feet to the top of her tangled hair, and she could feel the color flood her pale complexion, the curse of a Scandinavian mother. Even Simon seemed momentarily distracted by her appearance.

"Why shouldn't I know what Vittorio looks like?" Granita said loftily. "Don't I look at him every night before I go to sleep?"

Marielle couldn't bring herself to question that statement—she didn't know if she wanted to hear the answer. Esmerelda must have seen her expression, for she sniffed audibly.

"It's not as mysterious as it sounds," she said flatly, doing her best to deflate Granita's pretensions. "The old phony found a portrait of Vittorio in the basement and before anyone knew what was happening she'd hung it in her bedroom."

"Old phony?" Granita shrieked, sitting bolt upright and forgetting that she was supposed to be recovering from shock. "If anyone's a charlatan around here..."

"You still haven't told me what happened," Simon interrupted the squabble with the long-suffering air of someone who'd intervened many times. "You heard a noise in the dining room and what?"

"I went in, of course. I thought it might be one of my spirit guides." Granita fixed Esmerelda with a warning glare, but the other woman was momentarily silent. "The light wasn't very good, and at first I thought it might be rats or squirrels or something. It was just a sort of scrabbling sound."

"Like I heard the night before," Marielle said gloomily.

"But when I looked in I saw someone kneeling by the fireplace in an almost prayerful position. He was dark all over, like a fiend from hell...."

"I thought you didn't believe in hell," Esmy said.

"Be quiet, Esmy," Simon said, concentrating on Granita. "What happened then?"

"Well, of course I uttered a little mantra for self-protection. And then the creature turned and looked at me, and his features were all dark and blurry. But even so I could recognize Vittorio. I was so startled I must have screamed. He ran, and I kept screaming until you all ran in here."

"Old fool," Esmy sniffed. "You should have welcomed him. How can we ever expect anyone to cross over if people spend their time shrieking? Think of the things he could have told us about the afterlife. Think of the knowledge lost by your silly hysterics! There are times, Granita..."

"Ladies," Dennis interrupted with his engaging grin. "I would give anything to see a portrait of that old mobster. I've heard stories about him, and my brother-in-law filled me in on some of the history of the house, but I've never actually seen a ghost, even a portrait of someone before he became a ghost, if you know what I mean."

"Certainly," Granita said, rising with somewhat unsteady dignity. "I'd be more than happy to show you. Though you must realize the bed isn't made."

"He's not interested in an old maid's bed," snapped Esmerelda, trailing along behind them. "He just wants to see Vittorio."

"I didn't say you could come along." Granita stopped at the doorway.

"Try and stop me." Esmerelda was nothing if not persistent.

"I wouldn't lower myself. Come if you must." Granita swept through the doorway, then paused once more, tossing a brief phrase over her shoulder as a sort of afterthought. "And who says I'm an old maid?"

Marielle found Simon's dark gray eyes watching her with a certain solemnity. For all practical purposes they were alone once more—the sound of the two old ladies arguing, with Dennis's gentle comments interspersed, floated out from the bedroom, and the Meltirks milling around in the hallway couldn't understand a word of English. Simon could say anything he wanted to her.

"We'd better check the fireplace," he said, rising, ignoring the question in her eyes. "I expect it's the same people who broke into your place the night before."

"I suppose so." She didn't move, and neither did he. "Uh, Simon..."

"Yes."

An unhelpful response if ever she heard one, Marielle thought, standing her ground. "About last night."

"Yes." If she didn't know better she'd think there was a faint light of amusement in those steely gray eyes. But Simon Zebriskie wasn't someone who was easily amused, and while her discomfiture might be enough to tickle his morbid sense of humor, she decided to give him the benefit of the doubt.

"I must have fallen asleep." It sounded pretty lame when it came out, but without his cooperation this conversation was doomed to failure anyway, she thought.

"Yes."

"Why didn't you wake me up?" She lobbed the ball neatly back into his court.

"I must have fallen asleep myself."

Damn. There was no way she could keep skirting the issue. The Meltirks were growing more restive; the prince consort, a portly young man in a puce sweat suit, was peering in the door and describing the situation in voluble detail to his royal wife, and Marielle had a distinct suspicion that she could hear a goat in the apartment above.

"I'm sorry I ended up crying on your shoulder," she said, trying to sound rueful, ending up sounding stiff and uncomfortable. "I was just looking for a place to be alone for a while so I could feel properly sorry for myself, and your hallway seemed to be the perfect spot, complete with a comfortable chair for crying in. I wouldn't have come up if I'd thought I'd wake you. I won't do it again."

"Won't feel sorry for yourself or won't come upstairs again?" Simon countered, crossing the room and standing much too close to her. The prince consort had edged into the room, too, so that he was only a few inches behind her, listening to their conversation with avid interest. Simon ignored him, something Marielle had a harder time doing. "A little self-pity is a healthy thing every now and then, as long as it's not carried to extremes."

"Last night was extreme." The prince was breathing down her neck. Marielle turned to give him a discouraging smile, but the poor man panicked when she tried to meet his gaze, scampering from the room like a frightened rabbit. The noise in the corridor increased, then all the Meltirks vanished into their second-floor apartment, and the sound of the goat blended with the unmistakable noise and odor of chickens before the door slammed shut.

"Maybe," continued Simon, not the slightest bit distracted by their neighbors. "Or maybe it was a normal reaction that was long overdue."

"Normal or not, it won't happen again." The words came out in not much more than a whisper. No one could see them now, the conversation in Granita's bedroom was lively and loud, and Marielle wished, for some reason she couldn't begin to fathom, that Simon would touch her.

Simon did no such thing. Nor did he give her the denial she wanted to hear. Her own words had been half wishful thinking, half a challenge. Either way, Simon seemed to have lost interest.

"Let's check out the fireplace," was all he said, turning from her and moving silently across the room. And letting out her breath in a soundless, pent-up sigh, Marielle followed him.

The rubble-strewn fireplace here didn't look much different from those in the other two vandalized apartments. Someone, or something, Marielle thought with an effort to be fair to the supernatural elements, had chipped away at the mortar, removed some of the bricks and pulled away some of the twigs and dead leaves that had fallen down the chimney. Whether that someone or -thing had found anything of value or use she couldn't tell. She moved closer, planning to lean over Simon's kneeling figure, when she stepped on something sharp and let out a yelp of pain, falling against him and knocking him into the rubble.

She lay there on the floor of Granita's apartment, sprawled on top of him, for a long, silent moment. He was looking up at her, and for a brief second she thought she saw a flare of pure, physical desire of such intensity that it frightened her. As soon as she saw it it was gone, leaving her wondering if she'd only imagined it, if it had been the result of paranoid nightmares. Or wishful thinking.

"I thought we weren't going to do this," his deep voice drawled, his expression now carefully masked.

She still didn't move. If she were fool enough to fall in love again, she could fall in love with that wonderful voice of his. And the lean, wiry body beneath hers wasn't too bad, either. Not to mention his ridiculously sexy mouth. And his eyes, which could be absurdly kind.

She rolled off him, scrambling to her feet and limping slightly as she hurried to get away from insane tempta-

tion. "We're not," she said. She contemplated reaching
out a hand to help him up, then thought better of it. Simon didn't need her help for anything.

Slowly he sat up, brushing the rubble from his black T-
shirt. He stayed that way for a moment, resting his arms
on his drawn-up knees, watching her, and this time there
was no mistaking the expression in his eyes. "If you say so.
I wouldn't count on it, if I were you."

"Simon..."

"Just go," he grumbled. "Or come back upstairs with
me."

Marielle went.

Dennis raised an eyebrow at her when she practically ran
into the tiny bedroom, but didn't say a word.

"There you are, my dear," Granita greeted her. "What
do you think of the old rascal?"

For a moment Marielle thought she meant Simon, and
she could feel herself flush. And then she followed the
direction of Granita's gesture to the very bad oil painting
that was hanging over another, still-untouched and
bricked-up fireplace.

Vittorio Farnum was a surprisingly handsome man, apparently in his mid-fifties. He had a hawklike nose, a wide-
lipped, sensual mouth, and piercing brown eyes set under
heavy, beetled brows. He was painted wearing, of all
things, a monk's robe, with a heavy jeweled cross resting
against his barrel chest and a tattered-looking Bible in one
long-fingered hand. The technique was lousy—Vittorio's
eyes surely couldn't have been two such disparate sizes,
and the color was muddy and drab, leaving Vittorio's skin
tone more a pea green than a Mediterranean olive.

He also looked hauntingly familiar.

Marielle stared up at him, squinting her eyes, tilting her
head to the right and then to the left. "Where have I seen

him before?'' she murmured, then mentally slapped herself when she realized she'd spoken the words out loud.

"You've seen him before?" Granita pounced on the statement. "I didn't realize you'd actually had a visitation. This is most exciting. Esmy, did you hear...?"

"I heard," Esmy said, looking at Marielle thoughtfully. "When did you see him, dear?"

"I have no idea." She was acutely aware that Simon had now come into the tiny room and was standing much too close to her. So close that she could see the fine grains of plaster dust clinging to his bare forearm. "I certainly haven't seen any ghosts lately," she added in a more forceful tone.

"I think we have to do it," Granita said mysteriously.

"I'm afraid you're right, dear," Esmy agreed. "Tonight?"

"Tonight," said Granita, fastening her pale blue eyes on the others. "You'll all participate, of course."

"Of course," said Dennis.

"Yes," said Simon in a resigned tone.

"Participate in what?" Marielle questioned.

Granita looked up, way up into old Vittorio's dark brown eyes. "A séance," she said. "If you haven't seen Vittorio Farnum before, you'll see him tonight."

And Marielle, following Granita's gaze, shivered, moving an unconscious, instinctive step back toward Simon. "No, thanks," she said hastily. "I'll pass on this one."

"No, you won't." Simon's hands reached up and caught her arms, holding her in place in front of him. "If I have to put up with it, so do you," he added in a muttered undertone.

"Simon understands these things." Granita smiled at him. "We need everyone's cooperation for the powers to be in tune."

"You don't need a skeptic at the table," Marielle said.

"Nonsense. No one could be more cynical than Simon, and he's never interfered with the vibrations. If anything, his attitude has helped matters. Maybe," Granita said in a soulful hush, "we'll actually be able to talk to Vittorio." She smiled, a beatific grin. "Wouldn't that be absolutely splendid?"

Marielle didn't have the heart to raise any more objections. At least it could do no harm. "Splendid," she echoed gloomily. And she stepped away from Simon's enticing, imprisoning hands.

THE CHILDREN WERE EATING Cap'n Crunch cereal and watching *Muppet Babies*, a safe enough occupation, when Marielle finally returned from Granita's apartment. They greeted their mother's early morning return with their usual enthusiasm, and there was no trace of last night's tears on Emily's rosy face.

Julie looked equally sanguine, both about Marielle's unexplained absence during the long hours of the night and about the séance. "They're harmless," she said carelessly. "Miss Granita shakes and moans a bit, and Esmy tries to outdo her, but it's all in their heads. The most that's ever happened was when Miss Granita keeled over in a dead faint, and Esmy passed out on top of her. Of course, Esmy was faking and Miss Granita had forgotten to eat for two days, but the whole thing was very exciting."

"I still don't like the idea," Marielle mumbled into her own bowl of Cap'n Crunch. She knew better than to eat such empty calories, but she'd always had a sneaking fondness for the old Cap'n, and this morning she needed all the comfort she could find, even if it was in a box of presweetened cereal.

"Don't worry. I'll watch the children for you. I bet you find it entertaining."

"How about if I watch the children and you go? At this rate they've hardly seen me in the last few days." Marielle could see that the moment the words were out of her mouth she'd deeply offended Julie, and she quickly hurried to undo the harm she'd caused. "I don't want to take advantage of you, Julie."

"I don't mind. It's something to do, and you've got real special kids. I . . . like them," she said with her usual diffidence.

Marielle swallowed a smile. "They like you."

"Besides, Esmy says my pregnancy upsets the vibrations, so she wouldn't let me be around, anyway. If I know them they're counting on having you there. It's not often they get someone new to perform for."

"Two people," Marielle said wryly. "Dennis promised to go, too."

At the mention of Dennis's name Julie's face went carefully blank. "He should find it interesting."

Marielle's brain finally began working. "As a matter of fact, you might want to go down and check what happened to Granita's fireplace," she said with a diffidence that matched Julie's.

She didn't have to be a psychic to read Julie's mind. The younger girl opened her mouth to ask Marielle if Dennis was still down there, and then shut it again, afraid to know.

She should know better than to matchmake, Marielle thought, particularly in Julie's tangled circumstances. Look at how infuriating Simon's heavy-handed machinations were. But then Simon had a hidden agenda. Marielle simply wanted Julie to be happy.

"Go on down," she said again. "You never know what you might find down there."

And Julie, with a last, indecisive frown, went, leaving Marielle to wonder if she'd made a very big mistake.

Chapter Eleven

It was after nine that evening when Marielle knocked on Granita's scarred wooden door. She did so with great misgivings. She was dressed in an old black evening gown that had been unearthed from heaven only knew where. It smelled of mothballs and old perfume, and it had been worn by someone with a great deal more height and girth than Marielle was blessed with. The wispy black folds dragged along the floor, obscuring her practical Nikes, the sleeves drooped over her knuckles, and the low-cut, lacy neckline gaped over Marielle's less than abundant charms. Simon had returned her black shawl, and Marielle had it firmly wrapped around her overexposed figure, but she couldn't help feeling like a Halloween character.

She wished she hadn't had to join in this preposterous séance. The last thing on earth she wanted to do was spend the evening around a table with two eccentric old women trying to call forth ghosts. At best she figured she'd be heartily bored. At worst, if the séance actually worked and Vittorio showed up, she'd be scared witless, probably pack up the kids and run straight back to...

She didn't know where she could run to. There was no one in New York, and she wasn't in the habit of turning to other people for help. People usually turned to her, even her own parents. She was always so calm, so stable, so peacefully maternal that no one ever considered the fact that there were times when she needed to be mothered herself.

And she wasn't ready to leave Chicago, to leave Farnum's Castle, even if it did turn into something out of *Ghostbusters*. Her need to stay had something to do with the tenuous, gradually increasing feeling of self-sufficiency. It had something to do with the weird, wonderful people inhabiting the place. And it had something to do with the man who lived above her. What, she wasn't quite sure. She just knew she didn't want to risk never seeing Simon Zebriskie again.

The Meltirks had been uncharacteristically quiet when she'd passed their apartment on the way down. As usual the strange, smoky smells were issuing forth, and Marielle had no idea whether it was a ceremonial fire or simply Baluchistani cooking. She wasn't sure if she wanted to find out, particularly if the latter proved to be the case and she was forced to partake of something that smelled like that. She paused for a moment outside their door, but there were no voices, no sounds of animals. Maybe she'd imagined the goat and the chickens. Or maybe they were dinner.

She wasn't too keen on the smells coming from Granita's apartment, either, and for a moment she wondered whether she could get away with sneaking back upstairs and pretending to be sick. But no sooner had that delightfully devious thought entered her mind than the door swung open, revealing Granita in all her Stygian splendor.

She was draped in black from her veiled head to her large, flat feet. She was even wearing black support stockings, Marielle noticed. Music—if you could call it that—was issuing from the candle-lit living room. A small cassette recorder was putting out strange, atonal sounds, and the incense burning on the table smelled like rotting watermelon.

"Perfect." Granita's brisk, no-nonsense British accent was at odds with the theatrical setting. "You look perfect."

"She looks like the bride of Dracula," Simon drawled. "Where did you get that outfit?"

With a grimace Marielle picked up her trailing black skirt. "Don't you like it? Granita said it would be just the thing to summon Vittorio."

"I would say so," Miles Van Cortland said, stepping into view, his handsome face wreathed in an appreciative grin, his blue eyes oddly assessing. "That dress was worn by Vittorio's wife just before she died. I've seen old photographs of it. Where in the world did you find it?"

Marielle dropped the skirt with a startled screech. "You didn't tell me that!" she exclaimed accusingly, wishing there were some way she could get the clinging folds off her.

"I didn't know that," Granita replied calmly. "Miles is the great expert on Farnum's Castle, not me. That's one of the reasons I invited him to join us."

"Besides, she didn't die in the dress," he said, his beautifully sculpted mouth curving in a smile. "She died of pneumonia a few months after she wore it. And she never looked half as beautiful as you do in it."

Marielle's initial distaste began to fade, particularly when she noticed the absolutely ominous expression on Simon's face. "Not the bride of Dracula?" she murmured.

"Simon never had any taste in women. Look at his ex-wife."

"Ex-wife?" Marielle echoed, clutching the shawl around her more tightly. The room was warm, too warm, but there was no way she was going to let her modesty shield fall. "I didn't realize Simon was married."

"Simon is getting damned tired of this," Simon said, his gray eyes flinty. "Can we get on with it?"

"In good time, dear, in good time," Esmy soothed, bustling into the room in the same black garb as Granita. Even Simon was in black—a black T-shirt again, though not the one she'd pulled out of shape with her hungry, clinging hands. And black jeans. She'd better not start looking at his jeans, she told herself.

"We're not all here yet," Granita intoned, sinking gracefully into her chair. The requisite round table was covered with something that resembled a gypsy shawl, and the crystal ball sat squarely in the middle.

Where in the world did people find crystal balls nowadays? Marielle wondered, pulling the shawl still more tightly around her and ignoring the flush of heat that was climbing her cheekbones. Since she couldn't be tactless enough to ask that question, she went for another. "What happened to your wife?"

"I drowned her in the bathtub," Simon snapped.

Miles, his black wool suit impeccably tailored, moved up beside her and cupped her elbow with his strong, smooth hand. "Don't pay any attention to the man. It was a very civilized divorce. He was married to a career woman who wanted someone a little more ambitious. Didn't Sharon try to pay you alimony?"

"You're treading on thin ice, Miles. It's only because of Granita and Esmy that I don't use the language I'm longing to," Simon snapped.

"Oh, go right ahead, dear," Esmy said with an airy wave. "Granita and I are used to it. We deplore it, of course, but there are times when a good solid cuss word is so satisfying."

Simon smiled faintly. "I agree. However, I think Marielle's a bit more sheltered."

Marielle could feel the heat rise to her face, and she squirmed beneath her smothering shawl. "I'm not as sheltered as you'd think," she said, knowing it was a lie. She was probably even more innocent than Simon suspected. She moved away, sitting down at the table across from Granita, and pressed a faintly trembling hand to her cool, damp forehead.

"I wish to heavens the furnace would work right," she said. "It's miserably hot in here."

Esmy leaned over her, clucking sympathetically. "It's not really that bad, you know. It's better than being icy cold."

Before she realized what was happening, Simon's long fingers reached down and plucked off the hot woolen shawl. "If you're hot you don't need...this." The words trailed away as he realized how remarkably indecent Mrs. Farnum's black ball dress actually was. "My, my," he said. "I didn't realize old Vittorio had been married to such a temptress."

"I think she had a little more to hold it up," Marielle said, striving for an air of unconcern.

Miles sank down beside her, flashing that beautiful smile, his observant blue eyes never dropping below her chin. "She wasn't nearly as gorgeous as you are."

Simon sat down on her other side, and Marielle thought she could hear his teeth grinding in rage. "I'm so glad my matchmaking worked out," he snarled, his attempt at an affable smile failing miserably.

"Sorry to disappoint you, Simon," Miles said. "The lady keeps turning me down."

The expression of outrage, relief and confusion on Simon's long, narrow face was too much for Marielle. Quickly she ducked her head, biting her lip.

"You lied to me," Simon said, his deep voice accusing.

She looked up at him, trying to keep her expression innocent, then spoiled it all by giggling. "No, I didn't. I said you got what you wanted. You didn't really want me going out with Miles, and I didn't want to go out with him."

"Could we change the subject?" Miles requested in a pained voice. "I'm really not used to being considered so dispensable."

Marielle smiled at him, and Miles smiled back. "It's nothing personal. I'm not interested in getting involved with anyone at all. Simon knows that, but he won't listen."

"I could change your mind, you know," Miles said gently.

She looked at him, arrested by the soft promise in his voice. She looked at his wickedly handsome face, his beautiful mouth and aloof blue eyes, and shook her head. "No," she said, just as gently, just as sure, "you couldn't." If Simon couldn't, no one could, she thought. And Simon couldn't.

"It doesn't seem as if I'm going to get a chance to try." There was still the hint of a question in Miles's voice.

"The lady said no," Simon rumbled, clearly forgetting he was supposed to be in favor of the match.

"Message received, over and out."

"Am I too late?" Dennis appeared in the doorway, dressed in the requisite black, his red hair and open, friendly expression at odds with the funereal clothing. He looked around the room, his eyes fastened on Marielle's neckline and he let out a long, appreciative whistle. "If Vittorio won't come back from the grave for Marielle then nothing'll get him," he said, taking a seat beside Granita.

Marielle looked over her shoulder for her protective shawl, but Simon had tossed it out of reach. She could feel the blush reach her exposed chest, and there was nothing she could do but sit there while everyone stared at her exposed collarbones.

"Anyone else?" Simon asked, his voice impatient. "I'm due at the station by eleven-thirty, and I don't know if my boss will understand if I'm late."

"Jackie can always work a little over if you don't get back in time," Miles said, and a trace of malicious humor lit his eyes. "She'll just put on that thirty-minute song by Musclebound and take a nap."

"No!" Simon said, his voice strangled. "I'll be there on time."

"I wish I knew what you had against Musclebound," Miles said plaintively. "Their last album went platinum, they've been around for years and years, and you steadfastly refuse to play any of their records. It doesn't make sense."

"It does to me," Simon said stubbornly. "Just ancient history."

Marielle looked from the man on her right to the one on her left. Simon looked hostile, defensive and completely furious. Miles, on the other hand, looked almost smug. Not for one moment did Marielle believe that Miles didn't know what was behind Simon's attitude, despite his disclaimers.

She was still feeling hot, uncomfortable and short of breath. The kids had already fallen asleep by the time she'd put on her costume and trailed her way downstairs, and she wished she could be lying up there too, even in Vittorio's nasty carved bed, and Julie be down here in her place.

The final participant in the séance appeared at the door, and for a moment Marielle thought it was Julie. But her serene highness, Mrs. Meltirk wasn't as far advanced in her current pregnancy as Julie was, despite her imposing bulk, and she moved majestically into the room, nodding at her neighbors with her usual dignity. As she seated herself beside Dennis, Marielle caught the faint, unmistakable odor of goat, and her dizziness increased.

"Now we're ready," Granita announced with an air of satisfaction.

Marielle looked around the table. There were seven of them—Dennis, Granita, Esmerelda and Mrs. Meltirk on one side, Simon, Miles and herself on the other.

Miles was sitting too close; she could swear there was no need for him to hover over her like that. Simon was sitting too close. His jeans-clad leg wasn't touching her thigh, but she knew it was close, enticingly close. For some twisted reason she moved closer to Miles. She had no interest in Miles—he held no threat. She wasn't interested in Simon either, she reminded herself. She just didn't trust her own incomprehensible reaction to his nearness, she thought, wishing there were a little more air in the overheated room, wishing Granita had better taste in incense.

"I thought Julie's pregnancy interfered with the vibrations," she said somewhat desperately, looking for a final escape. "What about her highness?"

"Julie is an adolescent," Esmy explained. "Adolescent girls are full of undisciplined energies, pregnant or not. We couldn't risk upsetting the spirits...."

"She's eighteen," Dennis announced flatly. "And she's more mature than most thirty-year-olds I've met."

Everyone turned to look at him, surprise, calculation and hope among the predominant emotions. Dennis accepted their interest with equanimity—and with just a trace of defiance.

"Okay," said Simon, his slow, deliberate tone almost comical. "Shall we get on with this?"

Granita nodded her head. "If you would all just hold hands, we may begin."

And Marielle, fighting the wave of dizziness, lifted her black silk arms to the men on either side. Miles's clasp was cool and dry, light and just faintly possessive. Clearly he didn't like to give up easily, and whether he really wanted her or not, he didn't take no for an answer.

Simon's hand was much larger, warm and strong and pulsing with energy. Her hand disappeared within his grasp, and her left side felt warm, safe, tucked into him. Her right side was cold and lonely, despite Miles's encroaching thigh.

Maybe she was coming down with flu, she thought desperately. Maybe she should have remembered to eat something in the last two days besides sugary cereal. And maybe this time she was going to outdo Esmy and Granita and be the first to pass out.

The grip on her left side, Simon's side, tightened momentarily. She turned and looked at him out of slightly hazy eyes. For all his determined cynicism he seemed surprisingly kind, watching her out of worried gray eyes.

"Are you okay?" he whispered, and his voice seemed to rumble along her backbone.

She summoned up her best, falsest smile. "Just fine," she whispered, turning her attention to Granita, ignoring the strange sensation of someone touching, stroking her hair. She could see the hands on the table. It had to be her imagination.

The old woman's face had taken on a pale glow, and her milky blue eyes were shining with excitement. "If everyone is ready," she said in her schoolmarm voice. There were no more whispers. "Then let us begin."

And in a low throaty growl she began to moan.

GRANITA WAS RUNNING pretty true to form, Simon thought as he sat poker-faced in the uncomfortable folding chair. The moans, the incantations, the shaking of the table were all standard. The only difference tonight was the woman beside him, her cold, damp hand trembling in his.

And then there was Miles on the other side, breathing down that absurd excuse for a dress. If Simon had seen the dress that Granita had given Marielle he would have put a stop to it before Miles could run his lascivious eyes over her. He'd been half tempted to wrap the shawl back around her like a mummy, but had resisted the impulse. The other half of him couldn't stand to cover up such a delectable expanse of flesh, particularly when she blushed so charmingly. And it was nowhere near indecent, just slightly, irresistibly daring.

Nevertheless, tomorrow morning he was going to get that dress away from her and hide it. She shouldn't be allowed out in public in it—it was too tempting. If it were up to him he'd keep it around for her to wear when no one else was around. No one but himself.

But it wasn't up to him—it was none of his business. The only thing he could do was get rid of the damned thing, so she didn't get into any more trouble she couldn't handle, he told himself with a shade of self-righteousness he knew was absurd.

Miles wasn't paying any more attention to Granita's mumbo jumbo than he was, which was surprising, considering this was the first time he'd been invited. Simon had been at least vaguely interested the first couple of times he'd been forced to sit through one of these. But Miles seemed far more interested in peering down Marielle's dress, something that Simon would have found extremely annoying if it hadn't been for Marielle's discomfort. She had the good sense to see Miles for the lecherous fribble that he was. So instead of wanting to strangle Miles, Simon decided he'd be satisfied with bashing his perfect teeth in.

That crack about the rock group Musclebound was another thing, Simon thought morosely. It had to have been a coincidence, an unfortunate slip of the tongue. There was no way Miles could know anything about that whole sordid, damnable period in his life.

Except that Simon didn't believe in coincidences. And Miles had an uncanny ability to know things that no one else could possibly know, and he took absolute delight in using that knowledge for his own advantage.

Maybe he'd been hiding his head in the sand too long. Maybe it was time to have it out with his manipulative boss, find out what he really knew and what, for that matter, he thought about it. Not that Miles's opinion meant anything. Miles was such a manipulative sleaze he'd probably have more respect for Simon if he knew how low he'd sunk in the past.

Granita's moans increased and Mrs. Meltirk began to moan in counterpoint. Her highness always enjoyed these evenings, even though she understood not a single word. Esmy was making her own unique little gruntlike whimpers, and Dennis was following all this with complete, sober fascination. But then, Dennis had delusions of being a writer. He probably thought all this would be fascinating in a book. Little did he know how boring it would swiftly grow to be.

Simon moved his head a fraction of an inch so he could see Marielle's profile. She was very pale, her thick blond hair hanging down around her face, and her eyes had a haunted look. Not enough sleep, he told himself with a forced lack of sympathy.

Though actually she'd slept quite well in his arms, once they'd finally decided that that was all they were going to do. She was a surprisingly restful woman in certain ways; the way her body molded so sweetly to his, the way she looked after her children, the staunch way she'd been accepting the harsh blows that fate had dealt her.

On the other hand, she was surprisingly disruptive. He knew without any doubt that he was going to have a hell of a time stretching out on that old couch without missing her body. Even his bed wouldn't be safe. She'd never been in the bedroom, yet he knew when he tried to sleep he'd be imagining her there with him.

Even in the broad daylight or the dark of night, when he was busiest doing other things totally unconnected with her, the memory of her face, the way she tilted her head, that troubled, lonely expression in her eyes would sneak up and hit him, and he'd find himself mooning over her like a teenager whose hormones had run amok.

She seemed to have that effect on a lot of people, Miles included. It was a good thing Dennis was immune, or he'd be going even crazier than he was already. But Dennis seemed to have his eye on Julie, unlikely as that might seem. Maybe there was a chance for a happy ending after all. At least for them.

But not for himself. He turned his gaze back to Marielle, allowing himself the dangerous luxury of lowering his gaze to her scantily covered breasts. He could remember how she felt against his hands; now he could almost see what he'd touched. Sometime, just once before he died, he'd like the chance to see and touch at the same time.

If Granita was worried about adolescent hormones wreaking havoc with the vibrations around the table, she hadn't reckoned with his own libido and Marielle's effect on it. He pulled his mind back, trying to think chaste, depressing thoughts, but all he could see was Marielle's soft, sweet mouth.

Her hand definitely felt cool in his, almost cold. And her face was too pale, with sweat beading her high forehead. He was almost ready to say something, to stop the séance, when there was a loud crashing of glass as one of the windows in the living room caved in, bringing in huge gusts of wind that immediately extinguished all the candles.

"Don't break the circle!" Granita shouted in a hoarse, strained voice.

Indeed, most of them were too stunned to move. In the darkness of the old living room came an unearthly light, a grayish-green glow, centered in the broken window. And in the center of that glow, beady brows, hooked nose and all, shimmered the shadowy, shifting planes of Vittorio Farnum's cruel face.

The first scream came from beside him as Marielle's icy cold hand slipped from his as she slumped over the table in an undeniable faint. The second came floating at least three stories down from the top of the building. And it could only have come from Julie.

Chapter Twelve

Simon caught Marielle as she tumbled sideways toward him, her body limp in its flowing black silk. The hideous apparition in the broken window had vanished, the room was pitch-black, and it was several seconds before someone had the sense to stumble towards the light switch.

Dennis was already out the door, racing up the flights of stairs. They could hear the faint sounds of children crying, and Simon rose, cradling Marielle against him, desperately torn. He needed to find out what had happened, but he had to make sure Marielle was all right before he went.

Esmy came up beside him. "Put her down on the sofa, Simon," she said, her raspy little voice efficient. "We'll take care of her while you make sure the children are safe."

"But..."

"Go ahead, Simon," Miles said, moving with his usual grace and taking one of Marielle's lifeless hands in his own. "You'll do better grappling with whatever demons of the night are up there. I'll keep watch down here. I think our visitations have departed for now."

Simon's lip curled. "Coward."

Miles's smile was very pure. "Absolutely."

Simon allowed himself one last, worried glance at Marielle's pale figure before he ran after Dennis, taking the steps three at a time. The tableau that met his eyes on the fourth floor was both worse and better than he'd imagined.

Another window was broken, letting in blasts of cold air. The door to Marielle's apartment was splintered and hanging from one weak-looking hinge, but Simon suspected the mayhem had been caused by Dennis in his zeal to get to the source of that bloodcurdling shriek, not by whatever midnight intruder had ventured forth.

Julie was sitting on the couch, trying, not very successfully, to hold two wailing children in her almost nonexistent lap. Dennis was doing his best to help, sitting beside her and dabbing at the scratch on her forehead, and the children seemed equally frightened, although neither of them looked as if they'd been hurt.

Without thinking, Simon held out his arms to the miserable children. And to his amazement they both ran to him, Christopher clinging to one knee with fierce abandon, wailing in relief, Emily flinging herself against his chest and hanging on like a monkey.

He collapsed in an uncomfortable chair, taking the children with him, and his big hands were soothing, reassuring as he eyed Julie's sorry appearance. "What happened?"

"I was watching TV, and the kids were asleep," she said, her voice still shaky. She didn't seem to notice that Dennis had his arm around her shoulder, that his expression was an odd mixture of concern, anger and fierce protectiveness. "I thought I heard a noise in the chimney. It sounded as if it was coming from upstairs."

Simon's reaction was short, intense and not suitable for the ears of a five-year-old and an eighteen-month-old. "And you weren't smart enough to stay put?" he demanded, worry making him angry.

"Leave her alone!" Dennis fired back. "All she did was open the door. Some damned mugger was creeping down from your place. She screamed, he hit her, the children woke up and he got away.''

"Damn," Simon said more mildly, remembering the children's ears. "Are you all right? Should we take you to the hospital?"

"I'm more frightened than hurt." Surreptitiously she was pressing a hand to her swollen stomach, and Simon had a sudden, horrifying fear.

"You're not going into labor, are you?" he demanded.

"Don't worry, Simon, I've got three weeks to go. He's just kicking." She patted her stomach with a wistful fondness, unaware that Dennis was watching her, lifting his own hand to touch her swollen belly, pulling it back before she even realized what he'd almost done. He stood up abruptly, his eyes met Simon's, and a rueful acknowledgment passed between them.

"I'm calling my brother-in-law," he said shortly. "And then I'll drive Julie to the emergency room. Anyone this close to term shouldn't take chances."

"You aren't by any chance an obstetrician as well as being a plumber and an electrician?" Simon drawled.

Dennis's grin was self-deprecating. "Nope. But I did serve a stint as a medic when I was in the navy. I've been in a few delivery rooms. When it comes right down to it, it's all plumbing."

"Thanks a lot," Julie grumbled.

"On a much grander scale," Dennis said quickly, not missing the offended tone of voice. "Let me call Francis, and then we'll head out."

Simon listened to all this with decidedly mixed feelings. On the one hand he wanted to protest, to tell this young upstart that Julie and everyone else in Farnum's Castle were his responsibility, and if anyone was going to drive her to the hospital it would be himself.

On the other hand, Julie looked at Dennis as if the sun rose and set in his eyes and she'd much prefer having him by her side. And Simon's reasons for taking care of the lost souls at the castle were supposed to be for their sake, not his.

"Anyone know what he did to my apartment?" he asked instead.

"I think we should wait till Francis gets here to check. There might be fingerprints, evidence."

"If you're going to call anyone," Simon said evenly, "you're going to have to go upstairs. And if anyone's going upstairs it's going to be me."

"Me too," Emily said, clinging tightly.

"Me too," said Christopher, chewing on Simon's knee.

Simon looked at Dennis. "You call," he said wearily. "I'd better go down and see how Marielle is."

"What's wrong with Marielle?" Julie demanded, rising stiffly on unsteady feet.

"She fainted at the séance. I didn't have time to see if she was all right...." To his complete and utter horror Emily began to cry again, loud, piercing wails, and Christopher immediately joined in. "Oh, lord, I forgot," he muttered over Emily's loud demands for her mother. "Listen, your mother's fine. She just got a little dizzy. We'll go down and see her, right now. Okay? Okay?"

On the second okay the screeching stopped, Emily nodded her head, managing a semblance of her usual beatific smile, and Christopher uttered a watery chuckle as Simon rose, hoisting his small, wiggling body into his arms.

They felt surprisingly good to him, those two small packages of humanity leaning against him so trustingly. He'd never thought he wanted children, but then he'd never thought he wouldn't. Somehow during his long, misspent life the subject just hadn't come up. But there was something about them, the clean, fresh smell of them, the sweet faces, even the tempestuous tears, that was insidiously touching. If he didn't watch his step he'd find himself seduced just as thoroughly by Marielle's children as he was by their mother.

Marielle was sitting up on the sofa when they reached the bottom floor, and some of her color had returned to her pale cheeks. And her pale cleavage, Simon couldn't help but notice, mentally slapping himself. He set down the children, watching as they catapulted themselves across the room and into Marielle's arms.

He waited until the noise level abated somewhat before filling them in on what happened upstairs. Granita nodded, still so pleased with her visitation from Vittorio that she couldn't really concentrate on the simultaneous break-in. Esmy looked more thoughtful, but said nothing, and Marielle, her blue eyes horrified, kept her mouth shut as she cuddled her children.

It was up to Miles to respond. "This place sounds like a booby trap," he said with his usual lazy charm. "I think you should all get out of here before something even worse happens."

"And where do you suggest we go, Miles?" Simon demanded. "You going to put us up at the expensive penthouse on Lake Shore Drive?"

"It may have escaped your notice, but you live in a penthouse too, Simon. Of course, a haunted penthouse in Farnum's Castle is a far cry from my apartment. I wouldn't be caught dead spending another night here, after all you've been going through. When I think of that apparition in the window..." He shuddered, and Simon almost believed him. Almost. "Surely there are city agencies that can help find places for most of you. And Simon, I know that even with the pittance I pay you, you can afford a better place."

"Where do you suggest we go?" Marielle demanded, her faint voice slightly tart.

Miles smiled his glorious smile at her, and Simon controlled the urge to kick him out the broken window. "Now I think I might be able to find room for you."

"And my kids?"

"They must have grandparents somewhere," he suggested hopefully. "Aunts and uncles?"

"Forget it, Miles," she said, dismissing him as completely as Simon could have hoped. "We're staying."

"Well, I hate to be so trite, but don't say I didn't warn you," he practically purred.

Enough was enough, Simon thought. "Dennis is taking Julie to the emergency room," he said, moving into the room. "Do you want to have them take a look at you, too?"

Marielle looked up, startled. "What's wrong with Julie?"

"Just a bump on her head. She's fine, but Dennis thought they'd better check her out, anyway. What about you?"

She shook her head. "I've been pushing myself too hard. A good night's sleep will take care of it."

"And a few decent meals," Julie said from the doorway. "Cap'n Crunch is not enough to keep any grown woman on her feet."

"It has added vitamins," Marielle defended it faintly. "You look terrible, Julie."

"So do you."

Dennis cleared his throat, barely swallowing his grin. "Francis and his partner will be right over. He said to keep off the top floor."

"I'll keep out of the entire house," Miles said. "And if the rest of you had any sense you'd do the same. I presume you aren't going to make it into work tonight, Simon?''

"Not if you can find someone to take my place." Simon knew perfectly well he'd have no trouble finding a replacement. Miles kept a lengthy list of would-be disc jockeys who'd pay him for the chance to fill in. "Just so long as they know the rules."

Miles emitted a long-suffering sigh. "No playing Musclebound on your shift," he repeated wearily. "Someday, Simon, you'll explain that to me."

"Someday, Miles," Simon returned with utter calm, "you'll admit you know more than you have any right to know."

"And someday," Miles said, "you'll learn not to underestimate me, Simon. I always know more than I have any right to know. I'll get someone to cover for you. Let me know what happens, will you? And if you need any help finding places for people to live, I know a few people with influence. You can count on me for help."

"We'll be just fine," Marielle said, and there was no missing the defiance in her voice. Miles only smiled.

Simon waited until he heard the front door close, waited until the sound of Miles's footsteps was swallowed up by the night before he turned he spoke. "I hate to admit it," he said slowly, "but Miles is right. It's dangerous here, and you'll all be better off someplace else."

"Where would we go?" Granita demanded, some of her delight vanishing. "I don't want to go back to some wretched home—I don't think I could bear it. I don't think any ghosts are going to hurt me."

"You're going to get pneumonia from that broken window," he pointed out.

"Nonsense. I know perfectly well that you'll fix it, as you've fixed things before."

"No, he won't," Marielle said, pulling herself upright and reaching for the shawl. Simon watched with great regret as she proceeded to envelope herself in its voluminous folds. "I own the building. I'll do the repairs. Just give me a few moments to change my clothes and . . ."

"And who'll stay with the kids?" Simon countered. "Not to mention that someone, probably Dennis, smashed your door down. That should be repaired before the night's out, too. Face it, Marielle, we're all going to have to pitch in. I'll board up Granita's window—there's some old plywood in the basement that will probably cover it. I also have every intention of going over the frame with a fine-toothed comb. Much as I hate to disappoint you all, I don't think that was Vittorio Farnum peering in at us. He wouldn't have needed to break a window to do it. It was a trick of some sort, and I intend to find out how it was done and who did it."

"It wasn't a trick!" Granita insisted. "Couldn't you feel the vibrations, the hunger in the air?"

The only hunger in the air had been his, for Marielle, but he decided not to mention that in front of the assembled group. "If it wasn't a trick it won't do any harm to check, now will it?"

"You could offend the spirits," Esmy said. "It might make them feel unwelcome, drive them away."

"Good." Marielle lifted her head, brushing the thick tangle of blond hair away from her face. "I hate to break this to you, but the spirits aren't welcome here, and I'd like nothing better than for them to get as far away as possible."

"You don't realize what a golden opportunity you're throwing away," Esmy said earnestly. "You saw him as well as we did. You couldn't have any doubt who it was."

"It was an apparition that looked uncannily like Vittorio Farnum," she agreed. "Like Simon, I'm just not sure it wasn't a carefully manufactured one."

"But who would do such a thing?" Granita demanded. "And why?"

"Don't be a ninny," Esmy snapped. "The treasure, of course."

"And we could have asked Vittorio himself!" Granita moaned. "If only you hadn't fainted, my dear. I know you couldn't help it, but next time if you could try to control your dizziness..."

"Next time?" Marielle echoed faintly.

"Dare we try for tomorrow night?" Esmy suggested. "No, perhaps we ought to wait a bit. The moon will be new next Monday—perhaps that will be auspicious."

"Why not do it Halloween?" Marielle said, fully as sarcastic as Simon could be. "It's only a couple of days away...."

"Perfect!" breathed Granita, taking her absurd suggestion seriously. "We'll count on your assistance."

Before Marielle could speak Simon interrupted. If he had his way there would be no need for another séance on Halloween. He had every intention of finding out what in hell was going on around there well before then. "In the meantime," he said, his deep voice immediately gaining their attention, "I don't think anyone should be staying alone. There's definitely something peculiar going on around here, and I want people to double up. Granita, do you want to move in with Esmy or the other way around?"

The two old women glared at each for a long, combative moment. "I suppose she might as well move back in with me," Esmy said grudgingly. "After all, my windows are intact."

"Graciously put, but I prefer to remain here," Granita sniffed. "You have Julie to keep you company, and I, for one, am not afraid of Vittorio."

"Granita." Simon didn't need to say another word—just her name was warning enough.

"Oh, very well. But that doesn't account for the others. What about Marielle?"

"We'll put Julie in with Marielle—that way there'll always be someone to stay with the kids, and there'll be Dennis below and me above. No ghost in his right mind would go near the Meltirks.... Where is her highness, by the way?"

Marielle laughed wryly. "According to Esmy she thanked us all for an entertaining evening and went home to bed. I gather ghosts are a common occurrence in Baluchistan."

"Maybe the Meltirks are responsible for the sudden increase in supernatural visitations," Esmy suggested. "All the spirits want is a welcome."

"There's no welcome here," Marielle said. Christopher was sitting in her lap, his curly golden head drooping against her shawl-covered chest, and Emily's yawn seemed about to split her face in two.

"Let me help you get these kids back to bed," Simon said. "Granita, you move in with Esmy for tonight. I'll board up the window, but I'm not sure how quickly I can get to it. I imagine Officer Muldoon will want to talk with all of you, so don't go to bed quite yet." He reached down and hoisted the sleeping Emily into his arms. She rested her head quite comfortably on his shoulder, and he extended a hand to help Marielle to her feet.

She was staring up at him, openmouthed in amazement. "What magic spell did you use?" she questioned softly, adjusting her own eighteen-month-old burden on her shoulder. "She doesn't like strangers."

"I'm not a stranger."

She didn't move, apparently oblivious to the avid old ladies watching and listening to every word, every nuance. "No," she said finally, "I guess you're not."

If she could ignore the audience so could he. "And unlike her mother," he said, "she has excellent taste in men."

The smile started slowly, that delicious smile that tilted the corners of her blue eyes and wrinkled her short nose. "Oh, I didn't do so badly last night."

There was a pleasantly shocked intake of breath, but Simon's attention was all on Marielle's first, tentative flirtation. "You don't listen to warnings, do you?" he murmured.

"I'm willing to take a few chances. Aren't you?"

"No," he said flatly.

"Liar," she said, laughing up at him, her color and humor restored.

"My dear," said Granita, "I had no idea something like this was going on. Why didn't you tell us?"

"Nothing's going on, Granita." Simon was suddenly all business. "And nothing will."

Granita ignored him. "What do you think, Esmerelda? A Christmas wedding?"

"Don't be a ridiculous old woman," Esmy snapped, fully contemptuous.

"I knew I could count on you to be sensible," Simon said approvingly.

"They'll be married by Thanksgiving," Esmy announced.

"Let's get out of here," Simon said, giving up. "The kids need their sleep and you need to get out of that contraption you're wearing."

By this time Marielle had gotten a little cocky, probably from the aftermath of fear as much as anything. "Oh, I decided I rather liked it. It's fun to watch people's eyes bulge out of their heads."

Just for a moment he considered mentioning what else happened to bulge at the sight of that ridiculous dress, but the present company was too young and too old and altogether too innocent to hear such a thing. "Come along, earth mother," he grumbled. "Any chance you'd be willing to trust the elevator?"

"I'd be more likely to fly up there on my broomstick."

"That's the spirit," said Esmy. "Now you're fitting in to Farnum's Castle."

"She doesn't need a broomstick," Simon drawled, starting out the door and trusting she'd follow.

She did, trudging up the stairs after him, only slightly out of breath as they climbed flight after flight. "I'll try to get Muldoon to wait till tomorrow to talk to you," he said, pausing between the third and fourth floors. "But I can't promise."

"I don't think I'm going to be able to sleep tonight, anyway. If you could just keep him at bay until after the children are settled again, that would be relief enough."

"I can do that." He followed her into the apartment, past the splintered door and into the children's bedroom. Emily was already asleep in his arms, her heavy breathing and angelic expression leaving no doubt. He set her down very carefully, but she did nothing more than curl up, hand under her chin, breathing a deep, heartbreaking sigh.

Marielle turned from the Porta-crib, an odd expression on her face. "You do that quite well," she whispered. "You must have lots of practice."

He felt his mouth curve in a faint smile. "First time," he murmured back. "I must be a natural."

A sudden, strained silence filled the room. It was too enticing, the warm, sexy woman in front of him, the sweetly sleeping children, the whole domestic life that he'd learned he wasn't cut out for. Standing there in the shadows Marielle no longer looked fifteen, she looked like a woman. Like a woman he wanted quite desperately to kiss.

"I'll keep Muldoon away," he said, backing out the door, as big a coward as Miles Van Cortland ever was. And before she could say another word he was gone.

Chapter Thirteen

Marielle rubbed the woolen shawl over her suddenly chilled arms. She followed Simon's fleeing figure out of the children's bedroom, flicking off the light as she went. A blast of cold air rushed from the hallway through her apartment, and she surveyed her splintered door with a resigned shake of the head. She could only hope they were able to rout Vittorio's ghost or his present-day counterparts before winter set in. It was cold enough in October—December in Chicago with broken windows didn't bear thinking about.

For a moment she wondered why she hadn't confided in Simon. The eerie sensation during the séance still lingered in the back of her mind. Someone had touched her, someone had placed a gentle, almost loving hand on her back at a time when she could plainly see everyone's hands. The first time she'd ignored it, the second was when the ghostly image of Vittorio had appeared in the smashed window.

But she knew why she hadn't told Simon, or anyone else. For one thing, she didn't want to feed their fantasies. For another, she didn't want them to scoff. And lastly, and perhaps most importantly, she didn't want to think about it, even for the length of time it would take to tell someone. She would dismiss it from her mind as the figment of her imagination she knew it was.

Marielle had no idea whether Simon had headed upstairs or back down to Granita's apartment, and she decided she was better off not knowing. She closed the door
as best she could, setting it into the splintered frame, and
sank onto the sofa that wasn't even remotely as comfortable as Simon's ancient, overstuffed couch. She should do
something about the broken window in the hallway, but
the police would probably prefer her to wait. So wait she
would, curled up on the sofa, wondering why she felt
abandoned and bereft.

Maybe she should start thinking seriously about New
Mexico. While the offer for Farnum's Castle hadn't been
particularly overwhelming, it would at least provide her
future with a decent start. If she were at all reasonable
she'd think about getting out before things got any worse,
before someone else got hurt. Before her children got hurt.

The very thought sent a shiver of horror racing through
her body. Did she have any right to take chances when the
welfare of her babies was at stake? It was one thing to hold
out against superstition and coercion, another to endan-
ger everything that was most important to her. Maybe she
had no business doing anything but taking the children and
running.

There was, of course, another alternative. She'd promised her parents that the children would come visit them in
their safe, comfortable condo not twenty miles from Disney World. Greg's parents were only another hour away—
she could send the children down, do her duty to the
grandparents, and keep her children safe at the same time.
They could have their week visiting their adored grandparents, and she could have a week to get to the bottom of
the haunting of Farnum's Castle.

There was only one major flaw in the plan. She didn't
want to let them go. They were everything to her, her reason for living, her reason for most of the myriad deci-

sions, good and bad, that she made nowadays. They were
all she had, and she couldn't bear the thought of sending
them away.

But she couldn't stand the alternatives, either. She
couldn't go with them, give up on Farnum's Castle and its
hapless inhabitants. And she couldn't keep them here and
put them in danger.

They'd survive the separation probably much better
than she would. While she sat around moping they'd be
having the time of their lives, cosseted by doting relatives.
And within a week they'd be able to return to a safe envi-
ronment.

If they couldn't find out what was going on at Farnum's Castle and put a stop to it in that week, then her
choice was clear. She'd take the offer Liam O'Donnell's
client had made, take it and run, and to hell with Granita
and Esmerelda and Fritzie and Julie. Simon could take
over once more.

But that wasn't going to happen. They'd find out who
was vandalizing the apartments, who was appearing as the
shade of Vittorio Farnum. And since she was about to ask
a favor of her parents, she might as well go ahead and accept some of the money her well-to-do in-laws kept trying
to force on her. Guilt money or not, she might as well take
advantage of it.

She heard the modified rumble of footsteps and voices
as the police arrived and climbed the endless flights to Simon's apartment. She sat there watching the ceiling as she
listened to them move from room to room, their voices a
muffled soporific, and slowly her head began to nod. It
was after eleven, she was still dressed in that ridiculous, ill-
fitting, immodest dress, and she needed her sleep. It was
too late to call her parents now—tomorrow would be soon
enough. Soon enough to make the plane reservations, to

deal with the thought of being without Emily and Christopher.

She could barely summon up the energy to crawl into the bedroom. She'd never fainted before in her life, and if she wasn't intimately aware of how little she'd eaten, how little she'd slept and what time of the month it was, she'd be worried. She always felt a little wrung out when her period was over, and this time was no different. And she couldn't control her insomnia, not with burglars and ghosts popping in and out of windows at any time of night. But she could remember to eat properly, particularly when her children's well-being might depend on it.

She managed to slide out of the dress, leaving it in a graceful heap of silk on the wooden floor beside her bed. The gargoyles were shadowed in darkness, and she told herself that they wouldn't be leering tonight. Even carved satyrs would have pity on a woman on the edge of collapse. She did collapse, onto the too-soft mattress, too tired to climb between the sheets. If the police needed to talk to her tonight it would be up to them to wake her. Right then she didn't think Vittorio Farnum and all the fiends of hell could rouse her from the deep sleep her body was craving.

She surfaced for a few brief moments when she heard her battered door fall open, but the whispering voices belonged to Julie and Dennis, and she sank back into sleep. At one point a shadow moved through her room, picking up the discarded silk dress, pulling the heavy quilt over her body, brushing her hair away from her sleeping face. She was tempted to wake up and confront the intruder, but her instincts, even while she was sleeping, told her she was safe. It was probably just Julie, restless in her advancing pregnancy.

The touch on her face was so light that she could scarcely feel it, but there was gentleness and affection in that feathery caress. She knew without opening her eyes that it was the same hand that had touched her during the séance, and that it meant her no harm. Marielle settled deeper into sleep.

SHE'D HALF HOPED her parents wouldn't be able to take the kids, that some desperately important tennis tournament or bridge play-off would be keeping them too busy. She should have known better. Her mother jumped at the possibility of a visit like a starving woman at a feast, and instead of complaining that Marielle couldn't accompany the children, she seemed to be particularly delighted to have them all to herself.

"Now don't you worry about a thing, Marielle. A little bit of sunshine and doting grandparents is just what they need. Are you sure a week is long enough? Why don't I make the plane reservations for ten days apart? That would give us a little extra time...."

"One week, Mother," Marielle said in the tone of voice her mother always obeyed. "If things haven't improved around here by then, I'll come down and join you. There must be someplace I can stash a sleeping bag."

"Of course, darling. I do wish I could call you—this telephone situation is impossible. We'll pick up the tab for the airfare, of course. I'll make the plane reservations, then wait to hear from you. We'll do it tomorrow if there's space on any of the flights."

"Tomorrow?" Marielle gasped. "So soon?"

"It sounds as if the sooner they're out of there the better. Listen darling, if you can't trust your own mother, whom can you trust?"

Whom indeed? Marielle thought, replacing the receiver. From her seat in Simon's hallway she could see directly into his apartment. It was a disaster—books and papers strewn everywhere, posters torn off the wall, their glass frames smashed, the previously sealed-off fireplace a mass of rubble. She was half tempted to go in and start cleaning it up, but resisted the impulse. For one thing, it was none of her business. For another, she had enough to keep her busy without taking on new projects. If she knew her mother the children would be flying out some time tomorrow—Virginia Watson could be as ruthlessly efficient as a general in pursuit of what she wanted, and she wanted Marielle's children.

In the meantime she should be preparing the kids for their imminent departure, trying to get their clothes packed, to find what kind of laundry services the old building boasted. She probably didn't want to know. It would doubtless turn out to be one more thing that needed to be repaired.

Of course, she was forgetting her live-in plumber. And if he was feeling too caught up in Julie's welfare she could always remind him that Julie had laundry, too. She didn't really expect to have any problem getting Dennis to work, though. He seemed more than willing to help out.

The coffee would be ready by now—she needed to head back downstairs to the apartment and see what she could do about her splintered door. But there was one last thing she needed to check in Simon's deserted apartment.

He'd gone out early that morning—she'd heard the creaking and jerking of the elevator while she was struggling to find something a little more nutritious than Cap'n Crunch. Julie was still sound asleep on the living-room couch, the bandage on her forehead partially obscured by her hair, and the children were still snoring faintly, well past the time for *Sesame Street*. She'd crept upstairs barefoot, dressed in old jeans and a sweater, calling her parents before she could change her mind, instinctively knowing it would be hours before Simon would return, hours that would give her enough time to figure out how she was going to deal with him.

She suspected even weeks wouldn't be enough. She wasn't going to be able to deal with him until she learned to handle her own, incomprehensible reaction to him.

But she'd face that later. Right now she wanted to know one thing and one thing only. Had the vandal trashed Simon's celestially comfortable sofa in his orgy of destruction?

She tiptoed in, knowing there was no need for silence, being silent anyway. The place really was a shambles—it looked more as if a poltergeist had been at work than a thief. Most of the destruction looked wanton—flour and ground coffee strewn over the floors, furniture upended, obscene, incomprehensible messages scrawled on the bare white walls. She stared around her in shocked dismay.

"They did a thorough job, didn't they?" Simon spoke from directly behind her.

With a great effort Marielle controlled the start of surprise that his sudden reappearance engendered. "Who are Musclebound?" she asked instead, looking at the name written in what seemed to be blood, but which on closer examination smelled like ketchup.

Simon's short bark of laughter was far from amused. "Weren't you listening to Miles's sniping comments last night?" he asked, moving into the room and picking up some of the scattered papers. "They're a rock group, a very successful one, as a matter of fact. And I don't play their records."

"I know that. I mean, I've heard of the group. I wondered why the name is painted on your walls. Why don't you play their records?"

Simon kept his back to her. His graying black hair touched his collar, and she had the sudden, inexplicable urge to brush it back. Instead she knelt on the floor, scooping up papers, her eyes still watching his averted profile.

"Why don't you ask Miles?" he muttered, dumping a pile on the desk and leaning down for more.

"I don't think he knows." She sat back on her heels, the papers resting in her hands. "And I don't want him to tell me. I want you to."

He turned and looked at her then, and she was shocked at the dark pain in his eyes, the cynical twist of his mouth. "You really want to know?" he asked. "Then maybe I'll tell you. You won't like it, but then it's a sordid enough little story."

Marielle's heart twisted a little. "I can survive sordid details."

"Can you? It's no great tragedy, of course. Human greed, human venality, human weakness are all pretty standard for people in the modern world. I used to think I was invulnerable but I learned the hard way that I wasn't." Bitterness and self-loathing made his deep, beautiful voice raw and ugly, and he turned away from her, moving to the window to look out over the overgrown yard.

She sat without moving for a long moment. "So what did you do, Simon?" she asked gently. "Take a bribe from a record company?"

"Fairly obvious, isn't it?" He still wouldn't look at her. "Payola's a nasty crime. People lose their jobs, lose their licenses, lose their freedom if the courts so choose. If they happen to get caught. I didn't get caught."

She rose silently, leaving the papers scattered around her. "They paid you money to play Musclebound? I would have thought a group that successful wouldn't need to resort to payola."

"That's the incredibly stupid thing about it. If they'd just gone about it through normal channels they would have been as big a hit as they are now. But they took the sleazy way."

"And brought you down with it." Her voice was very gentle. "How long ago was this?"

"Nine years ago. I was at a big station in New York, and I was greedy. I thought it was all right to take a generous gift from the sales rep. No, scratch that. I knew it wasn't all right. I just decided to do it anyway. Everyone else was doing it, I needed the money, and I said yes. And I played Musclebound every hour for a week."

"But you stopped, didn't you? Isn't that something?"

He still kept his back to her. "Half the disc jockeys at the station got caught. Some ended up with their licenses suspended, one ended up with a six-month sentence. The station lost its license, and I was out of a job. But no one realized I'd had my hand in the cookie jar, too. I had too noble a reputation. So I never got caught. I moved back to Chicago, worked for a while at a big station, and then quit. I took a job with Miles's two-bit station, and I've been here ever since."

"Penance," Marielle said softly. "You said something about penance a few days ago. Is that what you're doing here?"

"Among other things." He turned then, leaning against the wall and looking at her. "So where's the Mary Sunshine absolution? Aren't you going to tell me I'm making a big fuss over nothing, that I've punished myself long enough? Come on, Marielle, tell me what a fool I'm being over a minor indiscretion."

She crossed the last few feet to stand directly in front of him. Inches away, her bare toes touching his well-worn running shoes. "You betrayed your principles. That's not a minor indiscretion. You don't need me to forgive you. You need to forgive yourself."

He looked down at her, his mouth curved in a mocking smile. "What if I don't think I'm worth forgiving?"

"Then that would be another major mistake on your part," she said. On impulse she reached up, pressing her cool lips against his. There was no response, though she could feel a faint tremor ripple through his body, and she drew back.

"You want to kiss the boo-boo and make it better? I'm not one of your children, Marielle."

"I can't help it if you act like a five-year-old." She reached up again without thinking, and pressed her mouth against his, increasing the pressure this time. She was shocked to feel his mouth open beneath hers, and she put her hands on his shoulders to brace herself. Suddenly she decided to shock him in return, to prove to him that she wasn't the skittish little coward he seemed to think her. Reaching out with the tip of her tongue she touched the firm contours of his lips, teasing the edge of his teeth, exploring, very gently, very shyly.

She was unprepared for the intensity of his reaction. He'd been standing there completely passively, hands at his sides, when a strangled groan caught at the back of his throat and he pulled her into his arms, his tongue meeting hers. He picked her up and turned her in his arms, pressing her against the graffiti-covered wall of the apartment as his tongue took up where hers had left off.

She didn't know people kissed like that. She didn't want it to stop; she wanted him to pick her up and carry her over to the sofa before she could start thinking again. Maybe a little disappointment in the end would be worth it, if the beginning was as astonishingly delightful as this.

And then he moved away, mere inches, his hands pressed against the wall on either side of her, imprisoning her. His breath was coming in strangled rasps, as was hers. They looked into each other's eyes for a long, startled moment.

"Why do we always end up doing this?" Marielle asked when she got her breathing back under control. "We can't be alone for more than five minutes before this starts."

The smile that curved his mouth was very small, but it was free from the bitterness that had twisted it moments before. "Maybe it's too big to fight."

"Nothing's too big to fight," Marielle said fiercely.

Simon simply stood there for another moment, then dropped his arms. "What are you doing here?" he asked, moving away and scooping up more of the scattered papers.

She couldn't very well tell him she'd wanted to see if the couch was still in one piece. It would prove she was far too interested in it and in what had almost happened on it two nights ago. "I was looking for you," she said, knowing deep down that it was the truth. "The children are going to visit my parents in Florida."

She tossed out the statement, determined not to show him how torn she felt, but she underestimated his sensitivity. "How do you feel about that?" he asked, dropping the papers once more.

"At this rate we're never going to get your apartment cleaned up," she joked, avoiding his question.

"To hell with the apartment. How do you feel about sending the children away?"

"Who says I'm sending them away?"

"Of course you are. It's a very wise idea, given that things have escalated around here in the last few days. If you want them to be safe you should send them away. You should go yourself."

She knew that was coming. "I'm not going."

He grinned then, a fully fledged, resigned grin. "I know that, too. I just thought I'd suggest it. What are you going to do while they're gone?"

She smiled faintly. "It's really quite simple. I'm going to make this place safe for all of us, the children included. With your help, or without it."

"Oh, with my help," he said promptly. "And how are you planning to perform this enormous feat?"

"It's quite obvious, really," she said. "We'll just find Vittorio's treasure before anyone else does."

Chapter Fourteen

She heard no groan of protest. "It sounds logical," Simon admitted. "If the treasure turns up, then no one would have any need to search for it. Assuming, of course, that the treasure actually exists and isn't part of some Chicago folklore."

"It exists," Marielle said flatly.

"What makes you so certain?"

"Someone's going to a great deal of trouble to get us all out of here. Night after night they're breaking in and trashing the apartments. They're setting up elaborate phony ghosts to scare us and they're absolutely relentless in their determination to find Vittorio's treasure. No one would go to all that trouble on the basis of folklore."

Simon dumped a pile of papers on the bleached oak table, then scooped up more. "A reasonable enough assumption. But what if you're wrong? What if the ghosts aren't phony? What if the break-ins are the responsibility of one of Vittorio's long-dead victims, come to wreak havoc on his old enemy?"

"You actually used to watch those old movies, didn't you?" Marielle said admiringly. "This isn't the night of the living dead, Simon. This is Chicago at the end of the nineteen-eighties. If the ghost of an old gangster were

going to rise up and cause trouble don't you think he
would have done so long ago?''

"Maybe something set him off. Maybe all the pregnant
women in the building... You're not pregnant, are you?''

The question took her by surprise. "Of course not!" she
snapped. "Not that it's any of your business.''

He shrugged. "Women don't usually faint unless they're
pregnant.''

"They do when they're confronted by a ghost.''

"I thought you didn't believe in ghosts,'' he shot back.

"I don't know what I believe in. I just think the trouble
at Farnum's Castle is more likely caused by greedy hu-
mans than otherworldly visitors. You can't seriously believe that Vittorio or one of his victims trashed your
apartment.''

"No. But I can always hope.''

He was baiting her, and she'd been much too quick to
rise to the provocation. "You're just as sick as Granita and
Esmy,'' she said with a weary sigh. "I'd just as soon be
spared the ghosts. Give me a Chicago thug any day.''

"That's precisely what Vittorio was,'' he pointed out.

She floundered, searching for a suitable response, then
gave up and stuck out her tongue at him. "Why are you
giving me a hard time?'' she demanded, suddenly much
more cheerful than she'd been half an hour ago. "I know
perfectly well that you're even more skeptical about ghosts
than I am.''

"It keeps you on your toes,'' he replied, unrepentant.

"Why are you pushing the idea of a ghost? Is it simply
to drive me out of here, or did you find something last
night when you boarded up Granita's window?''

"What makes you think that?'' Simon's narrow, clever
face was completely blank, but Marielle was beginning to
see behind the facade.

"You did find something!" she said. "What was it? Ectoplasm?"

"Ectoplasm?" Simon echoed in disgust. "Where's your skepticism when we need it? I found traces of fluorescent paint, piano wire, nails embedded in the window frame. All sorts of nice little bits of fakery. Even more interesting—it was all gone this morning when the police checked."

"A setup," Marielle breathed, pleased. "And we know there have to be at least two of them. One was upstairs trashing your apartment while the other was lurking outside Granita's windows. I don't suppose there were any nice muddy footprints?"

"Life isn't that convenient. At least we know our hideous apparition of last night was caused by flesh and blood and not ectoplasm."

"So why were you trying to convince me it was a ghost?"

"To see if I could persuade you to leave with the children."

It was absurd, the tiny little dart of pain that shafted through her. She'd always known he wanted her gone. "I'm not leaving, Simon," she said evenly.

"I know." His tone was resigned. "Are you sure I can't talk you into going with them? You wouldn't want the kids to travel alone, would you? Why don't you take a nice, safe, warm vacation while the rest of us sort this out?"

"Why don't you...?" She swallowed the retort. "Never mind. And you haven't had the dubious pleasure of meeting my mother. I have no doubt she'll fly up to meet the children and accompany them back. If I know her she won't even leave O'Hare."

"So what are you worried about? Wasn't she a decent mother? It sounds like she'll be a perfectly doting, overprotective grandmother."

"Who says I'm worried?"

He laughed, a short, cynical laugh. "I may not know your mother, but after five days I know exactly what's going on in that devious little brain of yours. You're sick at the thought of sending the children away, but you're too levelheaded to put them at risk. That doesn't mean you still won't be miserable while they're gone. Which is exactly why you should go with them."

"Simon . . ." Her voice held a definite warning.

"I know, you're not leaving," he said wearily. "Where do we start looking for this famous treasure? There are at least seventeen fireplaces in the building and our friendly housebreaker has only trashed half a dozen. Want to start with them, or do you prefer to be more subtle? Maybe checking out the basement?"

"What I need to do is get the kids' things packed. If I know my mother she's going to have them on a plane in less than twenty-four hours."

"That sounds like a good idea. I need some sleep if I'm going to manage to work tonight. Let me grab a few hours and then we'll start."

She was halfway across the littered room, looking at him, feeling strange, unaccountable emotions churning inside her. Maybe he was right. Maybe getting out of Farnum's Castle, out of Chicago, away from Simon Zebriskie was the smartest thing she could possibly do. After all, she didn't want anything from him, despite her seemingly irresistible urge to kiss him at the oddest moments.

No, ghosts and burglars and criminal treasure hunters weren't going to drive her away from the new home she was trying to make for her children. Nor was her inexplicable attraction to Simon Zebriskie. "A few hours," she said briskly. "We can start in the empty apartment beside mine."

"It's not empty. That's where all the old furniture is stored."

"Even better. We'll start by going through Vittorio's possessions and see if he left any clues. Maybe we should take down that old portrait."

"It'll be over Granita's dead body. Go away and let me sleep, Marielle," he said drowsily. "Even better, come sleep with me."

"I'll see you later," she said, ignoring the crazy little stirring inside her and hurrying out the door before she could even begin to contemplate temptation.

"Later," he agreed, his deep voice following her into the hallway and down the stairs.

He must be getting punchy, he thought, watching her go. Another minute and he would have grabbed her. The odd thing was, he didn't think she'd have put up much of a fight if he had pulled her over to the couch and proceeded to finish what they'd started far too many times.

Despite her belief in the uselessness of sex, she certainly responded every time he was fool enough to touch her. Her response astonished her as much as it should have surprised him. But he knew better than she just how good sex could be, and he suspected that even he didn't know the half of it. He was experienced enough to recognize mutual attraction, even if Marielle chose to hide from it. He was also experienced enough to know that his attraction to Marielle was stronger than anything he'd felt in years. If ever.

It was too late—he knew it as well as he knew his own body. Even if he could manage the impossible and send her away, the damage had been done. He was probably a fool to fight it.

He crossed the room and shut the door behind her, leaning his head against the frame for a moment. He couldn't believe he'd told her about the payola. The ugly deed that had flayed him raw for nine years, his own nasty little guilt that weighed down upon him, never letting him free, had been a secret from absolutely everyone.

For some reason he felt curiously weightless. Maybe that old chestnut about confession being good for the soul had an element of truth. He'd told Marielle the worst about himself, and she hadn't flinched, hadn't shied away in horror. As a matter of fact, she'd responded by planting a very brave kiss on his lips. With a little time, a little tutelage, she could be quite astonishing....

Cancel that thought, he ordered himself sternly, throwing his weary body onto the welcoming sofa. They weren't going to have the time. He was going to keep on fighting it with every breath in his body. At least until the children were safely in Florida, he added honestly. And then, maybe he'd just see what happened when Marielle had no other responsibilities. Maybe her curiosity might overcome her doubts. And maybe there'd be no escaping the inevitable for either of them.

On that troubling, optimistic note he fell sound asleep in the midst of his littered apartment.

IF SHE'D EXPECTED, secretly hoped for a little reluctance, a little misery from her children when she informed them of their imminent departure, then Marielle was doomed to disappointment. While Emily managed a cursory interest in her mother's whereabouts during their upcoming vacation, her concentration quickly shifted to Disney World, and for the rest of the day her piping little voice could be heard informing a sanguine Christopher about the treats in store for them.

Even Julie seemed dangerously cheerful, despite the lump on her forehead. She'd checked out fine at the emergency room; the baby was fine, everything was fine. The usually reserved girl was whistling as she bustled around the kitchen, fixing the biggest breakfast Marielle had ever seen and forcing her to eat it, scrambled eggs, bacon, muffins, coffee and all. The food had its expected effect and Marielle had begun to relax, when a peremptory knock sounded at the damaged door.

In response the door caved inward, ripping off the remaining hinge and exposing Liam O'Donnell, as prissy and as neatly put together as ever, glowering in the entrance to her apartment.

Marielle's good mood vanished instantly. In her experience lawyers never came bearing good news. Slowly she began to rise, reluctant to hear whatever he had come to say, when Julie moved her pregnant bulk in front of her.

"Were you looking for me?" Julie's belligerence was back with full force, and this time Marielle couldn't blame her. O'Donnell could bring out the belligerence in anyone.

"As a matter of fact, I was." O'Donnell stepped over the broken door and into the room, unasked, ignoring Marielle. "I heard you went to the emergency room last night. I was concerned for your health."

"You were concerned for your commission from my baby's adoptive parents," Julie said bitterly. "Don't worry, the baby's safe. You'll get your ten thousand dollars."

"You know perfectly well we're not talking about that kind of money," O'Donnell said, his wrinkled little mouth pursed in disapproval. "I'm doing this out of the goodness of my heart, trying to help out a girl in trouble and a couple who's desperate for a child."

"I didn't think you had a heart," Marielle broke in cheerfully. "What's the money going to cover?"

"I'm charging a pittance to cover court costs." He glared at Marielle's interested expression. "Is there somewhere we can talk in private?"

"We can talk in front of Marielle. She's my friend," Julie said staunchly, dropping onto the sofa beside her.

"Have you met the adoptive parents?" Marielle questioned, tucking her feet beneath her and preparing to stay.

"I don't consider that wise," O'Donnell said stiffly.

"I don't think he's decided who's going to get my baby," Julie said, her voice low and miserable.

"It shouldn't be up to him, Julie," Marielle said, much to O'Donnell's outrage. "It's up to you. And if you want to meet them before you relinquish the baby, then insist on it. You're not doing anyone any favors if you give up this baby without making absolutely sure it's what you want to do."

"I don't have any choice in the matter. I don't have the money to support the baby, I don't even have my high school diploma yet, and a baby needs two parents."

"Mine only have one."

"That wasn't up to you. I chose to carry this baby, and I'm not going to weaken now. It's going to go to the best, happiest family I can find."

"I wouldn't trust Liam O'Donnell to know the best and happiest," Marielle said frankly. "I think he'll go for the most money. Don't you?"

"That's it!" Liam slammed down his briefcase, advancing on Marielle like a slender, infuriated rabbit. "You will kindly cease to slander me in front of my client! You have no basis for that kind of remark, no basis at all."

"You're right," Marielle admitted. "Just pure instinct." She turned her back on him. "Julie, I think you should look into an agency. They'd be sure to screen prospective parents carefully, they'd provide counseling for you and even help you look into alternatives if you decide to keep the baby."

Julie's face contorted in anguish. "I can't keep the baby," she said, her voice rippling with pain. "I've gone over and over it in my mind. There's no way I can do it."

Marielle opened her mouth to protest, then shut it again. There was nothing she could say that wouldn't make things even worse than they already were. It wasn't up to her to help Julie keep the baby. But she'd never forgive herself if she didn't do everything she could to make sure Julie made a choice that she could live with for the rest of her life.

"I'm clearly wasting my time here," the elderly lawyer sniffed. "I'd like you to come into my office so we can begin the preliminary paperwork, Julie. I'll send a car for you tomorrow morning. Say around ten?"

"I'm not ready to do that," Julie said.

"Really, my dear, we both know this is best for the baby. And I'm a very busy man. I can't wait till the last minute and then drop everything for a charity case."

"I bet the only charity that benefits from this is the Liam O'Donnell Mercedes fund," Marielle snapped. "Don't push her. If the paperwork is too much for you, I'm sure we can find a state agency that'll be more than happy to handle the matter. If Julie decides that's what she wants to do."

She could practically see the smoke coming out of his ears. With a noticeable effort he controlled his rage. "Very well. Let me know when you feel like dealing with it, Julie. But don't take too long. You want your child to grow up with every advantage, don't you? My clients are from a much higher level of society than any you'd find through a public agency. Who knows, if you go through the state your child might be adopted by truck drivers." He shuddered delicately.

"My grandfather was a truck driver," Julie said fiercely. "And you couldn't have asked for a better father."

"I don't seem to be able to say anything right," O'Donnell said stiffly. "I'll wait for you to get in touch. And Mrs. Brandt?"

Now it was her turn. "Yes?" Marielle managed a tight smile.

His answering smile was as sour as a lemon. "You've had another offer on this monstrosity. The client has gone up another five thousand, but he says that's the limit, and if you don't respond within forty-eight hours the offer will be withdrawn. I suggest you take it. I know the bidder's reputation, and this isn't an idle bluff."

She could take off with her children tomorrow and never have to think again about the motley crew she'd be leaving behind. She wouldn't have to worry about courting disaster and disappointment and eventual heartbreak with Simon Zebriskie. She'd be safe, free and reasonably solvent. She must be out of her mind.

"I don't need forty-eight hours, Mr. O'Donnell. The answer is no."

Wasn't there some sort of fairy-tale figure who went into such a rage that he vanished in a puff of smoke? She half expected to see Liam O'Donnell do just that. But he was made of sterner stuff. After one last stare of loathing at the two young women, he turned on his heel, stomping on the broken door and moving into the hallway.

"I hope he takes the elevator and gets stuck," Marielle said with a muffled giggle.

She couldn't coax an answering smile from Julie's mournful face. "I don't. That'd just mean he'd be around longer."

"You're right. The sooner he's out of the building the happier I'll be. Julie..."

"Don't start in on me," the other girl said, pushing herself up from the couch. "I've got to go now. I'll be back, okay? I just need a little space."

"Julie..." She didn't know what to say. "I'm so sorry."

"Yeah," said Julie, her mouth curved in bitterness. "So am I."

Marielle stretched out on the couch, listening to Julie's footsteps on the stairs. She could only hope she wasn't trying to catch up with Liam O'Donnell. That evil man was trying to rip her off; Marielle just knew it. He probably had half a dozen desperate couples on the line and was planning to sell Julie's baby to the highest bidder.

Marielle's sense of motherhood was outraged. Children were precious, not a commodity to be bought and sold by a weasel like Liam O'Donnell. She'd been willing to give the lawyer the benefit of the doubt, but no longer. Any man who'd be willing to manipulate people in this sort of situation deserved nothing. He'd get his profit, from Julie and the desperate people he was bartering with, and leave misery in his wake.

It was a damned shame. Julie was so good with children, a natural. Young as she was, she still deserved to have one of her own, one to fuss over and love. It just wasn't fair.

At first she thought Julie's footsteps had simply moved out of earshot. The muffled sound of voices might have come from someone's radio. And then she recognized the sound of Dennis's baritone, raised in frustration, and a hopeful smile wreathed her face.

Dennis was her one hope—Dennis of the plumbing and heating expertise, a practical knight-errant if ever she saw one. She'd watched the way he looked at Julie and the way Julie looked back, both of them unaware of the other's interest. It wouldn't be the most auspicious way to start a marriage, but she could think of worse ones.

She heard the tinny thump of Dennis's door. The voices more muffled now, were directly beneath her. Better and better. If Julie could turn to Dennis in her hour of need, it wouldn't take him too long to come up with a solution. All Marielle could do was lie there on her sofa and cross her fingers, hoping for a happy ending. And try not to think of the couch she'd rather be on.

It was a losing battle. She was getting more and more preoccupied with things that shouldn't matter in the least. Simon Zebriskie, Simon's couch, Simon's hands. She needed a dose of common sense, and she was going to make one last attempt at finding it.

She pushed herself off the sofa. She needed to talk to someone levelheaded, needed that very badly. So she rounded up the children and made the trek up the curving flight of stairs to Simon's hallway telephone, cursing the phone company once more. Christopher and Emily were uncharacteristically docile, sitting at her feet with paper and crayons while she once more dialed Abbie's California phone number.

She had little hope she'd be able to reach her old friend. Every time she'd tried in the past she'd either come up with a busy signal or no answer at all.

Abbie was the practical one, devoid of romantic sentiment. She was the only woman Marielle had ever known who'd had the sense of self-preservation to terminate a hopeless relationship. Surely she'd be able to help Marielle come to her senses!

She listened with only half a mind as the phone rang, so preoccupied that she almost didn't respond when Abbie's familiar voice answered the phone.

"Marielle, I've been thinking about you!" she cried when Marielle finally identified herself. "Why don't you have a telephone?"

"It's too complicated. Let's just say I'm working on it."

"How are the children? Do they like Chicago?"

Marielle laughed, happier than she'd been in days, wrapped in the familiar warmth of her old friend.

"They've discovered they like sugared cereal and nonstop television. I'm sending them to stay with my mother for a week or two. Things are really in an upheaval around here." It was the perfect opening, and Abbie dutifully prodded her.

"What's been going on?"

For some reason Marielle wasn't quite ready to confess. She didn't know what there was to confess—that she was getting irrationally absorbed in a man who wasn't interested in her, that she was dealing with vandals and ghosts and hidden treasure? It all seemed so unbelievable, so instead she stalled. "Did you hear from Suzanne?"

"About her cowboy? Sure did. Who would have thought a big-city sophisticate like Suzanne would be happy in the wild west?"

"And little Mouse is married," Marielle added. "Not to mention Jaime."

"Not to mention me."

"What?" Marielle shrieked. "I don't believe it!"

"Believe it," Abbie said. "The mighty have fallen, and fallen hard. We're not rushing into anything, mind you. But I don't have any doubts about it. T. J. is The One."

"He feels the same way?"

"Absolutely. You should see us, Marielle. We're so much in love it would amaze you."

"Nothing would amaze me," Marielle said, swallowing the unexpected lump in her throat. "You deserve every happiness."

"I still can't quite believe it," Abbie said with a little laugh. "But tell me what's been happening with you. I know your voice too well. Something's on your mind."

"Not a thing except your happiness," Marielle lied. Now was not the time to burden Abbie with her confusion and anxiety. "Am I invited to the wedding?"

"Of course. It probably won't be till spring, but you'll be the first to know." There was a pause. "Are you sure something isn't wrong?"

"Not a thing," she said staunchly. "I just wanted to make sure everything was going well with you. I'll be in touch."

"Wait. I wanted to talk with you. I still..."

"The kids are about to fall off the landing," Marielle said desperately, and her two quiet children looked up at her in surprise. "I'll call you back the minute I have a chance."

"Marielle..."

"Give my best to T. J. Tell him he'd better treat you right." Her voice was getting a little rough around the edges.

"Marielle, wait..."

"Goodbye, Abbie, lots of love." And she set the telephone back on its cradle.

Emily and Christopher were looking up at her out of solemn eyes. She couldn't just sit there and burst into tears. Besides, she was happy for her friends, truly, delightfully happy. It just had the unfortunate side effect of making her feel even lonelier and more bereft.

"Let's go back to the apartment," she said brightly. "If you guys are going to Disney World we'd better get you packed."

And with gentle hands she herded her small brood back downstairs, putting her momentary lapse into self-pity out of her mind.

Chapter Fifteen

"Ms. Brandt, Her Serene Highness the Crown Princess of Baluchistan requests your presence."

Marielle just stared at the neatly dressed young bureaucrat at her door. She'd been stretched out, half asleep, half awake while the children were enraptured by *Sesame Street*, when a shadow had appeared at her door. She'd blinked sleepily, only to realize it wasn't Simon, after all.

She sat up, setting her bare feet on the floor and running a careless hand through her blond hair. She felt sleepy, messy and completely comfortable, a fact that secretly amazed her. Being properly turned out at all times had been part of her job description as Greg's upscale young wife. Now that she was on her own she could wear what she wanted to wear, do what she wanted to do, and if young men in gray suits showed up at her broken door, then they were running the risk of seeing Ms. Marielle Brandt at less than her most stylish.

"I beg your pardon," she said belatedly.

"Sorry." The young man stepped gingerly around the door and held out his wallet with an official-looking identification card in it. "I'm John Davies, with the State Department. I'm responsible for the Meltirks, and her highness asked me to have you visit her."

Just what she needed, Marielle thought wearily. "Do you have any idea what she wants?"

"I never know what her highness wants," Davies said mournfully. "I've tried to move them to better quarters, but they adamantly refuse. I beg your pardon—you own this building, don't you?"

Marielle smiled. If John Davies was going to have a future as a diplomat, he was going to have to watch his tongue. "I wouldn't live here either if I didn't have to," she said, even though that wasn't strictly true. "I'll have to wait till my baby-sitter gets back. Do you think she's in any particular hurry?"

"The Baluchistanis don't know the meaning of the word hurry," Davies assured her. "Life goes on at an almost sedentary pace. I think the only reason the revolution succeeded was because the ruling family was too lazy to argue. Any time this afternoon will be fine. Mrs. deCarlo has offered to translate, though her highness has a way of being understood if she wants to. Or I could always come back."

It took a moment for Marielle to realize what was going on. John Davies was standing there, smiling an ingenuous smile, and she knew quite definitely that he wouldn't have offered to come back for one of the old ladies or for Simon. "I . . . er . . ."

"And if your baby-sitter was still around we could go out to dinner and discuss the Meltirks. I'm sure they can't be the easiest tenants, what with their refusal to learn English and those ceremonial fires going all the time. I could fill you in on all sorts of Baluchistani background. Their religious ceremonies, their moral standards. Maybe we could even go dancing afterward."

"And you could show me Baluchistani folk dances," she suggested wryly, a slow grin lighting her face. It was nice to be appreciated by a man, even in her current dishabille, even if she had no interest in him whatsoever. It was nice to suddenly feel free and wanted.

John Davies grinned back. "I could. Or we could try something a little slower, where you get to hold on to your partner."

"Sounds peachy," Simon grumbled from the doorway. "You want me to baby-sit?"

John Davies's handsome face turned bright red. He looked like a little boy whose hand was caught in a cookie jar. "Hi, Simon," he mumbled.

"John." Simon's voice was deep and disapproving, and it was all Marielle could do to stifle a giggle. Simon was acting like an overprotective father, John like a guilty teenager. If he was going to go any further in the State Department he was going to have to learn to control his blushes too, she thought critically. And Simon needed to realize that his own feelings for her weren't in the slightest bit paternal, for all his patriarchal air.

"That's sweet of you to offer, Simon," she said. "But I was about to refuse John's invitation. The children are leaving tomorrow morning and I want to spend all the time I can with them. I'm sure Esmy will manage to translate just fine for me."

"Your children are leaving?" John's expression brightened considerably. "What about Saturday or even...?"

"No," said Simon.

"No?" echoed John Davies.

"No," said Marielle, regretfully. "But I do appreciate the invitation."

"Oh," said John Davies. "Oh." He looked from Simon's glowering expression to Marielle's impish one. "I guess I've been obtuse. I didn't mean to trespass." He backed from the room, tripping over the fallen door, steering clear of Simon's menacing figure, disappearing down the hallway as fast as his neatly shod feet could carry him.

"He's not real big on diplomacy, is he?" Marielle questioned lightly.

"John's okay. He's just young." Simon moved into the room and picked up the fallen door, leaning it against the wall. "I didn't mean to scare him off."

"Didn't you?" Marielle was frankly, cheerfully skeptical. "You sure did a good job of it."

Simon opened his mouth to protest, then shut it with a snap as Julie appeared in the doorway. Her large brown eyes were still puffy and red-rimmed, but her expression was calmer, almost hopeful. Apparently Dennis had managed to work wonders. And Marielle felt her own hopes rise.

"I'm feeling much better," she announced, forestalling Marielle's question. "Esmy's waiting down at the Meltirks. Why don't you go ahead and I'll watch the kids?"

"I'll start going through the old furniture next door," Simon offered, and if Marielle hadn't known better she would have thought there was an apology in his voice. "That's where most of your horrific furniture came from, and there's tons more. Maybe Vittorio left a clue in a dresser drawer."

"And maybe the moon's made of green cheese," Marielle countered. "I don't suppose anyone knows what the princess wants of me, do they?"

"Maybe they want you to participate in one of their animal sacrifices," Simon drawled.

Marielle stared at him in dawning horror. "They don't really?" she demanded, aghast.

"Probably not. All I know is animals go in there and they never come out." He dropped his voice so that it was low and sepulchral, and she suddenly remembered Simon Zee and the horror movies.

"Don't give me the creeps," she said, shuddering.

Simon smiled blandly, pleased with himself. "Go ask her highness. I'll be in the next apartment rummaging through old sarcophagi."

"Cut it out!"

"Halloween's in two days," he said, unabashed. "Are you sure you wouldn't rather be in Florida?"

"Go to hell!"

She could still hear him laughing when she reached the Meltirks' apartment two flights down. The prince consort, this time wearing a Mickey Mouse T-shirt and silver lamé running shorts, answered the door, ushering her in with a spate of words that sounded embarrassingly fulsome. Apparently her serene highness felt the same, for she cut off his greeting with a short, admonitory word.

The room was smoky, redolent of strange herbs. Her highness was sitting in state in front of the grimy, diamond-paned windows, her purple turban slightly askew, her eyes watery from the ceremonial fire that smoked and burned in front of her in a brass brazier. There were no smoke detectors around, the fire hazard was probably enormous, and they would probably all die in their beds before the week was out, but Marielle was beyond worrying about such things. She sank down onto the cushion offered her, smiled at Esmy and waited.

"Her highness bids you welcome," Esmy said formally. "She wishes you peace and long life and a good strong man to give you many more children."

Marielle choked, swallowing the sound in a polite cough. "Tell her I wish her the same."

"Her highness says she hates to add to your troubles," Esmy continued after translating, "but she has gathered it is customary for there to be hot water in American apartments. She would like there to be some in hers."

"No hot water?" Marielle echoed.

"Apparently not. I already mentioned it to Dennis and he said he could take care of it very easily."

"Thank God. Did you tell her highness?"

"I will now. I know she'd rather hear it coming from you. She doesn't think too highly of the male of the species. She comes from a matriarchal society and considers males to be of only limited use."

"In the procreation of many children, I gather?"

"Exactly." She translated to Mrs. Meltirk, who nodded, a regal smile wreathing her full, unpainted lips. She began to speak then, long and earnestly, the rich vowels and consonants of her native language rolling over Marielle, wrapping her in a cocoon of words. Marielle swayed slightly, unaccountably sleepy. Maybe it was the combination of the long, mellifluous speech and the heady smoke, she reflected.

Her highness finally stopped speaking. With great effort Marielle roused herself and looked to Esmy for a translation. Esmy merely smiled, shrugging her plump shoulders. "She says she's glad you are here, and you should not let the wicked men scare you. The spirits mean you no harm; you should not be frightened of what you cannot see. You should take the one who is offered, even if he's not sure, and have babies."

"Do you have any idea what she's talking about?"

"Not the foggiest. I've learned it's better not to ask. In the Baluchistani religion members of the ruling family are considered to be oracles. Actually you've been given quite an honor. I'll express your gratitude.

"Do that. And if there's any way you could find out what she meant..." The words trailed off as a goat raced into the room, followed closely by a knife-wielding senior member of the Meltirk family.

"No!" Marielle shrieked, jumping from her cushion. Since the goat looked marginally less nasty than the butcher knife she grabbed the animal, catching the ungrateful beast around his shaggy neck.

A shocked silence filled the apartment, broken only by the hiss of the fire and the noise of the outraged goat as it struggled in Marielle's grasp.

"Marielle, you shouldn't interfere...." Esmy began.

"They can't sacrifice this animal," she said fiercely, rising to her feet and keeping a fierce grip on the goat's long, curly hair. "I'll put up with just about anything, with ghosts in the chimneys, apparitions in the windows, ceremonial fires, no plumbing and overdue electric bills, but I will not put up with animal sacrifice." She started toward the door, dragging the goat with her. The Meltirks were too stunned to move.

"I don't think you realize..." Esmy began again, but Marielle had already fumbled with the doorknob and was in the hall.

"Express my regrets to her highness," Marielle said. "I don't care if I cause an international incident. There will be no killing of animals here."

Her highness spoke then, in long, sibilant tones, her expression infinitely sad. Standing in the hallway, Marielle kept her grip on the goat, waiting for the translation.

Esmy shook her head. "Her serene highness wishes you well, and if you wish the goat you may have it with her blessing. He was going to provide their dinner for the next few days, but if you prefer, they'll eat the chickens."

"Good God!" Marielle groaned, wondering whether she dared stage a raid and rescue a bunch of noisy, smelly chickens.

"Her highness feels she must warn you, however," Esmy continued, looking decidedly unhappy with the message she had to impart, "that the gods will curse you if you don't get rid of the evil that haunts this building."

Marielle looked down at her sneaker-clad feet. The goat had just deposited a dozen olivelike pellets all over the floor. "The gods," she said glumly, "have already done so." And turning away, she led the goat down the stairs.

"YOU PUT THE GOAT in the garage?" Simon demanded, incensed. "He'll probably eat my car!"

"If I remember correctly, your car deserves to be eaten," Marielle said, perching on a carved mahogany table that wobbled slightly beneath her and munching an apple she'd grabbed from her apartment across the hallway.

Simon allowed himself a brief moment to admire her long legs before returning to his perusal of the ancient walnut chest of drawers. She was growing steadily more distracting, and his own behavior was surprising him. He'd always considered himself a reasonable, if somewhat bad-tempered sort of person, but his reaction to John Davies and to Miles had bordered on the violent. He'd actually wanted to take Davies and throw his little yuppie body out the window.

God, why couldn't she get out of here? With her long legs, and with her strong white teeth crunching into the apple, she was driving him absolutely crazy. You wouldn't think he was a mature man in his forties, old enough to know better. And you wouldn't think she was a mere child in her late twenties, young enough to be his . . . sister.

"I don't think they were actually going to sacrifice him," she added. "I think the animals were simply there as food."

"Still sounds pretty bad to me," Simon murmured, pushing and pulling at the various panels of the drawer, looking for a secret compartment.

"To me, too," Marielle allowed. "Still, I imagine we're being a little picky. After all, isn't Chicago hog butcher to the world or something like that? And the Meltirks are merely following their traditions. After all, we all eat meat—why should we be so squeamish about how that meat gets to the table? At least the Meltirks aren't hypocrites.''

"Take the goat back to them, then."

Marielle's forehead wrinkled in thought, and Simon found himself wanting to cross the room and kiss every line. He dived back into the drawer with renewed vigor.

"I can't do that," she said. "But maybe we could see if they could work something out with the stockyards."

"Sort of like cutting your own Christmas trees?" Simon said with a laugh. "Maybe that's where you can find enough money to support this place. Start a Slaughter Your Supper franchise. It should go over big with the NRA."

"Aging hippie," Marielle said without rancor. "I'm just trying to be open-minded about the whole thing. I want to respect their customs."

"I think their customs include multiple husbands for the ruling family. What do you think of that?"

"One is more than enough," she said, finishing her apple and looking around for a place to put the core.

"That's what I think. By the way, I haven't found anything."

"Nothing?" She sat there, swinging her legs, the apple core forgotten. "I was sure we'd find something. A secret compartment, a hidden drawer."

"Oh, I found plenty of those," Simon said, closing the last drawer and skirting the mountain of furniture to reach Marielle's side. "There just wasn't anything in them."

"Might you have overlooked something?"

"You're welcome to go over everything again," he said gruffly.

"I trust you." Her sigh was resigned. "Anything worth looking at in my place?"

"There might be a secret compartment in your bed. There were lots of them in the other carved furniture."

"What if there is something hidden that's too small to see. A microdot, or something?"

"Marielle, my sweet, they didn't have microdots in the nineteen-thirties."

"Who says the place is being trashed for Vittorio's treasure?" she countered brightly. "Maybe the Meltirks are Russian spies who've hidden secret information all over the place."

"And the goat is their go-between? Give me a break, Ms. Brandt. Let's check out your god-awful bed and have done with it."

"I suppose you're right," she sighed, hopping down from the table in one graceful movement. "But it sure would make things a little more interesting. Modern spies are easier to catch than ghosts."

"Says who? I'd prefer the shade of old Vittorio to a modern KGB agent any day. I just don't happen to think we're dealing with either."

"What do you think we're dealing with?" she asked, crossing the hallway into her open apartment.

"Someone very greedy, very devious and very manipulative," he said, then stopped for a minute, struck by an unpleasant thought. He knew someone who fitted that description to a *T*, someone he never would have suspected of being involved in the haunting of Farnum's Castle. It made no sense whatsoever, but the more he thought of it the more likely it seemed.

"Why are you looking like that?" Marielle demanded, suddenly alert.

"Like what?"

"Like you just swallowed a salamander?"

"Nasty thought. I just had an unpleasant suspicion as to who might be behind this."

"Who?" she breathed, her eyes lighting up.

"I have no intention of telling you. For one thing, I have no proof, no real motive, only a gut instinct. For another, I could be dead wrong and I'm not about to slander someone on a mere guess."

"Wrong, Simon. You're going to tell me," she said fiercely.

He just looked at her. She was comical rather than threatening, with her blond hair a tangled mess around her pretty face, no makeup and her clothes comfortable rather than stylish. He liked her a lot better than when she'd shown up looking like a Lake Shore Drive matron. Hell, every second he liked her a lot better, to a point where it was getting downright dangerous to his peaceful way of life.

"Or what?" he couldn't keep himself from taunting.

She glared at him. "Or else."

"Tell you what. Let me check out a few things, ask a few questions, and I'll tell you tomorrow."

"On Halloween? How fitting," she said icily. "What if your suspect decides to murder me in the meantime?"

"I don't think the villain I have in mind really wants to hurt anyone."

"And you're willing to stake my safety on it?"

"Sure," he said cheerfully. "After all, you're the one who refuses to go to Florida. You're up to facing a little danger."

"Simon," she said, "you're the one who's in danger now."

"Marielle," he returned, amused by her threat, "let's go check out your bed."

She opened her mouth in outrage, ready to blister him, then shut it again as she realized the prosaic meaning of his words. She sighed, suddenly deflated. "Yes," she agreed.

"Let's go find the bed." Simon almost wished she were still fighting him.

She tried to bring the children along for protection, but Emily would have none of it, and Christopher, as always, followed in his older sister's footsteps. "I'm telling Julie about Disney World," Emily announced with great dignity. "She's never been there."

"Neither have you," her mother pointed out.

"No, but Grandma has told me all about it," the child explained, as if to an idiot. "And I've watched a lot of TV."

"So you have, dear heart," Marielle said, and Simon could hear the resignation and guilt in her voice. "Come in and keep us company if you get bored."

"Yes, ma'am," said Emily, dismissing her mother.

She'd made her bed, he noticed when he walked into the tiny room. She had flannel sheets on the huge thing, blue with tiny white flowers. She had four pillows on the bed, too many for one person. She'd hung a poster on the wall, one of Monet's water lilies, and he stared at it for a long moment.

He should pay attention to such things, he reminded himself. While his walls held *Night of the Living Dead* and *Invasion of the Body Snatchers*, she had romantic paintings. It was as plain as the walls in front of him that they had no future together.

Slipping off her sneakers, Marielle climbed onto the high bed and clambered toward the huge, ornately carved headboard. "You check the bottom," she said, reaching up, her hair tumbling down her back.

He considered running back to his apartment. He considered his better judgment, said to hell with it, and climbed onto the soft high bed with her.

Upon closer examination the carvings on the bed had a distinctly salacious air. The nymphs and satyrs cavorted in a far from innocent manner, and he doubted Marielle would appreciate what the carved goats were busy doing. He pushed and pulled, poked and prodded, but nothing moved.

"No luck," he said, turning and walking toward the head of the bed. The mattress shifted beneath his weight, throwing Marielle off balance so that she landed against his chest. She clung for a minute, her eyes wide, her lips soft and parted, and he felt that all too familiar tightening in his gut.

Someone groaned, probably himself, as he dropped his head to meet hers. All he could think of was the blue sheets with the white flowers, her mouth and that half-stunned, half-expectant expression in her blue eyes.

Then she pushed him away, hard, as she scrambled off the bed, backing up against the wall. "What in heaven's name is wrong with me?" she asked, speaking more to herself than to him. "My children are in the next room, you don't even want me—you just want to get me out of Chicago, and I don't even like making love. What is happening to me?"

He stood there in the middle of her flowered sheets. "The same thing that's happening to me," he said glumly. "And who says I don't want you?" Without another word he climbed down off the bed and walked past her, out of the bedroom and out of the apartment.

Chapter Sixteen

Marielle's mother was usually the most flutter-brained, inefficient, charmingly helpless creature on earth—except when it came to something she wanted, and she wanted a few weeks of her grandchildren. The plane reservations for Orlando were set for nine o'clock the next morning. Virginia Watson was planning to fly out at six and be there waiting at O'Hare for Emily and Christopher, and she'd already taken care of diapers, a crib, food and toys.

Marielle had no choice but to let herself be swept up in her mother's uncustomary whirlwind, squashing her own indecision and regrets. She had no doubt about her parents' ability to take care of the children—they were born to be grandparents. Doting, responsible, strict only when absolutely necessary, they would provide the perfect cocoon of love and safety for the few days the children had to be away. If things went well, if they were able to clear up the mystery of Farnum's Castle early, Marielle had no doubt Emily would put up a loud and long protest at being ripped away from the wonders of Disney World before her time was up.

They took a taxi out to O'Hare, damning the expense. She knew Simon would be more than happy to drive them, but she deliberately lied about the time of the plane. She wasn't quite sure exactly why. For one thing, she wasn't

ready for her inquisitive mother to meet him. Virginia
Watson possessed a sixth sense when it came to men, and
she'd scent a romance where absolutely none existed.

And none did exist, Marielle told herself stubbornly.
They'd shared a few kisses, a certain odd camaraderie, but
that was where it ended. And she didn't need her mother
jumping to the same embarrassing conclusions Granita
had. The expression on Simon's face had been more than
instructive, and his speedy escape from her bed and the
apartment imprinted the message on her brain, a message
he'd already given her over and over again. He wasn't
going to get involved with her, he wasn't going to get married again.

She wasn't going to get involved with him, either, she
reminded herself sternly. Her brain knew that full well, but
her body and emotions seemed to be lagging behind in
understanding. With the children gone she'd simply have
to be more alert.

She also hadn't wanted Simon along as a witness to her
relinquishing her children, even for a few short days. She
made it through the departure, greeting her mother with
bustling good cheer, hugging and kissing the children, remaining calm even when Emily's last-minute doubts surfaced and she burst into excited tears as Virginia led the
children through the security gate. The last Marielle saw of
them, Christopher was waving at her over her mother's
impeccably tailored shoulder, and Emily was giving her
one final forlorn glance as she clung tightly to her grandmother's hand.

Marielle kept waving, a bright, encouraging grin on her
face. She waited until they turned a corner and disappeared from sight, and then promptly burst into her own
tears.

She'd brought her sunglasses and a huge wad of tissues,
just in case. She cried from the security gate to the side-

walk, she cried on the diesel-smelling bus that had the nerve to call itself a limousine, she cried from the center of the Loop all the way out to the residential neighborhood that held Farnum's Castle. And she cried for the last three blocks, finishing her last tissue as she reached the rusty iron gate of the monstrosity she'd inherited.

She stopped for a moment, looking up, way up at its seedy grandeur. It was only half past ten in the morning and the day, the whole empty, childless day lay before her. What she needed, she told herself, walking up her cracked, uneven sidewalk, was a shower, a nap and a new lease on life. The sooner she found out what was going on, the sooner her babies would be back.

Another yuppie bureaucrat was waiting for her in the downstairs hall. She closed the door behind her, shutting out the chilly October wind, and peered through the gloom at the visitor. Another State Department employee looking after the Meltirks? she wondered. Or more trouble? With her recent spate of luck it could only be the latter.

"Mrs. Brandt?" he queried, peering back at her.

She looked at him uneasily, expecting a summons. But his hands were loose at his side, and he held no incriminating papers in them. Besides, who would want to issue her a summons? She hadn't done anything wrong other than inheriting this decaying monstrosity.

"Yes," she admitted, wondering if she was making a very grave mistake, wondering if she was going to get her shower and nap.

"I'm from the tax assessor's office. I've been in touch with Mr. O'Donnell at Parker and Stearns, and he informed me you were no longer a client."

Marielle looked at him for a long, sickening moment. "Do I need a lawyer?" she asked. Her voice felt rusty from tension and an hour and a half of crying, but she kept her face very calm.

Her newest bureaucrat didn't crack a smile. "It might be useful. Taxes haven't been paid on this building since 1984."

"Really? I don't know when my husband acquired it...."

"Nineteen eighty-four," he replied. "And as his wife, you're liable."

"All right," she said faintly. "What's the damage?"

"Twelve thousand dollars, not including late fees, interest or the last two years."

"Twelve thousand dollars?" she shrieked, and the sound echoed up the stairwell. "On this dump?"

"Chicago real estate is worth a great deal, Mrs. Brandt. Even though the building is in compromised shape, the land beneath it is extremely valuable. Speaking of the condition of the building, I believe an inspector will be visiting you early next month. In a rental property there are codes that must be followed, and this building seems, even to my inexperienced eye, to fall well short of those standards."

Marielle allowed herself the luxury of a quiet moan. She would have burst into tears and embarrassed the dickens out of the tax man, but she was all cried out. All she could do was lean against the cracked paneling and stare at him wordlessly.

"You have thirty days, Mrs. Brandt," he said, taking her limp hand and pressing into it the paper she'd thought hadn't existed. "Let us know if we can assist you in any way." *Yes, you can call off your wolves,* Marielle thought dizzily. She was barely aware of the front door closing behind him, or the steady, almost mincing tread of well-shod feet from the floors above.

"I warned you."

Marielle lifted her beaten head to look into Liam O'Donnell's chilly eyes. She said nothing, knowing that screaming in rage at the man would get her nowhere.

But O'Donnell didn't need any encouragement. "You should have taken that offer when I presented it. This is too much for a woman to handle. If you'd had any sense at all you would have listened to me, accepted the very generous offer and gone straight back to New York."

She didn't trust the man. Not one inch, not one centimeter. For all his dapper appearance, his seemingly impeccable lineage and respected reputation, he seemed to be just this side of sleazy. "And now it's too late?" she queried.

It might have been the shadowy darkness of the ill-lit hall, her red-rimmed eyes might have blurred her vision, or it might have been sheer imagination. But an expression of triumph and avarice swept over O'Donnell's features before he could control it.

"I don't know," he said, and Marielle knew he lied. "I have a fair amount of influence. If you'd agree to the offer right now, today, I might be able to work something out. The tax liability is a problem, of course, and the indigent misfits living here are another, but with my powers of persuasion I imagine that I could get that offer repeated. I can't promise anything—you may have to settle for less than the original offer, but I'm sure it would be more than generous." He practically rubbed his dry little hands together. "Shall I get in touch with my client?"

For a brief moment, a mere millisecond, she was tempted. She was at low ebb, emotionally, physically, depleted by tears and sleeplessness and uncertainty. She looked into O'Donnell's papery white face, and from the distance she could hear the sound of someone crying.

She panicked, then realized with mingled regret and relief that it couldn't be her children. They were somewhere over Florida by now, not even thinking of her.

"Why are you here?" she asked instead, knowing the answer lay behind the muffled sound of crying that was floating down the stairs.

"That's privileged information," he informed her primly. "Between my client and me."

Julie, she thought. He'd been badgering Julie again. The rotten, money-grubbing, heartless bastard.

"Well," he prodded, clearly impatient. "What shall I tell my client?"

"You can tell him," she said, very calmly, "to go to hell. And you, Liam O'Donnell, can go with him."

How could she have thought his eyes were colorless? Now they were dark with a sudden flash of rage, and it took all Marielle's considerable strength of mind not to step back a pace.

"You'll regret this," he said very quietly.

"Maybe. But in the meantime I'd like you to get off my property. Now."

He drew himself up to his full height, a few inches shorter than Marielle's five feet seven, and positively bristled with fury. Without another word he pushed past her and out into the chilly autumn morning.

He left the door wide open to the brisk wind, and she was glad he had. The stiff breeze swept through the hall, bringing a few dead leaves with it, sweeping out the presence of the evil old man. She only wished it could sweep out the ghost of the other evil old man as thoroughly.

"Well done," said Simon, standing in the open door of the elevator.

"Thanks for coming to my rescue," she said sarcastically.

"You were doing just fine without my interference," he drawled. "I would have assisted him out the door if need be, but you managed to rout him quite effectively. We'll have to tell Julie you got rid of the old creep. It might cheer her up."

"Where is she?" Marielle headed for the stairs, but Simon slid a restraining arm around her waist, pulling her back.

"Dennis is taking care of her. They're better off alone." He looked down at her, still keeping his arm around her. "I must say you're a more successful matchmaker than I was. You lied about going out with Miles. You weren't the slightest bit interested in him, were you?"

"Nope."

"Why not? He's young, attractive, charming. A bit overextended financially, but then so are most people. I would have thought you'd make a perfect pair."

She looked up at him. "You thought wrong. I'm not interested in coupling in any sense of the word."

He looked down at his arm encircling her, their bodies resting against each other, her complete acceptance of the situation. "Okay," he said easily. "I'll believe you." And he released her, leaving her suddenly bereft in the windswept hallway. "Are you ready?"

"Ready for what?" she asked warily.

"The park."

"I beg your pardon?"

"You've spent the last six days cooped up in this old building. You need to get out and enjoy yourself, and I've been elected to the job of seeing that you do."

"Who elected you?"

He grinned then, the smile lighting his usual dark expression. "I did. Come on, kid. You need sunshine and distraction. We'll go to the zoo and feed the baboons, we'll go to the planetarium and you can watch the star show and realize how insignificant you are."

"Just the thing to cheer me up," she said grumpily. "I was going to go upstairs and go to bed."

"Well, we could do that," he allowed, "but I thought you figured it was a waste of time."

"Alone," she said, trying to keep from smiling.

"Sorry. You're not allowed to be alone today. It's too easy to feel depressed when you're alone. If you're lucky I'll introduce you to my favorite orangutan. He does have embarrassing habits, but he's an ape after my own heart."

"I'll go," she said, unable to resist him in his unexpectedly lighthearted mood.

"Now?"

"Now," she agreed.

"Good. Then you can tell me why you didn't let me drive you and kids to the airport this morning."

Her defenses were still down. *An hour and a half of public crying will do that to you,* she thought. "I didn't want you to meet my mother," she said frankly. "My mother has too vivid an imagination."

He raised an eyebrow. "You think I'd scare her?"

"I think you'd raise her hopes in a direction where they shouldn't be raised."

"I can't believe she'd think I was a suitable replacement."

"Then you haven't met my mother. She'd fall at your feet," Marielle said bitterly.

"Wouldn't she think I was robbing the cradle? Not to mention the fact that I've been divorced?" His tone of voice was distant, as if he were no more than vaguely interested.

"Not my mother. She'd figure you'd learned from your mistakes and would be even better husband material than a bachelor." They weren't talking about her mother anymore, and both of them knew it.

"What about the age difference?"

"I've always been mature for my age. Besides, my father's seventeen years older than my mother and they've always been divinely happy. I'm sure she'd be fool enough to think history could repeat itself."

"A foolish thought, indeed." His voice was low, abstracted, his eyes watching her lips.

"My mother's not very practical."

"It's a lucky thing that we are."

"Yes," said Marielle huskily. "Very lucky." And she lifted her face, waiting for him to kiss her.

He didn't. Instead he moved away, heading for the open door and the brisk autumn morning. "Let's go feed some baboons."

Why should she feel rejected? Why should she feel depressed and unwanted when he was taking her to see baboons? Plastering a bright smile on her face, she followed him out into the bright sunshine. And this time her sunglasses didn't cover tears but a very measuring, uncertain expression.

TOO LATE, TOO LATE, TOO LATE. The worn tires of the Mustang whirred out the refrain that echoed in his brain as he drove through the rain-slick late night streets of downtown Chicago. He couldn't even excuse himself on the grounds that he hadn't known what was happening.

He'd known from the very beginning. He'd taken one look at Marielle Brandt and known that he'd have to be very careful. And knowing that, he'd gone into it full tilt, paying no attention to the warning signals.

He pressed down harder on the accelerator and the venerable old car leaped ahead, jerkily, he had to admit, but with still a semblance of its old power. To give himself his due, he hadn't realized quite how dangerous she was, for the simple reason that in his forty-two years he'd never felt like this before. Not for Sharon, his hardheaded former wife who was only out for corporate advancement, not for the women who'd come and gone before and after his brief marriage. He'd loved them as best he could, but in retro-spect his feelings for them seemed very shallow. Nothing compared to the intense, tangled web of emotion that wrapped around him when he looked at Marielle Brandt.

The park had been one of his dumbest ideas. Watching her toss her head back and laugh at the orangutan's ob-scene behavior, he'd felt a curious piercing in his heart. Scuffling through the fallen leaves, not touching, they'd walked for miles through Grant Park, talking, laughing at times, at others in a silence so peaceful and natural that it gave him the creeps to remember. It wasn't fair that she'd be perfect for him. Not when it was impossible.

He didn't really have to go in tonight. He wasn't sched-uled to work, but he didn't think he'd last the night with-out going crazy thinking about her one floor beneath, no children to interrupt, no responsibilities to demand her attention. If only she hadn't spent the night in his arms, if only she hadn't kissed him yesterday morning, if only, if only...

The fine mist was coming down at a steady rate, and there was a nasty bite in the air. He had to admit he felt a lot more secure with Dennis in the house. For one thing, he could count on the heat lasting through the night. Dur-ing the cold snap last winter he'd gone crazy imagining the old ladies freezing to death in their apartments, unable to do anything about the temperamental furnace.

And he was glad Dennis was there for protection. Now that he was reasonably certain Dennis was only interested in Julie and not his winsome landlady, he could accept his tenancy with absolute pleasure.

God, what a fool he was being! What an addled, jeal-ous idiot he was! Without any warning whatsoever he pulled a U-turn, disregarding the sparse traffic and head-ing back to Farnum's Castle. This had gone on long enough. Ignoring the problem was useless—he spent all his spare time thinking about her. It was time to confront it head-on.

When he slid into the old garage, he nearly hit the damned goat. The animal lifted its ugly head to glare at him, then went back to munching on the bicycle someone, probably Dennis, had been fool enough to leave there. He cursed the animal, pulled up his denim jacket and headed for the house through the freezing drizzle.

MARIELLE WAITED UNTIL she heard Simon leave. The thinness of the walls and her hastily repaired door were mixed blessings. The door opened and closed again, if one was very careful, but it did little to shut out the various noises from the hallways, and it would provide absolutely no protection if whoever, whatever had been tormenting them chose to repeat his efforts.

Not that even a solid steel door would provide any protection from ghosts, she reminded herself with a touch of asperity. And mortal felons could always get in through the windows. *Let's face it,* she told herself, she wasn't safe no matter what she did, so all she could do was wait for their next visitation.

But her mind wasn't on visitations, not right now. She'd wasted her day strolling through the sprawling lakeside park with Simon Zebriskie. As always she'd allowed him to tempt her from her duty, and her lack of progress today meant her children would be away twenty-four hours longer. And it meant that she was even more tied to Simon, when all she wanted was freedom.

How could such a cynical, gruff, sarcastic man be so persuasive, so—she might as well admit it—seductive? How could she let herself be drawn to him when she didn't want any man? And how could she have forgotten her children for most of the sunny afternoon, letting herself enjoy Simon's dry wit and the wonderfully prosaic pleasures of the zoo and the planetarium?

She couldn't forget them now. Alone in her apartment, with a cold rain splattering the windows, all she could think about was the empty cot, the empty crib. Would they be missing her? Would her mother remember that Christopher could only sleep with his tattered Pooh Bear, that Emily liked one story and three songs before she'd settle down?

If anyone had cried more than Marielle that day it had been Julie. Her eyes were red and swollen when Marielle returned from a ridiculously filling dinner at an Italian restaurant over on Wacker Drive, and every now and then she'd let loose with another strangled sob. Marielle had greeted her departure for a visit with Esmerelda with relief, but once she was alone the quiet closed in, the loneliness settling around her like a velvet shroud.

Simon's disappearing footsteps had been the final straw. She'd held her breath, waiting for his knock on her door, but he hadn't even hesitated. Clearly he'd been able to put her out of his mind far more successfully than she'd been able to dismiss him. A blessing, she assured herself, wrapping her arms around her chilled body. Someone needed to be sensible, and it was becoming increasingly clear that it wasn't going to be her.

The first creak didn't alarm her. It was an old building—creaks and groans were to be expected. The second she also dismissed as part of the settling process, even though a mansion of some sixty-odd years ought to have settled by now. But there was no ignoring the eerie, translucent light emanating from the chimney, or the muffled, barely discernible moans that floated on the howling wind.

The scratching began again, but there was no one anywhere near the chimney. The lights flickered and dimmed, and she heard a crash in her bedroom, followed by another, louder one and a low-pitched whining that sounded like a slow-motion scream.

The door fell off the hinges as she yanked it open and dashed into the hallway. She tripped, sliding down the last five steps, and began pounding on Dennis's door. There was no answer, and she realized with frustration that he must be gone. She raced barefoot down the next flight, ignoring the Meltirks' tightly shut door, and on down the next, terror beating at her heart, panic strangling her lungs, running, running, smack into the immovable strength of a monster.

She screamed at the top of her lungs. The sound vibrated through the entire mansion and the monster shook her hard, choking off her second hysterical shriek.

"What the hell is going on?" it demanded in a voice from the tomb. And in the shadowy darkness, Marielle stared into Simon's smokey-gray eyes and didn't know whether she'd at last found safety. Or another kind of danger, even more devastating. At that moment she no longer cared.

Chapter Seventeen

They were standing on the second-floor landing. Marielle hadn't yet gotten around to replacing the light bulbs, and if the tax assessor had his way she wouldn't have the money to upgrade from twenty-five watts to one hundred. She took a deep, shuddering breath, dimly aware of Simon's fingers digging into her arms, glad of the discomfort. He was solid, flesh and blood—and there.

"There...there was something in m-m-m-my room." She'd never stammered before in her life, but she realized her teeth were chattering, both in panic and from the cold. Farnum's Castle wasn't warm enough to race around barefoot, but what with the banshees wailing in her chimney she hadn't had time to look for her shoes before she ran out.

"What?" Simon's tone was wonderfully down-to-earth, despite the sepulchral depth of his voice.

"Th-th-the ghost," she managed to say. "Crashing around in my bedroom, pounding at the chimney, wailing and howling...."

He shook her again, not as hard this time. "Did you see anything?"

"I just told you. There was crashing and pounding and wailing and I couldn't find anyone. Dennis and Julie..."

"Dennis is in the basement working on the blasted furnace. Julie's handing him tools. Seems like the ghost was all sound and fury. You didn't actually see Vittorio materialize before your eyes, did you?"

Marielle was slowly growing calmer. "No," she said. "I didn't."

Simon nodded. His hands were still holding her upper arms, but now the grip was gentler, almost caressing. "Let's go and check it out. Come on." He tugged her away from the stairs.

She pulled back. "My apartment is upstairs."

"We're taking the elevator."

"The hell we are! Nothing short of the devil himself is going to get me in that traveling coffin."

He laughed then, an unaffected bark of humor. "I've been called worse." And he pulled her down the darkened hallway to the tiny little elevator.

"You're not getting me in there," she warned him.

"I'm not climbing five flights of stairs," he answered, shoving her into the compartment and pulling the door shut behind them. He punched a few buttons, the dim light flickered, and the boxlike structure jerked and shuddered, inching upward.

Marielle had backed into a corner and stood rigid, her fists clenched at her sides. "I'm not in the mood for this, Simon. I don't need to risk entombment after the day I've had."

They were moving awfully slowly. Despite her distrust of the elevator she hadn't thought it was this bad. "You didn't have a rotten day," Simon said, bridging the narrow distance, his tall, lean body hovering over her in the shadows. "You had a rotten morning and a miserable evening, but the rest of the day was just fine."

She should have felt even more claustrophobic with him looming over her like that. Instead she felt light, liberated, full of an odd sort of anticipation, and her fear of enclosed spaces, particularly of faulty elevators, vanished. "You're right," she said, her voice low. "I liked the park and the planetarium."

"What about the company?" His knees were touching her, his breath was ruffling her hair, and all she wanted was to lean forward and rest her head against his chest. *Danger, danger,* she warned herself, still fighting.

"The company was acceptable." Her qualification would have been fine if it hadn't come out in a husky murmur just as his head dipped toward hers.

His mouth touched hers, gently, softly, a mere taste. She lifted her head but he'd already moved on, feathering kisses across her cheekbones, her nose, her eyelids. She could feel her heart shuddering and pounding, her clenched fists trembling as the elevator moved up, up, and Simon's mouth moved down, down. She pressed her fists against the walls of the elevator, anything to keep from touching him. She was wearing an oversize flannel shirt with a silk camisole beneath it, and Simon had somehow managed to unfasten the buttons without touching her skin. He kissed her collarbones, the soft swell of her breast, her fluttering heartbeat, and finally she could stand it no longer.

Marielle pushed herself away from the wall and into his arms, sliding her hands around his waist and holding on tight. "This is stupid," she murmured against his shoulder. "It's a waste of time. It'll only lead to disappointment and embarrassment."

"Mmm-hmm," he murmured in agreement, nuzzling her ear beneath the tangled sheaf of hair.

"It'll destroy our friendship," she said desperately, clinging tighter. She'd always had sensitive ears.

"We aren't friends," Simon said, kissing her neck. "We're two people spending too much energy trying not to be lovers."

She moaned in reluctant pleasure. She'd always had a sensitive neck, but somehow Greg had never found the right spot. Simon had, the very first time. She made one final protest. "We shouldn't do this," she said, pulling his shirt from his jeans and sliding her hands up his back, along the warm, smoothly-muscled skin.

"You're right," he said, his mouth moving along her jawline. She'd always had a sensitive jawline, too. The light overhead flickered and went out, the elevator shuddered to a stop and the door slid open, revealing the fifth-floor hallway a few inches above the elevator floor. Simon's hallway, she thought. Simon's apartment. Simon's bed.

He pulled away, a few inches, enough to give her breathing space. "Do you want to go back to your apartment?" The question was patient, but Marielle could feel the tension running through his tall body, could recognize it as the same tension that was thrumming through hers.

"What about the ghost?"

"He'll be back." He didn't push her, didn't kiss her. He simply stood there in the shadows, waiting for her to make up her mind.

She shut her eyes, misery and indecision sweeping over her. "Simon, I'm not good at this sort of thing. I don't enjoy it much. You'll be just as disappointed as I am."

If she expected him to persuade her she was disappointed. He didn't say a word, but just stood there, enticingly close—still waiting for her to make up her mind.

"Simon," she said weakly, "don't do this to me. Don't make me decide. If I had any brains at all I'd go back downstairs right now."

"Your problem, Marielle," he said gently, cupping her face in his large, strong hands, "is that you've got too many brains. And you spend too much time worrying and fussing about others, and not enough just taking for yourself. I'll make the decision for you, absolve you of responsibility. I'm going to take you into my apartment and make love to you, and if you're miserably embarrassed and disappointed it won't be anybody's fault but mine. You warned me and I didn't listen. Okay?''

She looked up at him, her heart in her throat, hammering, choking her. "Okay," she whispered.

He kissed her then, setting his mouth on hers, warm and wet and open, and she responded, shakily at first, then with growing delight. His hands released her face, sliding down her body, cupping her breasts through the thin silk camisole, her open shirt hanging loose around her. She wanted to get closer to him, pushing her breasts against his hands, vaguely aware that despite the heat between them her nipples had hardened under his touch.

He pulled away, looking down at her, his breath coming in labored rasps that matched her own. "You don't like that, do you?" he whispered. "You probably won't like this, either." And he leaned down and put his mouth where his hand had been, on her taut nipple, drawing her into his mouth, suckling her through the whisper-thin silk.

She heard the moan, knew it had to be her own, but it sounded distant, foreign. He moved to the second breast, and she could feel the dampness of the silk against her hot skin, the burning and aching between her thighs. She reached up and caught his head, meaning to pull him away, meaning to stop the torment that was burning her alive, but instead she threaded her fingers through his thick, straight hair and held him against her.

Marielle could feel his hard, hot hands beneath her camisole, on her flat stomach. She braced herself, expecting them to move upward toward her breasts, but instead the button of her jeans was deftly unsnapped, the zipper drawn down, and he was pushing down the jeans over her narrow hips, out of his way. Then he slid his hand inside her bikini panties toward the hot, damp core of her, and she tried to jerk away, releasing his hair and pushing against his shoulders in sudden confusion.

Simon paid no attention to her protests. He kissed her, his mouth covering hers and sealing her objections as his long, deft fingers stroked and caressed her. Now she was clutching his arms, fingers digging into his hard-muscled flesh. She wanted to beg him to stop—except that she didn't want him to stop. She wanted him to keep on, keep on forever, his hand between her legs invading her, arousing her, taking her from blind innocence to someplace dark and dangerous and overwhelming.

Marielle tore her mouth away from his. "No!" she choked. "No, stop! I can't stand it! I can't . . ."

"Yes, you can." He was relentless, and for just a moment she fought him, pushing against him. Then the first wave hit, a jolt of sheer, agonizing pleasure shooting through her with the power of an electrical charge. She went rigid in his arms, shock and reaction keeping her still for a moment. Then her body convulsed against him as wave after endless wave of response twisted her into a helpless rag doll.

Simon picked her up in his arms, leaving her jeans in a heap on the elevator floor as he carried her into the hallway, kicking open his unlocked door and moving through the darkened apartment with the sureness of the night creature he was. He didn't bother to turn on the bedroom light, and the street light shining in was filtered by the steady rain. He set her down on the bed, and she lay there silent and trembling as he stripped off her flannel shirt and camisole, tossed her panties onto the floor and proceeded to strip off his own clothes.

Marielle had a brief, shocked realization that he'd seduced and undressed her in the elevator. That he'd done
more than that in what was essentially a public place. Then
his hard, hot body covered hers, and she was beyond rational thought.

"I finally found a way to keep you quiet," he murmured in her ear, a note of laughter in his voice. "I should
have done that days ago." He took her arms and pulled
them around his neck, then kissed her, long and hard and
deep.

She had thought herself too weary to respond. But her
mouth opened beneath his, her tongue reached out and her
skin softened beneath his touch.

She had thought her body too unbearably sensitized to
stand any more. But he moved slowly, carefully, arousing
her all over again, and when his mouth found her breasts
she arched against him; when his hand slid down beneath
her thighs she let him part them, shivering in anticipation.

Simon took her hand and placed it on him, on the hard,
smooth length of him. He was big, more so than she'd
expected, and damp, and she realized he wanted her very
badly. She let her fingers trail across the silk and steel of
him, wanting more, yet afraid of it.

He groaned, pushing against her hand, showing her
what he wanted, where he wanted pressure, where he
wanted softness. She wanted to kiss him, she wanted his
mouth on hers, and she tugged at him. He moved then,
kneeling between her legs, hot and hard against her, and
she tensed, not knowing what to expect.

"Now is not the time to be frightened," Simon whispered in her ear, nibbling on her sensitive lobe, but she
could feel the tension running through him, the trembling
in his arms as he held himself in check. "I'd like to make

this last longer, but I don't know if you can take much more this time. And I don't know if I can."

She shut her eyes, still tense, still waiting. But he made no move at all, despite the power vibrating in his arms, despite the need covering his body with a fine film of sweat.

"Look at me, Marielle." There was a hoarse note of pleading in his voice, one she couldn't resist. Her eyes shot open. "Say something, Marielle. Anything."

"I thought you liked me quiet." It didn't sound like her voice. It was raw with need and wonder and emotion.

He still didn't move. "Not that quiet. Say something, Marielle. Say you want me."

A ghost of a smile twisted her mouth. "Of course I want you. I've never in my life wanted anyone the way I want you. I never thought I'd want anyone the way I want you. I want you, I need you, I . . ." His mouth silenced the last, dangerous statement that might have slipped out, and his body pushed into hers, settling deep.

She could feel the tremors shivering through her, the unexpected little shimmers of response that she thought she'd already used up. Simon's big hands cupped her hips, holding her still for his driving invasion, and she wrapped her legs around him, pulling him closer. This time was for him, she thought. This time her joy would be in giving, in holding him and taking his body and his pleasure into her, in savoring his delight.

But Simon had other ideas. She could feel her own tension begin to build once more, feel her own body covered with sweat, feel the inexplicable wanting taking over once again. She kissed him, short, hurried kisses that he responded to in kind, and she could feel his strong, undulating body grow even more taut. She waited in uncertainty, in anticipation, expecting nothing but his pleasure. Then he reached between their bodies and touched her.

She exploded, arching in a delight so intense it was almost unbearable. She could feel Simon all around her, tense in her arms as his body went rigid with his climax, and through the maelstrom of darkness and confusion all she could do was cling to him, for safety, for comfort, for love, as she shattered into a thousand fragments.

A long time later he pulled away. He'd grown heavy, but she hadn't minded. She didn't want to look at him, didn't want to say anything; she simply wanted to hide her head against his shoulder and never move again. He rolled onto his side, taking her with him, and his hand brushed against her face, coming away wet with her tears. His own breathing had settled down to a reasonable facsimile of normal, and if his heartbeat was still a bit too fast it was nothing compared to hers.

She tried to duck her head, to bury it against his chest, and he let her, cradling her, still gently stroking her. It struck her that Simon was a kind man. Despite his gruff nature and deep-rooted cynicism, there was a streak of gentle caring about him that was easy to miss. And she had the sudden, unnerving fear that the last hour had simply been another demonstration of his kindness.

"Listen," he said, his voice a low growl, "we'll get better with practice."

She couldn't help herself. At his words she raised her head and looked at him incredulously. "If we get any better," she said, her voice heavy with emotion, "I'll be dead before I'm thirty."

He laughed then, and she realized with amazement that he hadn't been quite sure of her reaction. It suddenly made him much more human, and she settled back against him with a pleasant sigh. "I wish you were thirty," he murmured. "Or thirty-five."

I wish you were in love with me, she thought. *The way I am with you. The way I have been for days and days on end.* "Give me time," she said, keeping her thoughts to herself. "I'll be there sooner or later."

He could have said something then, but didn't. He simply pulled up the cover around them, wrapped her tighter in his arms and went to sleep, his hands gentle and possessive even in his dreams. And Marielle had no choice but to do the same. Tomorrow would be soon enough to deal with the overwhelming turn her life had taken. For now she needed a few hours of rest. Tomorrow she'd face everything.

HE'D MADE SOME STUPID MISTAKES in his life, Simon thought, shifting carefully so he wouldn't disturb Marielle. Up to and including both his marriage, his idiotic acceptance of payola and his obsessive·forms of penance ever since. But falling in love with Marielle Brandt had to take the cake.

He hadn't meant to do it. Hadn't even realized things were getting quite so intense. Granted, he felt hollow and empty when he went for most of a day without seeing her. He knew it required an almost inhuman effort on his part not to touch her. He knew he was drawn to her as he'd never been drawn to anyone in his life.

But he hadn't realized it was going to be the *Big L*.

He'd been so damned sure of himself, so smug. He could take her to bed, show her how pleasurable it really could be, and then walk away. He'd shown her, all right. But he'd shown himself, too, that what he'd just expected to be good sex had turned out to be something much, much more—something he'd never experienced before in his long, misspent life.

He looked at the woman sleeping so peacefully in his arms, a trace of dried tears on her soft cheeks, and a reluctant grin twisted his mouth. She hadn't known what had hit her last night. If his ego had ever needed boosting, her shocked, shivering reaction had done just that. She had clung to him as if he were life itself, and he had relished it.

So what was he going to do now? Nothing had changed—she was still too young and innocent for him. If he had any decency at all he'd back off, give her time to find someone more her type.

The children wouldn't be a drawback—they were great kids. Tough, adaptable, loving—any man would be lucky to get them along with their generous, warmhearted mother.

But he didn't want some suitable man to become their stepfather. He wanted Marielle himself and he wanted her children. Hell, he even wanted to have children with her— children who would be theirs.

But the best thing he could do was put an end to it, now, before it was too late. He could manage to dredge up one more noble act from his weary old soul. He could set her free to find the kind of life she should have.

And that was exactly what he was going to do, he told himself, cupping the soft swell of her breast as the sun began to rise over the Chicago skyline. She made a low, sexy noise in the back of her throat and moved closer, rubbing against him like a sleepy kitten. Tomorrow.

Chapter Eighteen

When Marielle opened her eyes for the second time that morning the first thing she saw was Bela Lugosi leering down at her, a cape covering half of his face. She swallowed the scream that was instinctive, huddled under the covers, then realized it was just one more of Simon's old movie posters. If she had anything to say about it, it would have to go.

She looked around her, resting her chin on her drawn-up knees. She had no idea whether she'd have anything to say about it or not. Simon had never expressed any interest in a permanent relationship—on the contrary, he'd repeatedly told her to go away. Maybe last night had changed things—maybe not.

She was alone in the bedroom. It was an overcast, cloudy day outside. Fitting for Halloween, she thought. The room was part of one of the castle's turrets—it was octagonal, with windows on every other wall. The bed was large and rumpled, the covers tossed every which way. On one side of the bed there was a digital clock and a pile of books. There were a few scattered pieces of her clothing on the other side.

She reached for her flannel shirt, remembering with dismay that her jeans were probably still riding up and

214 *Cry for the Moon*

down in that lousy elevator. But no one in the building ever used it except Simon. They all had too much sense.

If she'd just kept off the elevator last night she probably wouldn't be where she was now, a flush of remembered pleasure covering her body, a tangle of doubt and worry assailing her brain. What was going to happen next?

It took all her courage to climb out of bed and retrieve her fallen pieces of clothing from where they lay. At the last minute she stole a pair of Simon's old jeans, rolling up the legs, closing the too loose waistband with a pin. Taking a deep breath, she stepped hesitantly into the living room.

Simon was nowhere around. The front door of the apartment was open, the elevator door was closed, and the smell of coffee brought forth Marielle's first sigh of relief.

She was half tempted to beat a hasty retreat to her own apartment, a pilfered cup of coffee in her hand. But she knew she'd be putting off the inevitable. She'd wait, long enough to drink her coffee, long enough to see if his departure was temporary—or if he'd fled the city, the state and the country in an effort to get away from her.

The coffee was wretched, but at least it was brewed, not instant. That was another thing in Simon Zebriskie's life that needed to be taken in hand. His coffee, his choice of artwork, his mornings, his evenings...

Marielle sighed, setting down the half-drunk cup of coffee and staring about her. He'd cleaned up most of the mess left by the vandals, but the walls were still a mess, and nothing short of a new paint job would take care of that. Maybe a shade with a touch of warmth to it to soften the lofty spaces.

She was in deep trouble. One night of sex and she was redecorating his apartment and reorienting his life! She'd better get back to her own apartment and her own life before she let her fantasies get out of hand. He hadn't said a word about love.

He hadn't even said a word about going steady, she reminded herself wryly. She took one more drink of the bitter coffee, left the cup in the kitchen sink and headed for the door, wanting only to escape. As luck would have it, Simon chose that moment to reappear, her jeans slung over his arm.

If she hadn't known what to expect, Simon's expression wouldn't have helped her out. He looked distant, unapproachable, as if last night had never happened—but Marielle happened to know damned well that it had happened. That closely shaven chin of his had scratched her last night—she still had the rash to prove it. His hands...

She looked away from them, away from him to some point over his shoulder in the hallway.

"I thought you might want your clothes," Simon said, his voice diffident. "I see you found something to wear."

"I hope you don't mind," she said politely.

"Not at all." He was equally courteous.

"I helped myself to a cup of coffee. It was horrible."

She didn't have to look to know he didn't crack a smile. "I don't mind it," was all he said.

"I'd better go." She waited for him to move closer, to say something, anything.

"That's probably a good idea."

Five words. Five cruel, nasty little words, spoken so politely as they knifed through her heart. She looked at him then, at his distant, emotionless face, at the mouth that had kissed her senseless. "You win," Marielle said quietly.

"I beg your pardon?"

"I'll leave Chicago." She was trying to force a response from him. She didn't get the one she wanted.

He laughed. Granted, there wasn't much humor in it, but the sound was like a razor on her soul. "You take things too seriously, Marielle. That's the problem with youth—everything's so earth-shattering. You don't have to leave Chicago if you don't want to. I always thought you'd be happier somewhere else, but that's up to you. You certainly don't have to leave on account of last night."

So much for redecorating his apartment and teaching him how to make coffee. If he could be distant, so could she. "You're right," she said briskly, moving toward the door. "I happen to like it here. Actually, I'm very grateful to you. Now that I know sex can be enjoyable, my best bet would be to find someone a little younger, someone with a little more youthful energy."

She'd really wanted to wound him.

Instead he laughed again, and this time the sound was less strained. "I didn't know you could fight back," he murmured, his tone oddly admiring.

It took every ounce of self-possession in her to walk past him without edging out of the way. Simon could have reached out and touched her, but of course he did no such thing. He simply watched her, his gray eyes hooded, his face expressionless.

She closed the door behind her, quietly, carefully, resisting the impulse to slam it. He'd simply condemn her as childish if she gave in to that overwhelming temptation. She heard something behind the door, a word; it could have meant anything. It shouldn't have given her a speck of hope, it should have hardened her heart. It had been a very solid, very heartfelt "Damn!" and it proved that no matter how hard he tried to convince her otherwise, he was far from unmoved.

She headed for the stairs, studiously ignoring the elevator. If she wanted to she could consider that "Damn!" a good sign. Or merely proof that his comfortable life had been disturbed. The less she thought about it the better. The less she saw of him the better. All she needed was a shower, and she'd feel free to face the world....

She heard the crash five flights below. She heard the cry, a piteous, weak thing, barely able to float up all those flights. She raced to the bannister, peering over and down, down. Lying in the middle of the first floor, the broken railing on top of her, was a huddled pile of dark clothing that could only be Esmy.

"Simon!" Marielle shrieked, dismissing her lingering problems as the minor inconveniences they were. "Come quickly!" And she stumbled down the stairs, still barefoot.

Simon passed her outside the Meltirks' apartment. Her highness was silhouetted in the doorway, a worried expression on her usually phlegmatic countenance, but Marielle couldn't take the time to try to communicate with the other woman. She kept running, holding up Simon's oversize pants with one hand.

He'd already managed to get the broken bannister off Esmy's plump body by the time Marielle reached them. Esmy's face was unnaturally pale, and she was moaning softly. Granita was pacing around, wringing her long hands, cursing Vittorio Farnum and his haunted house in loud, irritating tones. Julie was kneeling on one side of Esmy, Simon on the other, both holding her hands.

Simon looked up at her, through her for a moment, and she told herself it didn't hurt, it didn't matter. Then he focused on her. "Call an ambulance," he ordered. "I think she's broken something."

THE DAY REFLECTED HER MOOD, Marielle thought, tidying her already neat apartment, wandering to the window to look out over the rain-swept streets of Chicago, then back to the definitely sparse furniture. A coat of paint, a few posters, she thought, looking about her. Or a one-way ticket to Florida.

"You okay?" Dennis poked his head in the open door. He had a streak of grease on his cheekbone and a box of tools in his hand. He looked wonderfully normal, and Marielle could have hugged him.

"Fine. I'm just worried about Esmy."

"Now you know there's nothing to be worried about. Julie called from the hospital and said it was nothing more than a simple fracture. Given her age they want to keep her overnight for observation, but by tomorrow or the next day at the latest she'll be back."

"I don't know if she should come back. This place is dangerous."

"Feeling guilty, are you?" he said shrewdly, leaning against the doorframe. "You shouldn't, you know. Esmy's lived here for the past six years. This is her home."

"But things have escalated since I came here. I can't rid myself of the feeling that maybe this place is haunted, after all." She shivered slightly, wrapping her arms around her body. "This wouldn't have happened if I'd managed to keep the place in decent repair."

"Maybe," Dennis said. "But I don't think it was a ghost who sawed through that bannister. And keeping up on repairs wouldn't have much effect on a deliberate act of sabotage."

"What?"

"You heard me. Someone booby-trapped that bannister. Nobody uses the elevator in this place—they all take the stairs. Whoever sawed through the bannister knew he wouldn't have to wait long for someone to take a tumble."

"That could have been murder!" Marielle breathed, horrified.

"Not likely. It was the lower section of the stairs—not one of the upper floors. It was unfortunate that one of the old ladies fell—their bones are more fragile."

"What if it had been Julie?" she couldn't help but ask.

Dennis's face darkened, and Marielle was very glad he was on her side. "It didn't happen," he said finally, releasing his pent-up breath. "As a matter of fact, I wanted to talk to you about Julie. Indirectly, that is."

"Okay. Indirectly, what do you have to say?"

"I was thinking of applying for my Illinois licenses. I don't know if I'd qualify as both plumber and electrician—their standards may be more rigid than New Hampshire, but I stand a good chance of making at least one. I could make a pretty good living if I wanted to. Plumbers and electricians are hard to find, especially good ones. No one wants to work anymore—they all want to be lawyers."

Marielle smiled uneasily at his joke. She wasn't quite sure where this was leading. "Does that mean you don't want to do any more work on this building?" If that was the case, she was going to call a taxi to O'Hare and take the first plane to Florida. She couldn't stand another setback.

"Not at all. I'd have plenty of time to keep up with things around here."

"But what about your writing? I thought you wanted to be another Elmore Leonard?"

He shrugged. "I've got time. Hell, I'm only twenty-seven, I'm strong and I've got a lot of energy. I can do anything I want, if I work hard enough."

"That sounds fine."

"I thought I might do a little bit of work on my apartment. That is, if you're going to let me stay on there."

"Of course." She was still mystified as to the eventual destination of this rambling conversation.

"Would you consider giving me a lease? I could promise a certain amount of hours of work per week, with an eye on paying rent after a while."

"Certainly. Don't you trust me?"

He looked shocked. "Of course, Marielle. I just thought it might be nice to have a bit of security in our lives."

"Our lives?" Marielle echoed. Maybe today wouldn't be such a total disaster, after all.

"I . . . er . . . thought I might turn one of the rooms into a nursery. Fix up a changing table, bring in a rocking chair, that sort of thing," he said self-consciously.

For all Simon's insistence on her extreme youth, Marielle suddenly felt very old when faced with such naive enthusiasm. "That sounds very nice. Does Julie know?"

"I thought I'd better talk with you first. I didn't want to promise her anything I couldn't follow through on."

"Very wise. I think she's had enough promises broken. I'll give you a lease," she said. "In writing, notarized, the whole nine yards. I don't think Liam O'Donnell will serve as my lawyer, but I imagine Simon knows someone." Her voice was admirably cool when she said his name.

"That little sleaze," Dennis said bitterly, and for a moment Marielle was about to protest. Simon was a cold-hearted bastard, but not a little worm. Then she realized he meant O'Donnell. "He tried to get Julie to sign papers relinquishing the baby before it was even born. It's lucky he's been making himself scarce—I would have thrown him down the stairs myself."

"He does give the legal profession a lousy name," Marielle agreed. "When are you going to talk to Julie?"

"As soon as she gets back from the hospital. Granita's planning on spending the night there with Esmy, so there's no need for Julie to stay."

"Am I correct in assuming this offer is more than room and board?" she questioned gently.

Dennis drew himself up to his full five feet eleven inches, deeply affronted. "What kind of man do you think I am?" he demanded. "I want her to be my wife."

"Just wanted to make sure your intentions were honorable," she replied, feeling older by the minute. "Let me know what happens."

"You'll be invited to the celebration."

THE WIND HAD PICKED UP, lashing the rain against the windowpanes. It grew dark early, and by the time Marielle remembered it was Halloween it was too late to go out and buy candy for the trick or treaters. Still, it would be a foolhardy child indeed who'd brave the haunted premises of Farnum's Castle for something as mundane as a Hershey bar. She made herself a pot of decent coffee, curled up on her sofa and began to drink it, waiting for Julie to come home.

She wasn't waiting for Simon, she reminded herself. She had nothing to say to Simon, nothing that wasn't insulting. It didn't matter that her body was experiencing strange, mournful twinges, that her lips felt stung and swollen, that her skin still tingled in errant memory. She was alone and determined to enjoy herself, despite the mess her life was in.

Esmy was fine, Julie had assured her. The children were having a ball, her mother had said. Simon had returned from the hospital only to disappear more than an hour ago, the sound of the elevator signaling his departure. She couldn't care less where he'd gone, she told herself. He probably wouldn't even be back that night. He'd been neglecting his work recently. As far as she could tell no one at the radio station cared whether Simon showed up or not, but sooner or later he was going to have to put his job ahead of Farnum's Castle.

Unless part of his penance was to get himself fired from his two-bit job. She wouldn't put it past him—anyone with the need to punish himself like Simon was capable of anything. Maybe going to bed with her last night had been just as self-destructive for him.

She tried beating herself with that miserable theory, then rejected it despite its morose appeal. Simon had wanted her, wanted her enough for it to overcome his better judgment. It was too bad that the good judgment had reappeared the next morning.

It was going to be a nasty night. She wasn't going to risk calling anyone else on the off-chance that Simon might return and find her camped on his doorstep. She wouldn't be able to bear it if he touched her. On the other hand, she wouldn't be able to bear it if he didn't, if he walked past her and shut the door.

She'd better get used to the idea of being alone. Granita and Esmy would be at the hospital, Simon would be at work, Fritzie was still in northern Wisconsin on an antique-buying trip, and there was no question at all that Julie and Dennis would be wrapped up in each other. She would definitely be a fifth wheel where they were concerned.

That left the Meltirks, and she couldn't quite envision herself cozying up to her serene highness and the ceremonial fire. The best thing she could do on such a rainy, lonely night was forget the coffee, pour herself a glass of wine, indulge herself with something tasty for dinner, and dress up for no one but herself.

It was a crazy impulse that made Marielle pick up the black ball dress. This time she used safety pins to keep it reasonably chaste, dispensing with the woolen shawl. She put on black lace stockings and ridiculously high heels, very red lipstick and very black mascara, and swept up her blond hair in a haphazard, decorative knot, held in place by an ornate black comb that had been unearthed along with the dress. She sprayed herself with so much perfume that she choked, surveyed her wavy reflection in the unsilvering glass of the dresser mirror, and held up her wineglass in a toast that wasn't nearly as self-pitying as she'd expected it to be.

"Here's looking at you, kid," she murmured. Her mysterious reflection smiled back, a little mournful, a little smug, and then she wandered into the deserted living room, her long skirts trailing, in search of something a little more lively than Lean Cuisine for dinner.

Marielle didn't hear the elevator, didn't hear his footsteps on the stairs. His silhouette blocked out the dim hall light, and she wished vaguely she'd done something about the door, something to keep him out. She kept her back to the open doorway, waiting for him to say something.

"Good heavens!" was what he came out with. She turned, and dropped her wineglass in shock.

"Good heavens!" she echoed, staring at the apparition in front of her.

It wasn't Simon Zebriskie standing in her doorway, watching her. It was Simon Zee in full regalia. In his rough jeans and work shirts he always seemed very tall; in charcoal-gray, tattered evening dress he looked mammoth. The usual gray streaks in his dark hair were augmented by sheer white, and the black-circled eyes, dead white complexion and thin, hungry mouth were something out of a nightmare.

Except that she'd seen him like that countless times, years ago on television. And the effect, while eerie, was having another, inexplicable impact on her disordered senses.

"Why are you dressed like that?" Simon demanded, seemingly unaware of his own bizarre appearance.

"Presumably for the same reason you are. It's Halloween."

"This—" he gestured with a disparaging, white-gloved hand "—is part of my job. I have to show up at a couple of Halloween parties as part of a PR thing. What's your excuse?"

"Cocktail parties for your radio station's clients? I don't believe you."

"You don't have to. That's not what I said. I just said parties."

"Where?"

He shrugged. "Where do you think a noble character like me would go? To the children's hospital on Wacker Drive, among other places."

Maybe it was the two glasses of wine, or the roller coaster of emotion she'd been riding; maybe it was just time to take a chance and stop being so damned serious. Marielle lifted her flowing black chiffon skirts, just high enough to expose black lace ankles and spiky black shoes, and sauntered across the room toward a wary-looking Simon. "Saint Simon," she murmured, her voice low and throaty when she reached him, "am I another one of your charity cases?" And before she could think better of it she reached up and pressed her red-painted lips on his, her heady perfume enveloping them both.

His hands were on her waist, pulling her close, and she realized with surprise and triumph that he was hard against her. She swayed toward him, longing for him with a bittersweet ache that threatened to choke her. His mouth opened beneath hers, and suddenly he was kissing her with a fierce passion that should have frightened her. It only made her exultant, and she pressed herself against him, her hips, her breasts, her mouth, wanting to be absorbed into his very pores, wanting to merge and cling and blend with him so that there might be no telling where Simon ended and Marielle began. His mouth left hers, trailing kisses across her cheekbones, her nose, her chin, and his hands were just the tiniest bit rough as they pushed at her dress, sliding it down to her waist so that he could feel her breasts warm and soft against him.

She wanted to touch his skin, too, and she pulled the dress shirt from his pants, sliding her hands around his waist, along his heated flesh. She was about to rip at the tarnished shirt studs when he lifted his head, looking down at her, his dark-rimmed eyes suddenly intent as he said the very last thing she expected him to say.

"Do you smell smoke?"

Chapter Nineteen

Billowing black smoke was pouring from the basement doorway, thick and acrid. By the time Marielle had managed to dump her dangerous shoes and follow Simon he'd disappeared into the cellar. She stood uncertainly at the top of the basement stairs, when Dennis appeared out of the murk, coughing, choking, his face streaked with soot. In his arms he carried an ashen-faced Julie.

Simon was right behind him, striding to the front door and opening it. The nasty smoke was sucked out into the rainy night, and Simon stood in the doorway, taking in deep breaths of the cold night air. "Fire's out," he said, turning back to face Marielle.

Dennis had already maneuvered Julie into the narrow elevator. Even for Julie's sake Marielle wasn't about to join them, but she stood in the doorway, her eyes anxious.

"Is she all right?" Simon came up behind her, a solid, reassuring presence.

Julie managed a weak smile. "I just breathed in a little too much smoke."

"Don't you think we should take you to the hospital?" Dennis inquired, with the air of someone who had asked the question half a dozen times already.

"I'm okay, Dennis," she assured him but her face was pale beneath the smoky grime, and there were beads of sweat on her brow. "I just want to lie down for a few minutes. I promise, if I'm feeling worse I'll go to the emergency room."

Simon pulled Marielle out of the doorway, shutting it so that Dennis could activate the elevator. She listened to it begin its laborious journey upward, her face creased with misgivings. "What if they get stuck in there?" she demanded.

Without a word Simon pulled her into his arms. He smelled of smoke and rain and warm male flesh, and she leaned against him, shivering in sudden reaction. "It's all right, Marielle," he said, his voice a deep rumble beneath her ear. "The fire was very small, contained in an old metal barrel. Julie had it out before we even got there, and there's no chance of it spreading."

"Who started it?" she mumbled against his chest, keeping her eyes closed. "Why was Julie in the basement in the first place? What the hell is going on here?"

"I don't have the answers to those questions. I can make a few educated guesses, but guesses don't help anyone. Let's go make sure Julie's all right."

Marielle lifted her head to look up at him. "Dennis is going to ask her to marry him," she said.

He raised an eyebrow. If she thought he'd react in any way relevant to their own tangled situation, she was in for a disappointment. "Then he'd better hurry."

Marielle didn't have to ask what he meant. "You think she's in labor."

"You know more about such things. What do you think?" he countered.

"She certainly has all the signs of it," Marielle said gloomily. "And if she is, I'm not going to be much help."

"Why not? You've been through this before. Twice."

"I was knocked out. I had both of the children by cae-sarean, and my doctor didn't believe in mothers being awake during the delivery. Neither did my husband, and at the time I wasn't into arguing."

"Oh, that's just great!" he said bitterly. "I guess there's nothing we can do but check to make sure our suspicions are correct, and then call the hospital."

He still had his arms around her, a fact she realized with belated embarrassment. She stepped back and he let her go, too readily. The elevator had returned like a stately old lady to the ground floor, and the door opened.

Simon's expression was quizzical, but she could see the glint of humor behind his dark-rimmed eyes. "I'll walk, thank you," she said, turning her back on him and heading for the stairs.

"I'll ride—" his voice floated behind her "—I've got-ten rather fond of the elevator."

It was a good thing he couldn't see her face, see the bright red color mounting her cheeks. She kept her back-bone stiff beneath the trailing black material, moving with great dignity until she heard the elevator start to move once more. Then she picked up her skirts and ran up the three flights of stairs to Dennis's apartment, arriving moments before the elevator stopped.

She had just enough time to smooth back her tumbled hair and take a deep breath before the door opened. She moved past Simon.

"I never said the elevator was faster, Marielle," he said under his breath. "Just more fun."

Dennis answered the door. He'd washed the smoke and grime from his face and was in the midst of rolling down his shirt sleeves. He greeted them with faint surprise. "What's up?"

"How's Julie?"

"Fine, I think. She wanted to lie down for a while. She's probably asleep."

"I don't think so," Marielle said, moving past him into the apartment. He'd already been working on it—the cracked window panes had been replaced, the trashed fireplace cleaned out. She headed down the hallway, the two men trailing after her, and peered into the first bedroom.

The room was dark. Julie was lying on a mattress on the floor, unmoving, but Marielle knew she wasn't asleep.

She reached for the light switch, flooding the room with light. Julie quickly covered her eyes from the glare, but Marielle ignored the gesture, kneeling down beside her and taking her hand.

"How long, Julie?" she asked quietly.

Julie looked up at her, suddenly very young and very frightened. "A few hours. I thought it might be false labor. I thought if I just got home I'd be all right."

"Damn it, Julie, why didn't you stay at the hospital? I would have come down!" Dennis exploded.

"Don't yell at her," Marielle said quietly. "She didn't want O'Donnell to find her. Isn't that it?"

Julie nodded, miserable, and then her face creased in a spasm of pain as another contraction hit her.

"He won't get the baby," Dennis said, dropping to the other side of the mattress and taking her hand from Marielle's grip. "We'll get you to the hospital, get this baby born, and then we'll get married. Okay?"

Julie looked up at him through wondering, pain-glazed eyes. "Okay," she managed to croak.

"Better call the hospital, Simon," Marielle said, her voice raw with suppressed emotion. "This baby wants to be born."

He was already gone. Marielle rose, giving herself a tiny shake. "She'll be all right for now. Just hold her hand when the contractions come. I'll go find her suitcase. She's going to want her own things at the hospital. By the time I get it the ambulance should be here.''

Dennis nodded, barely noticing her, all his attention on Julie's pale, sweating face. "Hurry," he said, more a prayer than an order. "Hurry."

Julie's things were all over the old building. Marielle found a pitifully beautiful assortment of tiny, handmade baby clothes in the back bedroom of Esmy's apartment and a handful of clean, mended clothes that could only have belonged to a prepregnant Julie in a box under the bed. From her own apartment she took her best Austrian flannel nightgown, the one with buttons down the front, in case Julie wanted to breast-feed. She packed everything in one of her suitcases, throwing in the warm woolen shawl that was part of her Halloween costume. She found she was crying as she packed.

Babies did that to her every time. She loved babies, loved the magic of childbirth and everything about it. Another precious child was coming into the world, and it was coming into the world with a father and mother to love it and care for it. What more could anyone ask?

She was just leaving her apartment when she met Simon coming down the stairs. She only needed a swift glance at his expression to know things weren't going well. "What's wrong?" she demanded. "Won't an ambulance come to this part of town?"

"The telephone's out."

"That doesn't make sense. The lights are still working. Did you remember to pay your bill?"

"Yes," he said irritably. "And the phone's not broken. The line's been cut."

Marielle swallowed the retort that had risen to her lips. "The line's been cut?" she repeated in a sick voice. "And someone set a fire in the basement? What next?"

"Vampires, most likely," he snapped. "Go tell Dennis to get her ready. I'll bring the car around to the front."

"You think that'll be safe? If someone tampered with the phone lines, they could have messed with your car. The garage doesn't even have a door, much less a lock."

"It has a killer goat tied up there to scare anyone away. God, Marielle, I don't know," he said, running a harassed hand through his long, streaked hair. Some of the white came off on his hand. "But the alternative isn't terrific, either. I'm not ready to deliver Julie's baby. Are you?"

"Get the car."

By the time Marielle reached Dennis's door her legs were shaking. It seemed as if she'd done nothing but run up and down five flights of stairs since she'd moved into Farnum's Castle.

Dennis was in the hallway outside the bedroom, looking for her. "I don't know if we have time to wait for an ambulance," he greeted her, his face pale. "I don't know much about these things, but the pains are coming almost nonstop."

"Simon's gone to get the car. The phone's not working." She didn't see any need to add to his worries by telling him why the phone was out of order.

"Did someone cut the wire?" At her reluctant nod he swore. "We've all got to get out of here. I don't think Simon can keep you and a horde of unintelligible Meltirks safe from whatever wants to get into this place."

"Don't worry about us. Worry about Julie and the baby."

"What do you mean by that?" he demanded, his voice hoarse. "Is something wrong?"

"Nothing's wrong. She just needs your attention right now. The rest of us can take care of ourselves." A groan from the mattress caught their attention, and she gave him a little shove. "Go see how she's doing. I'll see what's keeping Simon."

Down more flights of stairs, she thought, her muscles shrieking a protest. If she kept this up she should qualify for the New York Marathon. Or whatever Chicago equivalent there was.

She met Simon one flight down, in front of the Meltirks' closed door. He was soaked with rain, and the expression in his eyes was far from reassuring.

"The damned goat ate my tires."

"What?" Marielle's shriek echoed through the hallway. The Meltirks' door opened, and her serene highness appeared, draped in fuchsia.

She greeted them in her own incomprehensible language, and over her shoulder Marielle saw the wizened features of Mrs. Meltirk's mother. Or mother-in-law, she wasn't quite sure.

"I'm sorry, your highness, but Esmy isn't here, and no one else can translate. We've got an emergency."

Mrs. Meltirk just looked at Marielle, her heavy features placid.

"Julie's gone into labor," Marielle continued, her voice desperate with worry and the frustration of explaining to someone who didn't understand a word she was saying. "The phone's dead, so we can't call an ambulance, and Simon's car is broken so we can't drive her to the hospital."

Slowly, ponderously her serene highness, the crown princess of Baluchistan, nodded. "There is no need for hospitals," she said in slow, perfect English. "My mother is a midwife. I myself have brought many children into the world. Julie will be fine."

Marielle stared at her openmouthed. "You speak English?"

Her highness shrugged her massive shoulders, gesturing to her mother to follow her as she moved out into the hallway with all the majesty of an ocean liner.

They moved up the stairs, a curious procession, Marielle not sure whether she ought to cry in relief or laugh at the ridiculousness of it all. "Why haven't you spoken before?" she asked as they plodded their way into Dennis's apartment.

"It didn't suit me," the princess replied with her customary dignity. "If your government knew I spoke English, they would have asked me all sorts of exhausting questions and wanted me to make inflammatory statements about the wild young men who overran my country. If I were to make such statements there would be no chance of my returning to my country without further bloodshed. Very few people outside of Baluchistan speak my language—so very few people were able to disturb us. It was working very well."

She turned to her mother, issuing a long, involved statement. Her mother nodded, sketched a tiny bow and moved to Julie's side, muttering under her breath and shooing Dennis away.

"My mother says things are going well. It won't be long. And," she added, "it will be a girl." The heiress to the monarchy of a matriarchal society smiled. "That is good."

"I just want the baby born safely," Dennis muttered, looking askance at the Baluchistani contingent.

"My mother has never lost a baby or a mother in all her years," said her highness. "A father, perhaps." And she began to wheeze, a low, rumbling sound that Marielle finally identified as a laugh.

The old lady was speaking to Julie, a litany of long, cooing sounds that must have been incomprehensible, but nevertheless seemed to soothe her.

"Damn," Dennis said, sitting back on his heels beside the mattress. "I'd wanted us to be married before the baby is born. It's too late for that now, but I'd hoped . . ."

"Why is it too late?" her highness inquired. She'd settled her impressive bulk on the only chair in the room, prepared to await the outcome in relative comfort.

"There's no priest," Dennis pointed out, half distracted, as Julie moaned. "Not to mention no marriage license, no blood tests, no banns posted. We can't even manage a civil ceremony."

"I can marry you," her highness announced.

"Really?" Marielle demanded in a moment of curiosity.

"Of course. It would be perfectly legal in Baluchistan, and this country would be forced to accept it. Your government does not say no to me," she added simply.

"Fine," said Dennis. "But this isn't Baluchistan. This is Chicago."

Her highness smiled. "Dear child," she corrected him, "wherever I am *is* Baluchistan. Do you wish to be married or not?"

He hesitated for only a second, then capitulated. "What harm can it do? How do we do it?"

"Take her hand, young man." And leaning back, Mrs. Meltirk began to intone.

The Baluchistani marriage ceremony was a long-winded one. Julie's labor was short—for a while it was a horse race as to which would finish first.

But even her indolent majesty had a sense of the importance of matters. Three minutes before Esmerelda Granita McMurtry arrived in the world, red-faced and screaming, Dennis and Julie were pronounced husband and wife. Or the Baluchistani equivalent thereof.

Marielle looked across the room at Simon. They'd both been banished to the living room as unnecessary either to birth or to marriage, and they'd spent the last half hour alternatively pacing and staring.

They both ran to the bedroom door and peered inside. "Everything is fine," her highness announced, heaving her bulk out of the spindly chair. "You can take them both to the hospital if you like. There is no need, but Americans like to be reassured."

Indeed, there didn't seem to be the slightest need at all. The newest Esmy was tiny, perfectly formed, and now that the indignity of birth had passed, was sleeping peacefully in her mother's arms. The new parents stared down at the little scrap of humanity with expressions of awe and wonder. Marielle backed out of the room and into the bathroom and burst into tears.

Simon followed her, shutting the door behind them, shutting the two of them in. He pulled her into his arms, holding her tight, and she bawled loudly against his absurd evening clothes.

Someone pounded on the door. Simon ignored it for a moment, then reluctantly released her, opening the door to see Francis Muldoon's beefy red face. "So suddenly I've got a sister-in-law and a niece," he announced. "I didn't realize Dennis had it in him. The boy can work fast when he has a mind to."

Marielle managed a watery smile. "That he can. What are you doing here?"

"Got a call that a prowler was seen outside the building. Combine that with the phone being on the blink and we thought it might behoove us to check the old place out. Did you have a fire?"

"Just a small one. Julie put it out."

"Arson?" Muldoon was suddenly all business, no longer the proud new uncle.

"Presumably," Simon said.

"We've radioed for an ambulance. Once we get them settled we'll call in backup and go over this place with a fine-toothed comb. We'll start with the grounds and work our way inward. They're making a mockery of the Chicago police department," Officer Muldoon said severely. "And we don't like that." He moved away, back to the delivery room, and Marielle could hear the low rumble of voices.

Simon was gazing down at her, a peculiar expression on his face. "You look," he said wryly, "as bad as I do." He turned her shoulders gently to the mirror.

Her makeup had run down her face in long black streaks. Sometime during the last few hours she'd bitten off her bright red lipstick, and her hair had fallen around her shoulders. "I'd better do something about this," she murmured self-consciously, pushing at her hair.

"Not on my account. You look like a perfect lady vampire." His voice was very gentle, almost loving. A trick, she thought. Wishful thinking on her part.

"I'd better go," she said again, pulling away. He let her go. Was she imagining his reluctance? she wondered.

"I'll make sure they get off to the hospital," he said. "And then I'll come up to your apartment."

"Why?"

"We have to talk."

"We already talked," she said stubbornly, refusing to meet his eyes.

His hand caught her chin, turning her face up to his. "Maybe things have changed."

"Maybe they haven't."

"It's Halloween, Marielle. Time for a little trick or treat," he murmured, brushing his lips against hers, his hand holding her face still when she would have turned her head away.

She couldn't help it. Her lips clung to his, almost of their own volition. He didn't deepen the kiss, keeping it gentle and sweet, and when he lifted his head she found she was smiling.

"Give me half an hour," he said. "And then I'll be up. Will you talk to me?"

"I can't keep you out. My door's still broken."

"You could keep me out. If you wanted to. Do you?"

She really didn't want to be pinned down, but Simon was insisting. "Yes," she breathed. "No. I mean, I'll wait for you."

He smiled then, a sweet, loving smile that lit the darkness of his gray eyes. "I'll be there," he said.

And she still didn't know whether he was about to break her heart.

Chapter Twenty

Farnum's Castle felt oddly empty as Marielle wearily climbed the last flights of stairs to her fourth-floor apartment. She could only be glad of the sensation. The Meltirks were once again snug in their second-floor suite and she realized the sense of being unobserved, unthreatened.

She looked out her apartment window to the grounds surrounding the old building, out toward the street. The ambulance was there, its lights flashing in a lazy circle, and she could see the outline of Muldoon's police car. Simon's tall, spare figure was silhouetted in the street light as he looked back toward the house. She didn't know whether he could see her, mooning after him from her tower window, and she didn't care. Crying for the moon, that was what she was doing. Moping around for something that was forever out of reach. Maybe Simon was right; maybe she was just a child believing in happy endings and true love.

She was crying again. She pulled herself away from the window and headed into the bathroom. Icy-cold water did wonders for her self-pity, even if it couldn't help her red-rimmed eyes. The streaked black makeup washed off on her white facecloth, leaving her pale and weary-looking, her hair in witch locks around her face. She would make a perfect bride for Dracula, she thought with distant amusement. Bloodless, lifeless, soulless.

In a last trace of defiance she repainted her mouth, twisted her hair back up and slipped on her high heels. Simon said he wanted to talk, so she planned to face him with most of her defences intact. She held out very little hope for the outcome of their conversation. He'd probably tell her again to leave, she'd start crying, and it would all end miserably.

Or maybe, just maybe, there might be a happy ending for her, too. Miracles did happen.

Dangerous as it might be, she headed for the bottle of wine in her refrigerator. Dutch courage or not, after such an evening, such a day, such a week, she was in need of a little support. She was taking her first, tentative sip of the icy-cold chardonnay when she heard the noise.

If her apartment door weren't still splintered off its hinges she wouldn't have heard anything. If her children had been around, with the TV incessantly blaring, no one would have ever been the wiser. If Dennis had still been in residence and not on his way to the hospital with his brand-new wife and baby, she might have just assumed it was he making noises downstairs.

But no one was within three floors of her apartment but the quiet Meltirks. Simon and the police were combing the grounds before they searched the house, and there was no one on the floor below. No one.

She set down the glass on the stained and scratched Formica and headed for the door. Her high-heeled sandals made a clicking noise, so she slipped them off again. Her black silk stockings were already shredded, so it didn't matter if they took one more interminable trip down the stairs.

Dennis had left his door open, lights still illuminating the rain-swept night. She poked her head in, listening, but there was nothing. She turned, looking at the door of the one apartment in her dubious inheritance she'd yet to visit.

It might be the ghost of Vittorio Farnum, cozily ensconced in his own residence. Or it might be nothing at all—another empty apartment in a building with too many empty apartments. Or it might be someone evil—someone so obsessed with finding Vittorio's fortune that he no longer cared whom he hurt.

She crossed the hallway, pressing her ear against the door. There was no mistaking the noises from within. The hollow chink of bricks, noisy, yet muffled breathing, even an occasional curse.

She should have raced down the next three flights of stairs. But she'd had enough of stairs to last her for at least twenty-four hours. Besides, if she left, there was a good chance that when the police and Simon returned the intruder would be gone—perhaps even taking with him the long-lost treasure.

She put her hand on the tarnished brass doorknob. It turned easily, silently beneath her fingertips. Once more she hesitated. Their villain had yet to do any real, deliberate harm. The fire had been set in a metal barrel—there'd been almost no chance of it spreading. And if anyone other than an elderly lady had fallen through the bannister, he or she would have escaped with a few bruises.

No, she wouldn't be dealing with a murderer. If she just kept her wits about her she could find out who was behind the sabotage. And suddenly that need to know overcame any concern for her own safety. Pushing the door open, she stepped into the last empty apartment.

Only it wasn't empty. There were rugs on the floor. The same kind of cast-off furniture that furnished her own apartment, which was stored in abundance directly above this apartment, could be seen from the long narrow hallway. A dim light was burning in the living room, and

Marielle moved slowly, quietly, leaving the door open behind her.

A dark figure was kneeling in front of the fireplace. Bricks and rubble were strewn all over the faded Oriental carpet, books were tossed this way and that. The figure in front of the fireplace had a stocking pulled over his head, gloves on his hands, and he was staring at the fireplace and cursing.

She must have made a noise, though she thought she'd been completely silent. He turned swiftly, staring up at her, and through the distorting mesh of the stocking her intruder looked uncannily like the portrait of Vittorio Farnum still hanging in Granita's bedroom. But she had already guessed who it was.

"Find anything interesting, Miles?" she questioned coolly.

He didn't move, his body coiled in tension, and for a moment Marielle wondered whether she'd misread his basic cowardice, whether he'd rush her, hurt her.

Then he reached up and pulled the panty hose off his head, revealing his beautiful blond hair standing straight up. He'd used something to darken his face and eyebrows beneath the mask, otherwise she never would have noticed the resemblance.

"I found my grandfather's treasure," he said with a bitter laugh. "A bunch of lousy Bibles. Trust the old skinflint of a fanatic. There's nothing so dangerous as a convert."

Marielle looked down at the books on the floor. They looked very old, heavy, with leather bindings. "I suppose they were a treasure to him."

"They're not to me," he said, sitting back on his heels. "Do you realize what I've gone through to get these?"

"Yes," Marielle said gently. "I do."

His mouth twisted in a wry smile. "Yes, I suppose you do. And I think I'd better get the hell out of here before Simon gets back. I have no intention of having my teeth kicked in." He rose, lithe and graceful as always, completely at ease even in this bizarre situation. "No one will be able to prove a thing, you realize. It'll be your word against mine, and I happen to have a lawyer safe in my pocket. A very devious, successful lawyer who isn't above resorting to a little financial incentive for the proper witnesses. Not to mentionn that he has a certain talent for hiring muggers and setting up fake ghosts. He's a very clever man."

"Liam O'Donnell."

"Exactly. And if that doesn't work, the station owner happens to have a brother who's a very influential judge. Plus a daughter who's deeply enamored of me. I have no doubt whatsoever that I could work something out in that area. Of course, you could always promise not to say anything." He smiled at her, that warm, charming smile that had doubtless melted harder female hearts than hers.

Marielle was both aghast and amused at his gall. "Why in the world should I do that?"

"Well, now that the 'treasure'—" he kicked a Bible with his black sneaker "—is found, there'll be no more reason to break into this old mausoleum in the middle of the night. No need to drive you out, to try to get you to sell to me. As a matter of fact, I've gotten off quite lucky. If you'd taken me up on my offer I would have been out a considerable sum of money, with absolutely nothing to show for it but a pile of worthless old books."

"I don't think you're going to get off so lightly, Miles. I have every intention of seeing you're prosecuted to the full extent of the law," she said very calmly.

He just looked at her for a long moment. "Then I guess I'd better get the hell out of here," he said abruptly, diving past her and down the narrow hallway. He hadn't heard what she'd heard—the sound of someone climbing the stairs.

It was over in a matter of seconds, with shouts, curses and the splintering of wood. It must have been a trick of the light, or of her confused and weary mind. For a split second Marielle thought she saw two of Miles, the second one older, darker, dressed in a monk's robe. And then they were both gone, and Miles lay in an untidy heap two flights down, his leg twisted beneath him, his face white with pain. Another sawn-through bannister pressed down on him while Francis Muldoon, ignoring his groans, proceeded to read him his rights.

Simon was only a few feet away from her. "What the hell are you doing down here?" he demanded, his voice hoarse with strain and worry.

"I heard a noise and decided to check it out," she replied.

She'd never seen him angry before, really angry. He didn't raise his voice much above a hoarse shout, and didn't leave her any space to break in. He merely explained in loud, definite tones why she should never, ever risk her safety in such a foolhardy way.

"Don't you realize, you fool woman," he rasped, "that there are people who love you, people who depend on you in this life, people who wouldn't survive if something happened to you!"

Muldoon had already yanked a sweating, grunting Miles out to the police car, disdaining the use of an ambulance for this particular felon. They were alone on the stairway, and if Marielle noticed the Meltirks' door had opened a crack, she ignored it.

"Such as?" she prodded.

"Such as your children. Such as the people in this building," he shot back.

"Not good enough, Simon," she said, very sure of herself for the first time in months, in years. "Who else loves me and needs me?"

He glared at her. "First you scare the hell out of me, then you make me say it," he grumbled, not as loudly.

The Meltirks' door opened a little wider, and Marielle could see the shadow of her serene highness's turban silhouetted against the wall.

"I'm waiting."

"All right, damn it. I love you. I need you. And if you ever do something as stupid as walking in on a criminal in the midst of a crime I will strangle you. Do you understand?"

She smiled at him, feeling as if her face would split in delight. "Is that it?"

"Isn't it enough?"

She would have liked a proposal. She would have liked him to look a little happier about the whole thing. "I'll take what I can get," she said, moving to the top of the stairs. He was standing two steps down; her eyes were even with his, her mouth was even with his. "So what's next?"

His eyes were smoldering, no longer with fear and rage but with an intensity that made her knees weak. "Next, I get out of this wet evening suit. I'm freezing to death."

"What about me?"

"You could always get out of that dry evening gown and warm me up," he suggested, almost diffidently.

She went into his arms, plastering herself against his wet body, pressing her mouth on his. "Sounds wonderful," she murmured. "Are you going to carry me upstairs like Rhett Butler?"

"I'm going to make love to you right here on the stairs if you don't get moving," he growled. And Marielle had no doubt whatsoever that he meant it.

IT WAS THREE IN THE MORNING before they made it back downstairs to the third-floor apartment. Marielle was wrapped in Simon's little-used red chamois bathrobe, Simon was wearing tattered gray sweatpants and a T-shirt. The heating system, thanks to Dennis's recent ministrations, was deliciously efficient, and the chill that always seemed to linger at the back of Marielle's senses had disappeared.

Simon knelt down in front of the fireplace in the third-floor suite, picking up one of the heavy, leather-covered Bibles in careful hands. "This is Vittorio Farnum's famous treasure? This is what fifty years of fuss have been about?" he asked.

"That was Miles's reaction. Total disgust," Marielle said, pulling the long robe around her as she sank to her knees beside him.

"The problem with Miles," Simon said in a meditative voice, leafing through the first Bible, "is that he seldom looks beyond the surface. He's all flash and no substance. He wouldn't know a treasure if it came up and bit him."

Marielle looked at him in surprise. "Is there something hidden in the pages?"

"Like hundred-dollar bills in Deuteronomy? No, my sweet. You're just as prosaic as Miles. Take a look at this." He held out the first Bible for her perusal.

"It's in German."

"Very old German. Unless I miss my guess, this is from some time in the late fifteen hundreds or early sixteen hundreds. From Martin Luther's Germany."

"Religious sentiment aside, are you telling me this Bible is worth something?"

"If it's just any Bible from that time period it would be worth a great deal. If it's the *Ein' feste Burg* Bible, it's priceless." He set it down very, very carefully, and picked up another.

Marielle eyed it warily. "What's that one—the Dead Sea Scrolls?"

"Looks like it's French, but not any French I can read. I couldn't even begin to make a guess on these, but I expect they're all extraordinarily valuable."

"Who owns them?"

Simon grinned at her. "Practical as ever. I expect you do. Unless they're stolen property and the statute of limitations hasn't yet run out, or something equally unlikely. When one buys real estate one usually buys everything involved. This was part of the interior of Farnum's Castle, therefore it was part of the purchase and belongs to the present owner. I doubt Vittorio's newfound grandson has the slightest claim."

"Did you ever have the faintest idea?" she questioned him, momentarily distracted. "Miles did seem to know an awful lot about the place."

Simon shrugged. "His father was Swedish. Until he darkened his face the resemblance was almost impossible to notice. And his mother had done everything to live down the connection. As far as I was concerned, he was just a Chicago aristocrat dabbling in city history."

"He's not going to be dabbling in much besides jail for the next few years."

"Don't count on it," Simon drawled. "He's going to get off with a slapped wrist. He'll throw himself on Abigail Harbison's mercy, she'll take him, and her father will pull enough strings to get him off."

"Damn."

"Look at it this way—he'll be in a cast for months, he's got a mild concussion, and he's going to have to marry someone he has absolutely no interest in, someone who's going to keep him firmly in line. Miles isn't in for smooth sailing by any account."

"I suppose that'll have to do," Marielle said mournfully. "I still would have liked some revenge, for Esmy's broken ankle if for nothing else."

"Esmy'll forgive him. You may as well, too." He sat back on his heels, watching her out of hooded eyes. "So what are you going to do about these Bibles? You could live quite a comfortable life on the proceeds of these. Travel, buy a house someplace warm and safe where it never rains." As if to punctuate his statement the rain increased, pounding against the windows.

"Still trying to get rid of me?" she inquired, resigned. She reached out and touched the French Bible. "This should take care of the back taxes. Sounds like the German Bible will provide a new elevator, a bannister, a few years' electric bills and even a new boiler."

"And then some."

"And the others—" she gestured to the half dozen other books lying scattered amid the rubble "—should cover any contingency that might come up for a good long time."

"It should." He had retreated again behind that distant, unreadable expression. "I've been married," he said abruptly.

"So have I," she said. "Want to try again?"

If she'd hoped to shock him she failed. "Marielle, we haven't known each other for very long. I'm fourteen years older than you. I've been a loser when it comes to marriage...."

"I've heard all this a dozen times, Simon," she said, feeling very calm. "I know that beneath your gruff cynicism is the kindest man I've ever met. Also the sexiest. And I'm not going to give that up without a fight. Come on, Simon. Marry me for my newfound wealth. Take me out of pity. Just take me."

He reached a hand behind her neck and pulled her, not ungently, into his lap. "You're crazy, you know that? You're asking for trouble."

She twined both arms around his neck, smiling up at him. "I hope you like kids," she said, broaching the one subject they'd never tackled.

"I love kids. Particularly yours."

"Want to have more? Seeing little Esmy born has given me a wicked case of the baby blues."

"Woman, are you never satisfied!" Simon said, rolling his eyes heavenward.

"Now you know better than anyone that that's not true," Marielle purred, sliding her hand under his loose T-shirt. "So how about it? Are you ready to take a child bride of twenty-eight?"

He looked down at her, his mobile mouth twisted in a grin. "How can I resist such an offer? And she's rich, too."

"And cute into the bargain," she added, snuggling closer.

"Not to mention that I'm in love with her," Simon murmured.

"Let's not get too mushy, or she might have to start telling you how much she loves you, and then this would deteriorate into the kind of saccharine scene that would turn an old cynic like you green."

He kissed her, a full gentle kiss on her smiling mouth. "Don't worry," he said. "I'll turn you into a cynic before I'm done."

"Maybe," she said. "But I bet I turn you into an optimist instead."

"I doubt it."

"Try me," she suggested.

And for the fourth time that day, he did.

Epilogue

It was a Thanksgiving wedding. The children had returned from Florida, and Simon didn't believe in long engagements. They were married in the recently converted first-floor suite. Granita and Esmerelda were peacefully sharing an apartment once more, and Esmy was getting quite mobile in her cast, given the aid of the brand-new, smooth-running elevator. She had no trouble zipping upstairs to check on her namesake and the newlyweds at the most inopportune moments.

Granita's old apartment was to be a community room, and that was where the wedding was held, with the smells of freshly sawn pine and new paint blending with the scent of flowers.

Little Esmy came out with her first smile as she sat in her father's lap, her mother watching her with indulgent eyes. Christopher and Emily were proud observers and Marielle's bridesmaids, Abbie, Suzanne and Jaime, had flown in from all parts of the country. They were all jammed into the only empty apartment left in the rapidly improving building, and the four of them had been up half the night, laughing and talking and crying.

Jaime was glowing with an ease and self-assurance Marielle had never seen before. She'd finally come to terms with her overwhelming mother, and she couldn't mention

Quaid, her new husband, without going all soft and sentimental.

Suzanne, on the other hand, was still her usual sharp-tongued self. She'd left her darling Billy behind in Wyoming. Apparently he divided his time between Suzanne's house in the city and his ranch, and he'd been ignoring his duties too long. Besides, Suzanne said, she wanted to enjoy being around her old friends without having to consider anyone else. And yes, Mouse was well on her way to making her a grandmother, damn it.

But of all her friends Abbie was the most changed. She suddenly seemed years younger, as if a huge burden had been lifted from her shoulders. Marielle had never realized how very solemn Abbie could be, until she saw her free.

She imagined she must look just the same—silly and happy and young, with tears and giggles and salacious gossip ringing in her ears. It was the last time they'd be like this, she thought. Reality would set in again for all of them, but for now, for this Thanksgiving wedding weekend, they could all be the best, the closest of friends, and the memory of it would last through years of infrequent letters and phone calls.

A good portion of Chicago showed up for the ceremony and the huge Thanksgiving dinner afterward. Even Miles had the gall to appear, debonair as ever in a walking cast, his possessive fiancée and future father-in-law along as protection.

It was all Marielle could do to summon a polite smile, and when Miles tried to kiss her she ducked, giving him the faintest, most surreptitious kick in the cast she could manage.

He managed to smother a groan as he hobbled away. Then unfortunately, she was faced with the task of offering good wishes to the next bride-to-be.

Simon was right; Abigail Harbison wasn't Miles's type. She was built along sturdy lines, with a wide, generous mouth, shrewd eyes behind her wire-rimmed glasses, and had a no-nonsense air that could have been intimidating.

"Don't look at me like that," Abigail said under her breath in a cheerful voice. "I know what I'm doing. I understand Miles far too well. That's what scares the hell out of him."

Marielle blinked. "I wish you every happiness."

"I expect we'll have a harder time than you and Simon," Abigail admitted frankly. "That's why I'm glad he's in a cast. It's easier to keep him in line." And moving on, she enveloped Simon in an exuberant bear hug.

"Poor Miles," Marielle murmured to Simon a few moments later. "You're right—he's going to be much more restrained than he would have been in prison."

"She'll be the making of him," Simon replied.

She looked up at her new husband, laughing. "I told you I'd turn you into an optimist," she said. "I just didn't think it would be this quick."

He dropped a kiss on her upturned mouth. "Wait till I start the day shift at the new station. Then you'll find out just how cynical I can be."

"But at least I get you all night long. That should cheer you up."

"It does," said Simon. "Enormously. As long as we've finished with visitations and nocturnal visitors."

"Vittorio's gone for good," she replied.

He raised an eyebrow. "Vittorio hasn't been here in almost fifty years."

"If you say so, dear." She smiled sweetly, remembering the gentle touch of a hand, the scene on the landing and Miles's convenient fall.

"Marielle, don't tell me you ever really believed in ghosts," Simon begged.

Marielle looked over his shoulder to the portrait of wicked old Vittorio, still hanging in state over the newly refurbished fireplace. His evil old eyes seemed to wink at her.

"Never for a moment, darling," she promised. And smiling up at Vittorio, she winked back.

ABOUT THE AUTHOR

Anne Stuart is a multitalented writer with an uncanny ability to write both heartfelt drama and witty repartee. With the series since its inception, Anne has published nine American Romances since 1983, always delivering the sizzling romance her readers have come to love.

Anne recently had a new house built in the mountains of Vermont, where she now lives with her husband, daughter and son.

Books by Anne Stuart

HARLEQUIN AMERICAN ROMANCE

52–MUSEUM PIECE
93–HOUSEBOUND
126–ROCKY ROAD
177–BEWITCHING HOUR
213–BLUE SAGE
246–PARTNERS IN CRIME

HARLEQUIN INTRIGUE

5–TANGLED LIES
9–CATSPAW
59–HAND IN GLOVE

Don't miss any of our special offers. Write to us at the following address for information on our newest releases.

Harlequin Reader Service
901 Fuhrmann Blvd., P.O. Box 1397, Buffalo, NY 14240
Canadian address: P.O. Box 603,
Fort Erie, Ont. L2A 5X3

ATTRACTIVE, SPACE SAVING BOOK RACK

Display your most prized novels on this handsome and sturdy book rack. The hand-rubbed walnut finish will blend into your library decor with quiet elegance, providing a practical organizer for your favorite hard-or soft-covered books.

Only $9.95

Approximately 16" x 8" when assembled

Assembles in seconds!

To order, rush your name, address and zip code, along with a check or money order for $10.70* ($9.95 plus 75¢ postage and handling) payable to *Harlequin Reader Service*:

Harlequin Reader Service
Book Rack Offer
901 Fuhrmann Blvd.
P.O. Box 1396
Buffalo, NY 14269-1396

Offer not available in Canada.

BKR-1A

*New York and Iowa residents add appropriate sales tax.

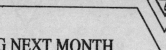

Harlequin American Romance

COMING NEXT MONTH

HARLEQUIN SIGNATURE EDITION

VIOLET WINSPEAR

HOUSE OF STORMS

Editorial secretary Debra Hartway travels to the Salvador family's rugged Cornish island home to work on Jack Salvador's latest book. Disturbing questions hang in the troubled air over Lovelis Island. What or who had caused the tragic death of Jack's young wife? Why did Jack stay away from the home and, more especially, the baby son he loved so well? And—why should Rodare, Jack's brother, who had proved himself a man of the highest integrity, constantly invade Debra's thoughts with such passionate, dark desires . . . ?

Violet Winspear, who has written more than 65 romance novels translated worldwide into 18 languages, is one of Harlequin's best-loved and bestselling authors. HOUSE OF STORMS, her second title in the Harlequin Signature Edition program, is a full-length novel rich in romantic tradition and intriguingly spiced with an atmosphere of danger and mystery.

Watch for HOUSE OF STORMS—coming in October! HOFS-1